Digby Marsh Berry

The sister martyrs of Ku Cheng

Memoir and letters of Eleanor and Elizabeth Saunders. Third Edition

Digby Marsh Berry

The sister martyrs of Ku Cheng
Memoir and letters of Eleanor and Elizabeth Saunders. Third Edition

ISBN/EAN: 9783337108601

Printed in Europe, USA, Canada, Australia, Japan

Cover: Foto ©Raphael Reischuk / pixelio.de

More available books at **www.hansebooks.com**

THE

SISTER MARTYRS OF KU CHENG

MEMOIR AND LETTERS

OF

ELEANOR AND ELIZABETH SAUNDERS

("Nellie" and "Topsy")

OF MELBOURNE

BY

D. M. BERRY, M.A.

CANON OF MELBOURNE, CHAPLAIN TO THE BISHOP

THIRD EDITION

COMPLETING FOURTH THOUSAND

London

JAMES NISBET & CO., LIMITED

21 BERNERS STREET

MELVILLE, MULLEN & SLADE,

MELBOURNE

PREFACE

THE history contained in the following pages is a history of scarcely more than a year and a half in China, but it shows an amount of work and experience crowded into that short time which is truly marvellous. The letters of the sisters, nearly all written to their mother, are so voluminous that they only required arrangement and a few connecting-links of explanation to form a complete as well as a lively and graphic narrative. The extracts are given exactly in the form in which they flowed from the pens of these ready young scribes, with the exception of the slight corrections and alterations necessary in unstudied compositions, which were never intended for any eyes but those of a mother. The editor's object has been to let the girls speak for themselves, and to let the reader see what manner of girls they were— bright and buoyant young spirits, and all the more bright and buoyant for having been brought to surrender themselves unreservedly to Him who is the Source of all true life and happiness.

CONTENTS

CHAPTER I

HOME LIFE

CHAPTER II

FROM BRISBANE TO MANILA

CHAPTER III

HONGKONG AND FOOCHOW

CHAPTER IV

FOOCHOW TO KU CHENG

CHAPTER V

CHRISTMAS AT KU CHENG

CHAPTER VI

THE NATIVE CHRISTIAN CONFERENCE

CHAPTER VII

ACTIVE WORK

CHAPTER VIII

SPRING EMPLOYMENTS AND JOURNEYINGS

CHAPTER IX

TOPSY'S SEASIDE HOLIDAY

CHAPTER X

NELLIE'S MIDSUMMER HOLIDAY

CHAPTER XI

THE MANDARIN'S FAMILY

CHAPTER XII

TOPSY'S AUTUMN WORK

CHAPTER XIII

THE BISHOP AT DONG GIO

CHAPTER XIV

NELLIE'S DECEMBER WORK

CHAPTER XV

JANUARY EXPERIENCES OF COUNTRY WORK

CHAPTER XVI

THE FEBRUARY CONFERENCE AGAIN

CHAPTER XVII

ALARM AND FLIGHT FROM KU CHENG

CHAPTER XVIII

TOPSY'S MARCH EXPERIENCES

CHAPTER XIX

NELLIE'S LAST WORKING DAYS

SISTER MARTYRS OF KU CHENG

CHAPTER I

HOME LIFE

"The Willows"—"Paddock children"—All things new—Consecration and service—Claims of China—Training—Separation
inevitable—The Letters a result—Leaving home—A tearless
parting.

On the outskirts of Kew, one of the most beautiful suburbs
of Melbourne, and on the slope of a hill which looks across
an undulating country to Mount Macedon and the Dividing Range some forty miles away, stands a comfortable-
looking red-brick house, surrounded by a shady garden,
and bounded by pasture paddocks, stretching away beyond
the row of willows from which the house takes its name.
In this home were spent most of the early years of our
heroines, Nellie and Topsy Saunders. Their father, a
Melbourne merchant, died when Nellie was five years old
and Topsy only three, and their mother was thus left in
charge of a family of three stepsons and two stepdaughters,
besides her own two little girls. Of the former family,
one member has followed the example of her half-sisters,
by offering herself for foreign missionary work.

Mrs. Saunders brought up her children as much as

possible to an out-of-door life, and the little sisters became known to the neighbours as "the paddock children." Consequently they grew up with simple tastes and a strong love of freedom, and with just enough of the harum-scarum in their nature to make them interesting.

In one of her letters from China Nellie observes :— "The Chinese are surprised at my agility in crossing their river bridges, but they would not be surprised if they could have seen me walking on the top rail in our paddock and climbing up the flagstaff."

The elder sister was the more robust and active, and the younger, who grew up tall and slender, was somewhat more thoughtful and dreamy. In the following pages Nellie will be found to be the historian and Topsy the philosopher and theologian of the story. Their mother— the widow of a sincerely pious husband—was herself a godly woman, but had never risen to the full understanding of the privileges and duties of the Christian calling until she and her daughters began to attend the ministry of the Rev. S. M., of St. Hilary's, East Kew. Topsy was at this time old enough to be prepared for confirmation, being fifteen years of age, and the instruction she received in view of this solemn rite was the means of opening her eyes to see her true position as one of Christ's redeemed. From the first she accepted Christ, not only as the author of her eternal salvation, but as the king and glory of this present life, as well as of the next.

Her earnest desire to see her elder sister also brought to the feet of Christ, was fulfilled after that sister had passed through a spiritual conflict which lasted nine months. From this time forward the mother and

daughters were of one heart and soul in counting all
things but loss for the excellency of the knowledge of
Christ Jesus, their Lord. Unlike so many ordinary Christians, whose faith seems to be only one element in their
lives, and that rather the sombre than the joyous element,
the very sunshine of their daily lives was found in Christ,
and all tastes and pursuits were strictly subordinated
to an entire devotion to His service. Nellie was passion-
ately fond of music, and had shown promise of being
successful in it as a profession, but she now began to
feel that the four or five hours of spare time, which she
used to devote daily to practising on the piano, were
required for occupations more directly connected with
the service of the Master, and therefore, after a severe
inward struggle, gave up her favourite employment, and,
feeling how strong was the attraction and temptation,
rigidly restricted herself to sacred music in order to keep
clear of it.

The mother and daughters now set themselves to do
some definite good work in the world as witnesses for
Christ. Removing for a time to the parish of St. Mary's,
Caulfield, they opened a Sunday-school at their house,
with the sanction of the Rev. H. B. Macartney, as well as
a Monday evening prayer-meeting, conducted by a lay
reader. Both these little institutions are still in existence.

In 1889, the founder of the China Inland Mission, Mr.
Hudson Taylor, and his assistant Mr. Beauchamp, made a
visit to Australia, and their account of Gospel work in
China so fired the enthusiasm of these ladies, that to go
and work in China became the great desire of their hearts
and a theme of constant planning and discussion. The

plan, however, did not take definite shape until the visit, in 1891, of Mr. Eugene Stock, Secretary of the Church Missionary Society, and with him the Rev. R. Stewart, a devoted and able missionary of sixteen years' experience in China. After consultation with these gentlemen, it was decided that the daughters should at once begin a course of preparation for the work, and that as soon as they were ready the mother, after disposing of her property at "The Willows," should accompany them, with a view to taking care of them, and possibly also of other young lady missionaries, in their work. Meantime their services were to be offered to the Church Missionary Society, and they were to go out and work at their own expense. Thus they proposed, but God disposed otherwise. The financial depression, which has afflicted Victoria now for about five years, deprived them of the means of working without remuneration, and the utter impossibility of selling or letting "The Willows" upon reasonable terms, made it necessary that the mother should remain at home. Meantime the daughters had been diligently studying for two years; much of their time was spent in the Melbourne Hospital, obtaining a knowledge of nursing, and theological instruction was given them by Canon Chase, a veteran Melbourne clergyman, whose heart was always in sympathy with missionary enterprise. It is remarkable that the news of their martyrdom reached Melbourne on the very morning that the remains of this true servant of God were laid in the grave. The writer of this memoir also had the privilege, for about six months, of giving weekly instruction to the sisters in Christian evidences and Church history, the latter subject being treated mainly by the light of the Book of

Revelation. Never can he forget the earnest look in the bright young faces, as they listened to his attempts to expound to them the meaning of those symbolic visions to whose faithful study a special blessing has been divinely attached.

When it became manifest that Mrs. Saunders could not for the present leave her home, the momentous question was put to them all—Will the mother give up her daughters to go without her, and will the daughters have the courage to go without their mother? This question was settled by each of the three between herself and God. It was never so much as discussed among themselves. They felt that the call had come for them, and that they dared not disobey. They had learnt to believe fervently in the near Second Coming of Christ, and that they must —to use their own phrase—"hurry up," in order to witness for Him to the world before His coming. The anguish that this sacrifice caused to the mother's heart (not to speak of the daughters') is known only to herself and God, but never for one moment has she doubted that it was the right course to take.

"I see now," she said to the writer, "why I was not allowed to go with the girls. If I had gone too, these letters would never have been written." She fully hopes and believes that these letters will be an appeal to the Christian Church which will bear fruit in increased effort for the evangelisation of the heathen world, and especially of China.

The particular kind of work in China for which the sisters were preparing will be explained later on, and we can promise the reader, who peruses their peculiarly interesting letters, that he will be left with no vague and indefinite conception of what they were about in that country. For ourselves, we almost feel as if we should know our way about in the districts that they traversed, and recognise by sight the places and people to whom they introduce us.

At length the day of departure arrived. The mother was to accompany her daughters as far as Brisbane, and they left Melbourne by the express train for Sydney on the 10th of October 1893. After two days spent in Sydney, they embarked on board the s.s. *Menmuir*, bound for Hongkong, and on the 15th of October, in the harbour of Brisbane, mother and daughters took a final leave of one another. The watchword between them was—"Jesus only;" and, as if by mutual consent, no tears were shed at parting. "What a want of natural feeling!" some will say. But they don't know, and we do. At a later period, when the captain of the vessel was no longer a stranger, he confided to the girls that he would never forget the night at Brisbane when Nellie said, in answer to the mother's petition that he would take care of them, "We have Someone better!" And then Topsy's head went down on the rail, and there was no sound for a quarter of an hour after the tender went away.

CHAPTER II

FROM BRISBANE TO MANILA

Heart to heart—Glorious scenery—Sunday services—The baby organ—Manila and its inhabitants—Topsy's reflections and difficulties.

NELLIE writes to her mother :—

" S.S. *Menmuir, Wednesday,* 17*th October* 1893.—Yesterday was the first day without my dearest Petsy; it is so horrid not to have you here, dear, but 'Jesus doeth all things well,' so we know that this is all right, for it must be His will. I couldn't write yesterday because I felt too sick, and I couldn't see properly. How are you, dear? I hope you won't be very lonely; it is not like the Lord's faithfulness if you are, but I know you won't be. We aren't any of us sick to-day; Toppy and I, being the worst of the lot from the first, remained bad the longest, but we are all right now. I was glad for one reason that Mrs. J. came for you that night, because I could think of you at M. I know where you slept, and it was much nicer than you being in a strange coffee-palace.

" Do you know, I feel so upheld that I don't feel a bit miserable, and I thought I should be wretched. And then I try to conjure up a picture of you sad and lonely, and I can't do that either, because I don't believe you are either one or the other—'Satisfied with favour, and full with the

7

blessing of the Lord.' I don't understand why the Lord has fixed things like this, but I don't want to, and I am content. And we don't exactly know when He will let us be together again, but Jesus we *know*, and He is on the throne. All power is given unto Him, and He can do all things. Dear Petsy, I don't believe it will be long, and anyway, it does not do for us to be wanting to choose the way that He shall make us witnesses for Him.

"I thought I should just be horribly desperate, but the Lord is so good; I cannot help contrasting the way we felt last year in Sydney, just as home-sick as possible, but the Lord's promise is sure, and *He is* good indeed. I feel it so much on board here that 'unto them that believe *He is precious,*' but unto the others, those that don't believe, He is just a *stumbling-block.*"

Topsy writes :—

"I woke up with the words in my head—'While to the cross I cling, rest is sweet at Jesus' feet while homeward faith keeps winging.' It is the only place one can hope to rest, and it is indeed very sweet. I can't say I have any definite guiding, but I don't think this witnessing time will be very long.

"I don't want to chronicle very minutely my experiences for the benefit of the Christian public. There is only one dear little missus that would feel interested enough to want to know what I had for breakfast, dinner, and tea.

"If my dear Petsy were here we should like the voyage so much! I don't think that He minds us thinking that. Neh. viii.—'Send portions to them for whom nothing is prepared . . . and the joy of the Lord is your strength.'

I think that is very good for us three; don't you, dear? You sent two baskets to carry some portions to those that have nothing at all, and the joy of the Lord is strength for us all. I think of my dear always praying for us, and I know there will be definite results from those prayers. I thought that I never should be able to look at the sea with a calm inside, but now I am beginning to enjoy it quite well. Still, I shall not be sorry when the voyage is over and we get right into the work. It is a very lazy life, and when your slippers are finished, and my hat is trimmed, there will be nothing to do in the way of work.

"Yesterday Nellie and I felt longings after a kitten, so Ellie went to look for one. She went and asked the captain if there were any kittens on board, and when they looked round and inquired, the quartermaster said it had been left in Sydney, and there was only the 'shilling pup' [a dog belonging to the captain], so he sent Ellie up to know if we would like the calf instead. Imagine us with a calf instead of Koteck! I wonder if Fuhning [Koteck's sister] is getting big and handsome.

"I was reading in Ezra viii. this morning about the journey up to Jerusalem, and the genealogy of them that went from Babylon. 'And Ezra weighed into their hands talents of silver and gold, and said that they and the vessels were holy. Watch ye, keep them until ye weigh before the Chief of priests . . . in the chamber of the house of the Lord.' We have talents given us to keep, to watch for and deliver up in that day. Do you think that is a nice dig, Miss? [A 'dig' is a search into the meaning of Scripture.—ED.]

"We are getting close to Port Darwin now. This morning we passed an island 150 miles long; it is all cannibals. One party that went there from Port Darwin got rather the worst of it. Captain said at breakfast that it was a good field for missionaries — sarcastically, of course; and we asked him to put us down, but he said he had too much respect for us. I wish I could describe to you the sunset we saw the other night—every colour, from the deepest crimson to pale lavender, and such glorious white clouds, and framed in by masses of indigo green clouds; and the sea was all one mass of gold. I never saw anything so beautiful; just like a little bit of the glory not yet revealed."

The scenery of the islands in the vicinity of Point Darwin is thus described by Nellie :—

"We seem to be sailing through a great smooth lake. The water is not blue, but the sweetest *eau-de-nil*, and it shades off into all the variations of blue and green and grey and purple near the islands. All round, as far as you can see, there are islands, and they are beautiful in the morning haze of sunshine. You can see the outlines, even of those which are miles and miles away, as clearly as possible, and the colouring and shades on them are exquisite. The weather is so beautiful, too—as clear and bright as possible. We are not at all sick now; we go down to meals, and eat like anything. I am afraid we shall get extremely stout.

"These islands are glorious; I keep on stopping to look at them. One we are just approaching now—an irregular mass of orange-brown rock, covered in places with dull green bush, mixed with a sort of reddish-coloured furze, bordered with a vivid white line of beach, and then the pale green colour of the sea all round it, while behind it you see another island, rising as a sort of background in neutral tint, and the sea, as you look past the first island, becomes the deepest of blue indigo, and the colouring of the whole blends so beautifully that you can't help exclaiming at it. And to think that our Lord made it all; that just enhances the charm of everything, does it not? 'Something lives in every hue Christless eyes have never seen.' The man that wrote that hymn knew what he was talking about, that is certain. Last night we had the baby organ out; it is such a grand little one. We sang hymns ever such a long time, and one officer, Mr. R., came and sang too. All the others, including the military gentlemen, camped just outside and listened, and never went away till we had done. And then the most unsaved of the lot came and helped to put the baby organ to bed."

There were three other missionary ladies on board the *Menmuir,* all belonging to the China Inland Mission, and on their way to China. The five girls intended to hold private devotional meetings on Sundays in one of their own cabins, but, before the Sunday came, not only was the fame of the baby organ established, but the joyous outspoken faith of the missionaries had made an impression, and some of the ship's officers said, "It would be nice to hear the young ladies speak!"

Nellie writes:—

"I really don't know how it all got arranged that we were to have a service yesterday morning, except that we just simply asked the Lord to arrange it for us, and we were perfectly quiet about it all, and never spoke to a soul about it, except Mrs. H., who has been used in this piece of work by the Master to speak to some of the men about coming to the service. Mr. G. was very nice about it, and the captain could not come, as he has to be on duty nearly all the time just now; and so we had it all in our own hands—or rather the Lord arranged it according to His own good pleasure. As the time drew on, Mr. G. was really so good in getting everything fixed for us, and seemed so interested, that I thought it would be nice to ask him to read the lessons. So after consultation, in which we all agreed we must ask him, though we hoped he would refuse, I did so, and he turned and promptly said, 'No, he was too shy.' So I said, 'All right then, don't.' Ellie M'Culloch was chairman, and sat at the end of the table, in front of a cushion covered with the Union Jack, and everybody all round was provided with a very musty Bible and Prayer-book; but, of course, we did not take the 'form of prayer.' We had four hymns, 'Jesus my Saviour to Bethlehem came,' 'Pull for the shore, Sailor' (which took like anything), 'There is a Fountain,' and 'Have you any room for Jesus?' and Topsy and Ethel Reid spoke.

"Several of the engineers came, and the solitary woman in the second class; also a real Chinese lady, who was shipped on at Cooktown. She is going back to China with her husband; they are saloon passengers. She can't speak much English, but we have been talking to her a little. The next Sunday service was held when the vessel was at anchor off Manila. I must begin by telling you about the service on Sunday. We have made great

friends by this time with the second and third mates,
as well as with Mr. G.; and on Sunday morning at breakfast, though nothing had been said about having a service, they all three appeared, got up to kill, with lovely
white shirts, and their dark blue coats with the gold
braid and buttons on; they don't wear any waistcoats,
'cos it's too jolly hot.' We wondered why this was thus,
and thought they must be going ashore, perhaps, to the
Roman Catholic Cathedral, as the passengers were doing.
Topsy spoke to Mr. G. about having a service, as the
engineers had said the night before they would like to
have it. He pretended to be uncertain about it, and
so Toppy said, 'Oh! of course, it is just as you like;
we would have one for ourselves in any case, but it is
just whether any of the men would like to come to it.
We don't want to make a nuisance of ourselves.' He
growled out, 'Who said you were, I should like to
know? I will put his eye in a sling if I hear any one
say it.' Then he said that they *had* intended going
ashore, but if we were going to have a service they
would not go. So 'once more into the breach, dear
friends,' to raise the banner that the Lord has given us
to be upheld. For the second time the table, cushion,
Union Jack, and the musty prayer-books made their
appearance 'topside.' Topsy in the chair, Ellie and
Hettie for speakers, I as organist, and Ethel, stop-gap,
alongside of me; we had a grand little service. Mr. G.
and Mr. C. had a conversation about it afterwards, and
came to the conclusion, as C. confided to Topsy, that if
it were possible for a man to believe as we did he would
be a jolly lucky fellow.

"In the evening they all demanded the baby organ and hymns. It is really almost touching to see those great big things, that spend most of their time playing poker and drinking when we are not about, listening to the hymns, and they do like them so. 'Now the Day is Over' fetched them all completely. I do think it shows there is such a lot of good in people, even when they have been knocking about in sin and all sorts of things through their lives; and they are all so eager to talk, we never have to make an opportunity of speaking, because they rarely want to speak of anything else."

On Sunday Manila was reached, the capital of the Philippine Islands, one of the few remaining foreign possessions and colonies of Spain. Topsy writes :—

"This morning, at 4 A.M., we anchored off Manila. It looked so pretty in the dim morning light; just the sort of place one sees in the old Spanish pictures, ever so many of those dome-shaped buildings. I don't know what they are; I must ask some old Don. There has been an old Spanish Don on board, and he came in to talk to us just now. He is the stevedore, and he told us that if they knew on shore that we were missionaries, we should not find it over pleasant to be there. The place is in utter subjection to the priests; every one bows down literally before them. They have the Inquisition here too. Does it not seem dreadful to think of the hold they have on the people?

"We had a grand time yesterday over in the town. You would have enjoyed it so much. We landed at a narrow stone jetty, which also does duty for a road, with shops all along, open-fronted, and crowds of men, women, and children, more or less in a state of nature, chattering like monkeys. The lower classes are a mixture of Spanish and Malay, and generations have produced queer specimens of humanity. They wear very bright-coloured skirts twisted round their bodies, and funny little muslin tops very loose and *dégagé*. We drove all round in two little carts, and nearly got jolted to pieces, the roads being paved with blocks of stone not over neatly put together. We went out in the suburbs, too, among paddy fields, and that was really the prettiest thing I have ever seen. The roads are like lanes, and thickly lined with bamboos and all sorts of trees that I did not know the names of, and the houses are all very old and covered with beautiful hanging-creepers. Such queer old houses, that open right through and close up with folding doors. The river winds in and out through it all, and one keeps getting little glimpses of water through the trees, and as the sun went down it was per-fectly lovely. We went to the Lunetta in the evening, and saw all the Spanish beauties out driving with their Beppo Stalianos, and heard the band play pretty tunes. All the different regiments take it in turn. They do play so well, and we liked it immensely. It is all quite dif-ferent to anything we ever saw, and just like a story-book."

Nellie writes :—

"The great thing about Manila is the Lunetta; that is, a sort of Rotten Row, about as long as the Esplanade, not far from the sea-shore. Down the middle there is a wide place for a promenade, with the band-stand in the

centre, and several beautiful, cool-looking fountains.
Each side there is a carriage drive, and the carriages go
round and round, and everybody looks as worldly and
pleasure-loving as you can possibly imagine. At six the
fun begins, and lasts till ten or eleven. So having strolled
round and seen the town, we drove to the Lunetta; and
our carts went round and round with us in them. At
one end there is a grass plot with little tables and cane
chairs, and we got out and sat down and demolished ice
creams; after which we promenaded, to the admiration of
all beholders. I *never* saw anything like the way they
stared; simply turned and stared and nudged one another
to look, not rudely at all, but just as though struck all of
a heap; it was very funny. None of the real Spanish
ladies were visible in the daytime, but they all came to
the Lunetta in their carriages. They don't wear any hats,
and much the same kind of dress as our evening dress.
I was informed that this is the Manila winter. You
could not wish for more beautiful weather; but it is
quite as hot as the summer in Melbourne, only they
don't have north winds. All the ladies were in cool
summer dresses, and the men in white that evening,
just like a summer night in the middle of January in
Melbourne.

"We had such a splendid feast of Nature on Thursday last. Mr. G. got the company's steam launch, and
we went up the Manila river to a lake inland. The
scenery was splendid, the best I ever saw—the river very
wide, with thick vegetation, mostly bamboos, such lovely
ones, and little settlements of funny little native houses
built on long sticks, some reaching out into the water, and

we could see them cooking on tins over the water; they all cheered us, and every one seemed so pleased that we noticed them. It seems to be perpetual washing-day here. All up the banks in front of the houses were men and women, with a pocket-handkerchief tied round their waists, but otherwise in a state of nature, washing clothes in the river, and beating them on the rocks. Another thing that makes it so beautiful is the colouring; the sunsets are gorgeous, and light up the water, making it so pretty. We went for afternoon tea to such a nice Spanish house where three Englishmen live; they are in offices here; there are only about one hundred Europeans in all. These three are English, and very important men, but they were very nice to us, giving us luncheon and showing us all their establishment, including five ponies, two deer, endless dogs, a tortoise, &c. The Spanish houses are built so nicely, rambling up and down stairs, and having great verandas as wide as our dining-room is long, in fact wider, I think, and finished up with chairs and hanging lamps and pot plants. They always have *chow* (breakfast) on the veranda."

Much of their time at sea was spent by the ladies in united Bible study, and many were the discussions which took place among them on the sublimest subjects. Something of this appears in the following quaint mingling of theology, humour, and pathos in which Topsy addresses her mother:—

"I have been endeavouring to solve a problem the whole day. I will tell you what it is, to relieve my feelings, as I can't come and argue the point, as usual. The many discussions we have had about Christians on this

B

boat raised a point in my mind that I cannot just yet satisfactorily settle. How far are believers released from the power and effect of sin in their lives? I believe that we are freed from *all* the guilt of sin as soon as the blood of Christ is applied by faith, but as to the extent that hereditary sin and acquired sin are driven from possession, I don't quite see. The theory is easy enough, I suppose, and I got a lift by remembering Mr. Berry on that subject, on Moule's Outlines; but when one comes to look into the *daily experience* of nearly every Christian life, one does not see the theory carried out; not even in the Old Testament characters, nor even in the New Testament ones; there does not seem to be one man who has not got a fair slice of self left in his composition; even Paul and Barnabas came to smash over next door to a trifle. Moule says it is the imperfect receptivity of Christians that prevents that. Well, I say, what prevents the receptivity? I suppose it is a form of unbelief, but if you ask for cleansing entire, one only gets it up to a certain point. I suppose growth comes in then. All this makes one think that we are not to look for a state here in which it is possible to be without sin; not that I want, therefore, to settle down and take it easy, but I think there is so much confused teaching on this subject that really I have nothing at all on the subject but some wild ideas of my own. I intend taking the subject up and going into it as straight as possible, and I am not going to leave off till I get something properly definite. I have relieved my feelings considerably, although I expect you think the sea air is having a bad effect on my brain, and that what little there was of it is evaporating. I suppose it is a case of live and learn. Then another thing about it is, that we take so many different views of what is right and wrong; that is another confusing point. Certainly the Bible is clear enough, but it is not easy to dig deep enough all at once to find out the real truth. I am convinced of one thing, *i.e.*, that we must grow—not jump—into things: first get planted, *of course*, but after that I believe it is 'shining more and more unto the perfect day.' Oh, I wish that day were here now. I do feel so weary sometimes of everything. You must not think I am groaning, dear, at being sent away. I know that it is all right, but I suppose it is my nature to live in the clouds and come dropping down to earth again occasionally, and it *hurts*. I would give anything I possess for one half-hour with you at home now! I know exactly what it is like, so quiet and peaceful; and we could sit on the veranda or on the grass, and the frogs in the pond would croak, and it would be so nice. And instead of that, we are here, in a boat, going further and further away every minute. 'Consider Him who bore such contradiction. Ye have not resisted unto blood.' Yes, I think we know what it is to shed heart's blood on the banner. I think it is good of God to use us; we are so unworthy. If He can lead one soul home through our sacrifice, what joy it will be, when we are at home, to think that here He called us to follow right in His very footsteps; to see those blood-marks all the way along that mountain-track, as He went to look for His lost sheep—those other sheep that must be brought in too; His kind, loving heart cannot bear to see one missing that He died to save. 'Except a corn of wheat fall into the ground and die it abideth *alone;* without Me ye can do nothing.' Death means a great deal. I wonder if there is a deeper meaning in the words—'I am crucified with Christ.' It was such a lingering death, wasn't it? 'Rest is sweet at Jesus' feet, as homeward, HOMEWARD, faith keeps winging.' Make haste, my beloved. 'Surely I come quickly. Amen. Even so come, Lord Jesus.'

" Do you think I am very dumpy to-night, dear heart? I don't think it is dumpy altogether, but it is all sorts of things that have not any names, so far as I know. My dictionary does not contain enough words to express all my feelings; so far, they are only things to be felt, and I can't always write my feelings. When we get right into the work it will not be so bad—not because I shall forget, but because there will be the responsibility of souls to look after for Him, and a definite work to do. It amuses me when people say that time wears off the edge. If time does anything for me, it is the exact opposite. I want you a great deal more to-night than I did that Monday night that you went away. I don't think that people know what they are talking about when they say things like that. The idea of a few weeks or years being able to extinguish *yourself,* because that is what it amounts to. I don't see how people can shut their eyes to this fact, that the Lord must come back soon. Perhaps it seems so to me more now because I want it. And others, weary of things many years ago, may have thought so too, just because they wanted it. But then, on the other hand, there is so much of that 'falling away' too; so much carelessness and disregard for good. On all hands one meets with that most painfully common form of unbelief, the disbelief in the divinity of Christ. It is just awful, I think. After all this growling you will want something nice, won't you, dear? But I know I am always safe in growling to my dear Petsy."

CHAPTER III

HONGKONG AND FOOCHOW

Terrors of the China Sea—Kindness of the officers—Leave-taking—
Hongkong to Foochow—The Stewart children—Archdeacon
Wolfe and Mr. Stock—A Chinese feast—Translating names—
Received one cat—Native conference—Need for workers—Mis-
sionary work in Fuh Kien province—Chinese Missions in general
—Mr. and Mrs. Stewart—Destination of the Misses Saunders.

NELLIE writes:—"Saturday, at 4 P.M., we left Manila.
That night we slept peacefully, and awoke on Sunday
morning to all the horrors of the China Sea. I never
knew before what it was to be *really* sea-sick. About
eleven I was dragged out on the lower deck and planted
in a chair, in which I remained till it capsized, and nearly
smashed me to atoms. Then I went inside and lay on the
bath-room floor, an utter wreck, till after dinner, when
Mr. C. came again and dragged me out; this time on to
the hatch. He and the captain were the only ones not
sick. You would have laughed if you had seen us—utter
wrecks, far too bad to be sick—lying on rugs and pillows
on that hatch. We remained there from Sunday night
till this (Tuesday) morning, when we reached Hongkong
at nine o'clock. I feel very bad still; *very weak*, and
scarcely able to eat at all. We are going ashore to-
morrow to the Mission place. Mrs. Bennett, the secretary's wife, was down here this morning, and we are

going there to-morrow. Anything like the kindness of the captain and officers you can't imagine."

Topsy writes:—" HONGKONG.—We are nearly dead! The run across the China Sea was indescribably awful. They said it would be rough, and so it was; the boat nearly rolled into the middle of next week. I feel almost too weak to write. They were all awfully good to us— brought our mattresses out on the hatch, and made us stay there all the time, and we had an awning rigged up to keep the spray off. The water was just washing the decks. No one could have looked after us better than our three cavaliers, getting arrowroot and all sorts of things. They all longed for a camera to take us. I dare say it did look funny. We were all camped on that hatch, where I took up my lodgings the first day, and from Sunday morning till this morning we only moved to interview the fishes. We were more sorry than I can tell you to leave the dear old boat."

It will be apparent from the foregoing extracts that quite a friendship had sprung up between our missionary ladies and the officers of the *Menmuir*. The girls never forgot their kindness, and the feeling on the other side has been shown by visits made to "The Willows," when the *Menmuir* was at Melbourne, and by many offers to convey parcels and presents to China. An officer of the *Haitan* has also borne recent testimony to the good impression made by our heroines during their short stay on board that vessel, between Hongkong and Foochow.

Topsy writes :—" Our luggage promised to be an awful nuisance when it was all got out. Captain said there was so much, they would charge us overweight on the *Haitan*, the Foochow steamer. However, we came out top there, as we generally do, because Mr. G. undertook to look after it, and went and interviewed the first mate, and we are not going to be charged at all. That is good—is it not? So we left on Wednesday morning; they hung over the side and looked so sad as we sailed off in our sampan. We promised to go back the next day and stay to *chow*. It was really necessary that we should do so, because our luggage had to go off in sampans to the *Haitan*, and though we knew they would do all that was necessary, still it did not seem nice to clear out and not go back again, when they had been so kind. That was without consulting our own feelings on the subject, which were much in favour of staying on board. The good people at the Mission are very kind to us. I think they consider us rather too independent, but being Australians accounts for everything."

At Hongkong the missionary party from the *Menmuir* were hospitably received at the house of the Rev. Mr. Bennett, local secretary to the Church Missionary Society, Mrs. Bennett going on board the vessel to welcome them. A few days were spent in this port, but exhaustion after the sea-sickness, and the necessary business of packing and transhipment, left but little time for sight-seeing.

Nellie writes:—"We left Hongkong on Sunday, the 19th November, at ten o'clock. Last year, on the 19th November, we went down to see Mr. Stewart off in the *Victoria*. This year, on the same date, we left Hong-kong for Foochow."

Our travellers had now taken leave of their three friends and fellow-passengers of the China Inland Mission, and

were joined by the four youngest children of Mr. and Mrs.
Stewart and their faithful nurse, Lena, who, with her
charge, arrived at Hongkong by an English steamer only
just in time to catch the boat for Foochow.

Nellie writes :—"The little Stewarts comprise two girls
and two boys—Mildred and Kathleen, Herbert and the
baby—a great big thing, rather more than a year old.
The girls are dear little things, very fair, and they have
nice gentle manners."

Topsy writes :—"At length on the borderland of our
work. We got in from Hongkong, as we prophesied,
more dead than alive. Some of the folks came down to
meet us. All the boats anchor down the harbour, and the
people came down in the house boat and the steam launch
for us. After *chow* we sailed up the river for one hour
and a quarter, and finally landed. There was a whole
crowd down to carry the new arrivals off to different
places. Miss Wolfe came for us. Mr. Stock has been at
them for the last four or five mails, to be sure and take
the greatest possible care of us, and a room was reserved
for us at the Archdeacon's all through the conference.

"We got four letters from Mr. Stock waiting for us
here, full of the most fatherly advice. We nearly had
forty fits when we read them all. He is a dear good man,
and it was awfully kind of him to write so that we should
get the letters just then. We have fallen head over ears
in love with the Archdeacon. He is such a nice old thing,
something like Archdeacon L., only not so fat.

"We have just returned from a Chinese feast. I must
tell you about it. It was held in the boys' school, and
little square tables were placed up the hall, holding about

six people each. In the middle of the table was a large bowl, replaced by another every now and then. I think we had eight centre dishes in all, and all round them were little saucers full of sweets, *i.e.*, smoked melon seeds, peanuts rolled in sugar, beef boiled and beaten till it looked exactly like pink tow. Each one was provided with a little dish and a sugar-spoon and chopsticks. It is manners to dip your chopsticks into the centre supply, and then stuff them into your mouths. It makes one's inside turn rather when one sees all the sticks fishing, and their not overclean mouths. Then we had bowls of stuff like vermicelli in brown soup to ladle into our mouths with chopsticks, or else rice; I took rice, as it looked to be the cleanest; it smelt just like the scullery does when it is full of the smell of steam and boiling clothes. However, we enjoyed ourselves immensely, and came home to a good wholesome meal.

"Miss Wolfe has some of her Bible women to tea this afternoon; they have such nice faces, so intelligent and kind.

"The Archdeacon has christened us; that is the first performance, and a very important one too, because if we get the wrong name, it is a great nuisance afterwards.

"Nellie is Sung Ku-niong, and I am Sung Ne Ku-niong. Ku means 'set apart, sacred'; Niong means 'lady'; Sung is Chinese for Saunders; Ne means 'second.' [Their Christian names also required translating, and were rendered—'Na-li' and 'To-si.' The latter is said to mean 'much silk.']

"We have got such a dear little kitten from the *Haitan;* Mr. Douglas sent it up this morning; it is to go up with us, and will be so useful to catch the mice. His name is

Grim; at present he is rolled up on my bed asleep. He
came up in the launch this morning, and a coolie brought
him up in a basket; we had to sign the delivery sheet for
one cat.' I think they had a most queer idea of what we
were like. Mr. Eyton Jones, one of the Fuh Ning missionaries, told us that he got a letter from Mr. F., saying
that there were two ladies coming from Australia who
would not work at all unless they could do it on their
own lines.

"There has been a native conference all this week. It
is splendid to see them gathered in from all parts of the
province in the big college hall. The catechists all speak
—some each night—and report on their year's work. Of
course it is a bit slow, not being able to understand; but
they have such splendid faces, some of them, and speak
with such conviction. Some of them require interpreters,
the dialects even in one province being so different. One
funny little man got up to speak, and no one could make
him out, so they called for an interpreter. Evidently what
he said was very funny, for the people laughed and laughed
till they nearly burst. The look of him was enough; he
did comedy man to perfection.

"I wish you would tell them all that there really is such
a lot to be done here, and it does not need wonderfully
gifted people, but just hard-working, patient, Holy Ghost
Christians; and medical missions, too. There is a hospital
in Foochow with a doctor, but no nurses. They scrape
along with a Chinese woman, and, of course, the place is
dirty; *que voulez vous!* Tell Matron that Foochow would
suit her all to nothing. They want every one, but men
particularly, though there is a great demand for women.

Such invitations from the natives to come and teach them, and no one to send! In the Ho-Chiang district there are hundreds of Christians, and one lady only who is able to visit them. When will the Christians wake up?"

The native conference referred to is an important annual Synod, and consists of about three hundred persons, representatives of thirteen thousand native members of the Church of England in the province of Fuh Kien. The other Protestant denominations have at least an equal number of baptized members.

While our travellers are expecting the arrival of Mr. and Mrs. Stewart at Foochow, it seems the proper place to give some account of the work in which they were about to take part. The province of Fuh Kien, of which Foochow, on the river Min, is the port and capital, is about equal in area to England without Wales, and has a population estimated at twenty millions. The cities are numerous and large, and several of them are the centres of missionary districts under the superintendence of Arch-deacon Wolfe. Ku Cheng, a city of about fifty thousand inhabitants, is situated about ninety miles inland from Foochow, and on the same river (Min), but at an elevation of about one thousand feet above the sea. It lies in a beautiful valley, flanked by lofty mountains, and imme-diately above it—about 1500 feet higher up, and about twelve miles distant—is the little village of Hua Sang, which the missionaries of the station have been accus-tomed to use as a sanatorium, but which has now an evil reputation from the terrible tragedy which occurred there on the first of August last. The head of the Church Missionary Society's station at Ku Cheng was the Rev.

R. W. Stewart, and under him was a staff of native clergymen, catechists, and schoolmasters, distributed over a district about as large as Yorkshire. But, inasmuch as men can do little or nothing for the benefit of the native women, there were, in addition to these, thirteen ladies of the Zenana Missionary Society, whose work in superintending the work of native Bible-women, and visiting and teaching in conjunction with these latter, was found to be invaluable, especially in the numerous villages of this great district. In Ku Cheng itself there is also a foundling institution, under Miss Nisbitt, of which a photograph is reproduced on another page; and a boarding school for girls, under Miss Weller.

Besides the Church Missionary Society, there are in the great province of Fuh Kien stations of the American Congregationalist and American Episcopal Methodist Churches, and in the south others belonging to the Presbyterians and the London Missionary Society. Fuh Kien, with its twenty millions, is only one of the eighteen great provinces of China. Protestant missionaries have been at work in this vast empire since 1844, and there are now about fifteen hundred missionaries and about a hundred thousand converts. The largest Protestant Missionary Society in China, though the most recent, is the China Inland Mission, founded in 1865; but we are not aware that it has any stations in the province of Fuh Kien.

Mr. and Mrs. Stewart arrived in Foochow from their furlough in England about the first week in December. The biography of these devoted servants of God will, no doubt, be written soon. They had laboured together for sixteen years in China, eight of which had been spent

in Ku Cheng. To this city and district they were now
returning after an absence of five years, during which
time their place had been taken by Mr. and Mrs. Bannister. After some deliberation, it was decided that the
Misses Saunders should accompany the Stewart party,
and spend the period of their probation at Ku Cheng.
It was intended that they should afterwards settle at
Ning Taik, a city in the eastern part of Fuh Kien, with
their mother to keep house for them. In the accompany-
ing map we have endeavoured to show the position of the
principal places mentioned in the following pages.

FUH-KIEN PROVINCE

CHAPTER IV

FOOCHOW TO KU CHENG

Embarking on the house boat—River scenery—Chinese lessons—
Various costumes—Walk by the river-side—An idol temple—A
photograph—Slow progress—A favourable breeze—Landing—
Early start next morning—Chair coolies—Travellers' difficulties
—A rapid march—A friendly crowd—Objections to English
dress—Chinese refreshments—Capsize of Nellie's chair—Native
bridge—Ku Cheng—A warm welcome—The Mission compound
—Sunday services—The question of dress.

NELLIE writes:—" Wednesday, the 13th December, we
started for Ku Cheng; our loads consisted of a pair of
native baskets, full of bedding, the baby organ, the
'kitchen,' and the spotted 'handkerchiefs.'[1] We went
down, and all the Wolfe family to see us off, to the Bund
(landing-place) at one o'clock, and found the M'Clellands
and Mr. Starr already there. We were supposed to start at
1.30, but it was quite 2.30 before the Stewarts appeared;
their luggage—piles of it—was coming on all the time.
Everybody came to see us off. I think Dr. Rigg is the
only notable one I have not mentioned." [Dr. Rigg had
recently been roughly handled by a mob, and had nar-
rowly escaped the horrible fate of being thrown into a
cess-pit.] "I am sure he is a splendid fellow. He has been
very ill, and so has his wife, but she is recovering now, and

---

[1] These were names of certain boxes. The latter were so called because
Nellie had protested against their purchase, declaring that the rest of her
belongings could go "in a spotted handkerchief."

when she is all right they are going back to England.
It is uncertain whether they will ever come back. He
came to see us off, and so did Mr. Lloyd, with a detach-
ment of Church of England Zenana ladies under his wing.

"At last we started. We have a large house-boat
and a small one. The party consists of the Stewarts,
their four children, and Lena (the nurse); Miss Johnson,
of Nang Wa, who has been in Foochow nursing Mrs.
Rigg; Mr. Starr, Topsy, and I. The house-boat we are
on belongs to Jardine's Company. The house part consists of a grand little saloon, with a bedroom and kitchen
at the back, and right aft there is accommodation for the
Chinese servants. The luggage is mostly in a sort of hold,
and forward there are hatches that one can sit on to
admire the view. Just at present that is where we are
sitting in the bright sun; and how am I to describe the
scenery? The river is very wide, but not deep, with the
mountains on each side towering above it. They are very
grand-looking, but give one unconsciously a sort of desolate feeling. Every here and there you see clumps of
olives and lichees (a native fruit tree), but for the most
part the mountains are perfectly bare, and you *do* miss
the gums so! I am writing rather under difficulties,
because on the other side of this hatch (two feet square)
there is a Chinese lesson going on. Mr. Stewart, with my
fur cloak on, is teaching Topsy, Ellie, and Kathleen to say
Chinese tones, and in between my thoughts and medita-
tions I hear 'Chung' (in a very high voice), 'Chung'
(lower down), 'Chaong,' 'Chank,' &c. It is very beautiful
to see the lights and shades on these mountains as the
afternoon draws on. The picture right ahead just now is

O

almost perfect; the hills rising one above another away into
the distance, all softened with a bluish grey mist, and
the river lying at the foot of these hills, with here and
there a native boat creeping slowly along under the light
evening breeze, and above the highest summit, far, far
away, the golden clouds of the sunset. I think the natives
must be rather amused at the variety of our costumes—
Mr. Stewart in his clergyman's clothes; Mrs. Stewart,
Topsy, and I in our ordinary things; Frances Johnson in
native dress; and Mr. Starr in a tourist's costume, with
a Norfolk jacket, knickerbockers, and magnificent plaid
stockings. In the morning Mr. Stewart and Mr. Starr,
we three Kuniongs, and Millie and Kathleen, went for
a walk. We got out of the house-boat, and, climbing up
the rocks on the river beach, walked along the little path
on the mountains leading by the river side. We enjoyed
it very much. There were a good many trees, and in one
place there were fields in which the natives were tying the
dry grass into bundles for the buffaloes, or else for burning, and it smelt just like hay, and the whole place looked
so pretty. Every now and then the path would lead us
out on to the top of some great cliff, or along the steep
sides, and then you could look over the edge on to the
rocks down by the river; and across the river you see the
mountains on the other side casting deep shadows in the
water. There are great clumps of grass and reeds, and a
sort of New Zealand flax growing among the rocks on the
sides of the mountains. Twice in the course of our promenade we came across heathen temples, the first being
on the edge of the rocks, projecting over the river. It
made such a pretty picture; the narrow path took us past

it, between the very edge of the rock and the temple wall.
The priest came out and wiggled his hands at us, and
seemed charmed when Mr. Stewart addressed him in his
own language. 'Ping ang!' he remarked. 'Ping ang!' said
Mr. Stewart, and then a conversation ensued which ended
in our being taken into the temple. I hate seeing them
—the idols are ranged along one side in three compart-
ments. The middle one contained the 'Three precious
ones'—three ugly grinning beasts, but made of brass or
something that looked like it, and with swell ornamenta-
tion round their distinguished necks. The others were
less important, and the last compartment contained *the
most frightful-looking horrors*, namely, the Jall (white
devil) and the short black devil. You *never saw* such
awful objects; they give you shivers only to look at them,
but I dare say they are a faithful portrait; Satan ought
to know what his servants look like. Then we came to
another temple, a much larger one, the outside of which
is painted red, with Chinese characters in gold and black.
There was a large bell hanging up, which is rung by a
piece of rope attached to a block of wood which strikes
against the side of the bell, making a deep solemn sound
that reminds one of a death knell. There was a huge
banyan just outside—such a beauty; in fact there were a
good many banyans along there, and any amount of tall
flax and climbing plants. In one part there was a great
quantity of a good-sized tree, covered with a beautiful
white flower, like quince-blossom, only white; and another
tall tree which looked very pretty, with its autumn coat of
red and yellow leaves, and clusters of white berries among
them. Mr. Starr is a great person for taking photos, and

he was anxious to take a group of the company in some
place which would give an idea of the scenery; so just
about this time we stopped in a very pretty place, and
Mr. Starr, standing with his camera in an elevated position, got us to look pretty in a good place, as foreground
in a most lovely view across the river. Imagine a path
curling over a deep creek, and enclosing a clump of trees
near a big rock overgrown with flax and fern, and close to
it a paddy field. A paddy field is generally more or less
of a bog, and this one had to be crossed from the other
side in order to reach the big rock, which was to be in
the foreground of the photograph. On the top of the
rock behold me and Kathleen Stewart in elegant atti-
tudes, with flax drooping gracefully at one side; Milly is
leaning against the front of the rock, and just on my
right, beside the rock, is Mr. Stewart; then farther on,
in the middle of the paddy field, behold Topsy with a
sun-bonnet on, looking truly picturesque; Miss Johnson,
holding a large white umbrella, is on Topsy's right, but on
a firm piece of ground. The amusement that was caused
by Mr. Starr's cool request, that Topsy would plant herself
in the middle of the bog, was long lived. We had really a
lovely walk. It is pretty hot walking in the middle of the
day, and we were very glad to have our dinner. In the
afternoon we sat on the hatches and wrote letters, and did
some Chinese with Mr. Stewart. He is a very good teacher.

"*Friday, 15th December.*—This morning we had another
lovely walk, but have been making very slow progress all
day. If the wind is with you you can get to Sui Kau in
three days, or perhaps a little less, but your progress
varies with the state of the wind. When there is no

wind the Chinese sailors, or coolies, or whatever you call them, row us along, or else 'pole' with long bamboo poles. This performance causes great contortions and a large amount of yelling and screaming, but you only get along at the rate of a quarter of a mile an hour, so that you have plenty of time for meditation. It is not *always* that one has such beautiful weather as we have had; scarcely a bit cold, though we are prepared for Arctic regions. Sometimes it takes a week to get to Sui Kau, and it *might* rain the whole time, as it did the last time Mrs. Stewart went up.

"This afternoon we had some hymn-singing, the baby organ coming in very useful. One hymn, that I never noticed before, we had first; it is a tremendous favourite of Mr. Stewart's—'God Holds the Key'—I think it is 592 in 'Consecration and Faith,' and such a beautiful hymn it is! He holds the key that is going to open the door for you, my dearest Petsy. I think it will be directly. I do long to see you again, my dear own Petsy. After some more Chinese with Mr. Stewart, we had afternoon tea, and then we went for a scramble over the rocks. All day there had not been a breath of wind, and eighteen more miles to Sui Kau. No human possibility of getting up to-night! But the Lord must have intended that we should get up, so as not to have to travel on Sunday. We had tea, and still no breeze! But about seven o'clock a smart strong wind came—so strong that we were nearly blown aground once or twice—and now, at a quarter to ten on Friday evening, 15th December, here we are at Sui Kau. All day to-morrow in chairs, and Ku Cheng on Sunday! This lovely river trip is over; I am sorry, for it was very nice. But now it will be real business. The inhabitants of the other house-boat have just left us. We have to pack our small belongings to-night, and get up at 5.30 to-morrow. I said I didn't think it was worth while going to bed, but no one seems to agree to that. Good night! my dearest dear Petsy! 'He is able to do exceeding abundantly above all that we can *ask* or *think*.'

"We got up and dressed by lamplight at five o'clock, and had breakfast at six or a little after, and by seven ourselves and our things were out on the river beach, with a group of admiring Chinks all round. The ground rises very much from the beach, and half-way up there is a Chinese village, from which proceeded a string of youngsters, dirty and ragged, to look at the foreigners. The group was really picturesque. The chair coolies are a most awful-looking lot. They are opium-eaters, and the lowest of all the classes. Mr. Bannister sent native chairs and coolies for us from Ku Cheng, and they arrived on Friday night; and the comical covered native chairs, and the awful-looking coolies, and the Chinese crew carrying the luggage off the house-boat, made a very remarkable scene.

"Poor Mr. Stewart had rather a time of it. Once when I looked round I saw him with the baby in his arms, trying to cram his wife and Herbert, with their effects, into a small native chair, talking at the same time to some of the coolies, who were all shrieking at the top of their voices at once; while behind him Mr. Starr, in the tourist garb, was doing his level best to extricate himself from some difficulties connected with his camera, which the coolies objected to, and at the moment I saw him he was appealing from behind to Mr. Stewart, imploring him to come to his aid with some Chinese. And Kathleen, meanwhile, plied the unhappy man with endless questions about everything, standing as nearly as possible right in his way. I captured her at last, and got her to come with me. The first part of the cavalcade started about 7.30. We could not have done it a moment sooner. It is very difficult to get a Chinaman to move; they don't seem to have any idea of the value of time. We walked on—Frances Johnson, the two little girls, and Topsy and I, and our chairs followed us. When we had gone about half-an-hour's walk we got to some height above the village, from which we could see the starting-place, and Messrs. Stewart and Starr were just leaving the place. We walked till about eleven o'clock—a narrow, little, stony path—over hill and down dale. Down ever so far below, you can see the river rushing along, and paddy fields, so trim and particular-looking, lying along the river-side. The mountains tower above right up into the sky, tier above tier, and if there were only more trees the scenery would be perfectly beautiful; but you do miss the trees. We had to get a certain distance done, and it was a case of hurry up, so there was very little stopping to look at the view. About twelve it got very hot, and we got into our chairs and were carried for a while. We had cut two pine saplings to help us to walk over the stones and up the hills, but they were not in the least elegant.

" Just about noon we passed through one village, rather a large one, and immediately there was a crowd round us —men, women, and children—whose curiosity was something astonishing. Frances was with us, and Mrs. Stewart, and they talked to them. I had on my thick woollen gloves, and presently I pulled one off, which was greeted

with a chorus of admiration. I presented it to one lady
to try on, which she did with great satisfaction. We
could only grin at them, but they seemed very pleased
with us. One thing one has to remember is this, that in
China you must not have a waist. They think an Eng-
lishwoman's figure nothing more or less than shocking.
It is much the same to them as if we were to see a lady
parading the streets in tights; so you must wear your
things very loose. Chinese dress, of course, obviates the
difficulty at once, but if you don't wear that you must
wear a loose cloak or dress that conceals the figure. Now,
though Mrs. Stewart and I knew this, we forgot all about
it, and both of us having on tight-fitting bodies were
much commented on. Topsy, having on her out-door
jacket, was all right, and Frances wears Chinese dress.
Mrs. Stewart, who understood what they said, took refuge
in her chair, with the baby on her knee. The Chinese
admire the little fair children very much indeed, but can't
understand how they manage to have white hair at such
an early age. For the next village I donned my big
jacket, and so passed muster, being decent. One man
noticed our sticks, and evidently their use was explained
to him by one of our coolies; but he didn't think they
were nice sticks, so off he went, and presently I saw him
coming through the crowd with a lovely ash stick—such
a smooth straight stick. He was so pleased with himself,
and we smiled and grinned at him, and he looked happier
still. At last, by walking pretty fast and riding in our
chairs a good part of the time, we got to the half-way
place about 1.30. We were very hungry and hot, and we
would have liked a little tiffin, but the food baskets were

miles behind, and, of course, we could not think of waiting,
so we went into a Chinese inn, and on a table in one of
the back rooms we had our bowls and chopsticks put, and
we each had a bowl of the most disgusting stuff, like
long strings of vermicelli, only made of Chinese flour,
and tasting very much like bad paste. This, with some
doubtful-looking cakes, and a drink of condensed milk—
which was the only thing Mrs. Stewart had brought with
her in the chair—was our mid-day meal! Oh! I forgot,
we each had an orange after. At each of these villages
our coolies—every man of them—went into one of the
opium places to smoke a little before starting again.
They hate having to do the whole distance from Sui
Kau to Ku Cheng in one day, but they understand pretty
well that if an Englishman says it must be done, he
means what he says. But you have to wait till they have
had a little smoke, whatever happens. When we came out
from having our luncheon, all the chairs were standing
about, and the coolies were having their smoke. Mr.
Stewart was sitting in his chair reading, and mine was at
the other side of the street, three feet away. It struck me
that I would fix my *meing* a little more comfortably, so I
crawled half into my chair and began tugging at the
meing to get it out, when I became aware that the whole
concern was capsizing—and capsize it did !—straight over,
with me inside. I heard an exclamation from Mr. Stewart,
and every one began making remarks, and Mr. Starr rushed
up from somewhere, but as he passed Topsy's chair—just
in front of mine—Mr. Stewart told him not to go near
me. He had not moved himself, knowing the Chinese so
well, and what they might say ; but Brother Starr came to

the rescue, and seized the side of my chair to haul it back, but I called out to him not to do so, as I could crawl out quite well, and I did so when I had finished giggling. They all laughed at me very much. The chair was right on the edge of a dirty gutter. Wasn't it a good thing I did not go in?

"After we passed that village the scenery got more and more beautiful. I can't describe it; but there is one place where you cross a native bridge, and where the mountains are covered with a tall feathery bamboo, and more trees than you can see in most other places, and they rise one above another ever so high. Just at your feet there is a most beautiful waterfall, and the river rushes down over the rocks foaming and gurgling, and the beauty of the whole scene is really like a fairy land. There is such a grand solemn quietness over it all, one cannot help being impressed by it. But it was a forced march, and we had not as much time as one would like to take it all in. Oftener than not the trip is done in two days, so that gives you an idea of how we flew. The Bannisters were not expecting us till Monday night next at the *earliest*, knowing that we would not travel into Ku Cheng on a Sunday, and thinking it quite impossible for us to be up on Saturday. But we did it, and about 6.15 we entered the city of Ku Cheng, and travelled along the path just inside the wall towards the ferry. About half-way along we were met by a number of Chinese catechists—about a dozen of them; the news that the party had arrived had flown like wildfire, and reached the ears of the Chinese Christians, and they came to welcome 'Su Senang' (their name for Mr. Stewart), their much-loved teacher of former years. It was so touching to see the greeting those men gave

him, and then they all accompanied us right along to
the gate which leads through the city wall on to the
river beach, where the ferry-boat is, and where there were
more Christians. Such a loving welcome from them;
they *were* so delighted to see Mr. Stewart again; some
of them had not known him before, but most of them
were old friends. Then the ferry-boat appeared, and Mr.
Bannister's hearty voice welcoming us. Topsy and Mrs.
Stewart and Kathleen had arrived before us and gone
across, and the rest of us got in and were ferried over.
The boys' school was down on this side of the river to
welcome us. 'But, you know, there are *no Christians
among the Chinese.*' Oh! we *did* eat a good supper that
evening, but we excused ourselves by relating our day's
experience. I don't think I *could* describe how tired we
were; my legs ached, my feet were *awfully* sore, and my
ankles felt as though they had been badly sprained, though
I wore boots. But we had a good night's rest, and were
very glad to be in Ku Cheng instead of in the Chinese
inn. The large compound here contains four houses.
The Bannisters', where we are now staying, will probably
be empty by the time you get this, as they are going to
Foochow College in January or the beginning of February.
Mr. Stewart's house is just a few yards away, separated
by a wall. It is two-storey, and a very comfortable-look-
ing one. On the same side, but lower down, is the baby-
house (for foundlings), under the charge of Ada Nisbitt
and Annie Gordon. The fourth house occupies the fourth
corner, and is known as 'The Olives,' being the Church of
England Zenana establishment. On Sunday morning we
attended Divine service in the Chinese church. It *was*

nice. Mr. Bannister and Sing Mi conducted the service, and Sing Mi preached; and then Mr. Bannister and Mr. Stewart conducted the Communion Service. The singing was very so-so, every one, except the two schools and the English people, singing a little tune of their own, with no particular time. The Chinese beat the record in the responses, and they gabbled the general confession faster than any one I have heard do it before; Mr. Bannister and Mr. Stewart came in at the end a bad second, 'Sik sing si ngwong,' which means, 'Amen, I truly desire it.'

"The next morning there was a wonderful performance. About twenty or thirty Christian Chinamen, with a string of lesser lights, came with a sound of music, making day hideous, to welcome 'Su Senang' (Mr. Stewart) back again. They brought two or three little scrolls, which they hung up on the walls, and there was a great speechifying, and afterwards a long palaver in the Bannisters' Chinese reception-room. In the afternoon we did some Chinese with Mr. Stewart, and this morning (the 19th) we had our first lesson with our Chinese teacher. I know six or seven characters quite well now; can pick them out, and I know how to say them properly. He is a tiny little shrimp. We have decided that as we shall probably be here for a year, it will be really a saving to keep our own things and wear native dress here, as all the other sisters do it. So we are going to have a red skirt each, which will come to about $2.30 each, and one coat made of native blue stuff, which will come to about $5 for the two. We think it will be more economical in the end, and came to this decision after much weighty confabulation with Mrs. Stewart and the Kuniongs."

CHAPTER V

CHRISTMAS AT KU CHENG

Chinese lessons and music lessons—Politeness of the Chinese—
Christmas decorations—Donning native dress—Farewell to Mr.
Bannister—The ferry-boat—Mission-school girls—A Chinese
congregation—Fire baskets—Praise of Mr. Bannister—Privations—Chinese delicacies—Topsy's studies—Furniture—The
doctor's orders—Topsy on love—Health and diet—Christmas
tree—Dress again—Thoughts of home.

NELLIE writes:—"It is so funny to think I am writing
this three days before Christmas, and that it will perhaps
be well on in February by the time you get it. I do wish
you could be here. Being Church Missionary Society, we
live with the Bannisters till the Stewarts get straight.
We began Chinese with our teacher, Wong Senang (Mr.
Wong), last Tuesday. It is so pleasant having Mr. Stewart;
he is in and out all the time, and he superintends and tells
us the English of things we don't understand. He is a
dear old thing; he parades round the place in a huge pith
helmet, and after meals you hear the melodious sound of
his cornet, playing hymn tunes, and occasionally he and Mrs.
Stewart have concerts. There was a terrible concert going
on this afternoon when I came into the Bannisters' drawing-room, Mr. Bannister with his violin and Mr. Stewart
with the cornet. I told them the police were coming!

Topsy and I go over first thing after breakfast to the
Stewarts, and we have our Chinese in their back rooms.
This afternoon we went for a walk over the hills with
Mrs. Stewart, and when the music had ceased to charm
them, Mr. Bannister and Mr. Stewart came up too.   Yesterday at four o'clock there was a prayer meeting held at
the Stewarts'.   It is a weekly affair, held turn about, here
and at the American Mission place.   There was a good
roll up, and we had a beautiful meeting.   Mr. Stewart
spoke on Philippians i. 4–11, and it was very good.   He
speaks always so simply, and yet with such power.   Then
he showed some places where the Greek ' Agonia ' is used
in speaking of prayer, showing the depth of earnestness
that St. Paul puts into his words.   On Friday we didn't
do much except Chinese.   When you get hold of a thing,
and you feel you have got hold of one end of the line, the
thing is to hang on and pull tighter till you get some
satisfaction out of it.   That's how you feel with Chinese.   It
takes a considerable time to see your way, but directly you
begin to see you want to get along quickly.   They all say
that we want to work too hard.   We begin as soon as the
Stewarts' room is ready, between nine and a quarter to ten,
and go on till the boy comes to lay the table at one.   We
know a little, and as soon as we know a sentence practise it
on somebody.   The Chinese about here don't laugh at be-
ginners, they are too used to it ; but they are very polite
everywhere, I believe, and never laugh at a foreigner's
mistakes, and they will always tell you you speak well,
whatever you may say.

"Frances Johnson says that when anybody who is
beginning says anything, but in somewhat indifferent

Chinese, they will say 'How *well* she speaks Chinese!
What is she saying?' all in one breath. Saturday we
spent doing Chinese all the morning, and in the afternoon, being half-holiday, we thought it would be nice to
do some decorating for Christmas. So Milly and Kathleen, Toppy and I, went out on the hills and got ever
such a lot of beautiful red berries and some autumn
leaves in long sprays, and anything we could lay our
hands on, and came back loaded with materials for deco-
rative purposes. We first did Mr. Bannister's drawing-
room—it looks so nice—and after tea we trooped across
to the Stewarts and did their drawing-room. Mr. S.
was seated in front of our baby organ, which has taken
up its residence there, playing with one finger and
keeping in tune with his cornet, which he plays to the
admiration of all beholders. He performed for our benefit
nearly all the time we were decorating the apartment.
Next day was Sunday, and in the morning, Toppy being
poorly, I went to church *in my Chinese clothes* for the
first time. Mr. Bannister having disappeared, and Mrs.
Bannister having expressed her intention of staying at
home, I went across to Mrs. Stewart, and was sitting
talking to her when the master of the house came in.
'Good morning, Kuniong,' says he, with a very low bow,
meant out of respect to my Chinese garments. They are
so pleased that we have got the dress. Mr. Bannister
and Mr. Stewart then walked solemnly to church, Mrs.
Stewart and I following behind. You mustn't walk with
a man if you have a Chinese dress on. I can distinguish
a few words in the service, and that is something for less
than a week's study.

"In the afternoon there was a large united meeting of Christians from the American and English Missions in the American chapel, in rather a low part of the city. This meeting is held every quarter, and this particular one had unusual interest, as it is the last at which Mr. Bannister will attend. They are very sorry to leave Ku Cheng. All the happy family in this compound are so united and so sympathetic, I don't wonder they are sorry to leave a place where they have been so much used. Mr. Bannister has worked splendidly here for the last five years. If there were another man to take Mr. Lloyd's place at the College in Foochow he would not have to go. The work will be very heavy for Mr. Stewart. The Ku Cheng and Penang districts are simply enormous. They want a chief each; but as they can't have that, one man has to do the work that could be easily divided among six. The Bannisters are taking their removal splendidly. You never hear a growl; in fact, you would think they quite liked it. But Mr. Bannister's face on Sunday showed how much he felt his farewell address at the quarterly meeting. The hall is rather a large one, and it was well filled — men one side, women the other. To get to Ku Cheng city from our compound you have first about ten minutes' walk down to the ferry; then you possess your soul in patience on the river beach for a while, and then you get into the boat—a long narrow one, with no seats, and very dirty in the bottom. If you have any luck you sit on the side of the boat and hold on like grim death as your skipper dashes round and the other gentleman twirls his pole in the air.

"As you step in you are invited by Mr. Bannister to

proceed to the first-class saloon, which means the far end of the boat, as that end will probably (but by no means certainly) touch the opposite side first. You may get stuck on a sandbank—we did—and then all the passengers rise in a body, and by means of shrieking and yelling, and nearly capsizing the whole concern, they manage to shove it off; but it probably takes some time. However, this only troubles the minds of foreigners, as the Chinese have not the slightest idea of the value of time. Once landed on the other side, you plough through some sand and go up some stone steps that take you to a path which runs all round the city wall. You tramp along till you get to what is called the South Gate, and then through dirty streets to the church. The girls from the compound school came over, some of them in our boat, and the rest in one before. They all marched in single file, some of them with tiny bound feet. How they can manage to trot along as they do passes my comprehension. We were ahead of the school some way—Mr. Stewart and Mr. Bannister first—when we came to a group of rough men who stood and stared, making what sounded rather rude remarks about us. Mr. Stewart stopped and told us to go back and walk with the native girls, as these men would probably insult them if the foreign ladies were not with them. He did not *say* that, but *we* thought that was what he meant. They stared fearfully at the girls, who did not seem to care a scrap, but there were no remarks made. Of course, such a sight as these girls walking through the streets is not at all a common sight, and only Christians do it: the heathen girls of that class are never seen out. We managed to attract a large

D

amount of notice, and they don't the least mind your hearing all their observations about you.

"The speakers were two catechists and Mr. Bannister. All three, but especially Mr. Bannister, were listened to with *great* attention. I noticed ever so many of the men leaning forward with their eyes fixed on him, listening eagerly, if you can use that expression with regard to a Chinaman.

"One old man made a speech in the middle, telling the company how this was Mr. Bannister's last Sunday, and how sorry they all were to say good-bye to him, and then introduced Su Senang, who was to take his place. Oh! it is wonderful to see how the Lord has worked with some of those men—it gives one such encouragement to go on—and it *is* so splendid to see that church full of Christians in the heart of a great heathen city!

"They are not the best-behaved congregation I have ever seen; the women bring their children, who are *utterly spoilt*, being allowed to go wherever they like; and these 'kids' walk round and make observations and converse among themselves on matters of general interest during the whole service. Occasionally a diversion is created by a dog walking in to have a sniff round. Nobody hunts him out, and perhaps he invites a friend or two in, and they have a look round together.

"The Chinese ladies—they are not any of them real ladies, but all of the common classes—seem to feel the cold immensely, and to ward off chills they provide themselves with the luxury of a fire-basket, being a basket open at the top, with a little earthen pot inside which contains the burning charcoal. They have a striking way

of warming themselves with this implement. They get
their hands inside their many coats and hold the handle
of the basket, and you can just see the bottom of it
underneath the coats. I forgot to mention that they all
bring their fire-baskets to church. There was a great
service that day. I sat among the girls—they are such
nice girls—ever so many of them. Directly they see you
in Chinese dress they seem so pleased, and you avoid all
the staring that is sure to fall to your lot if you appear
in your foreign costume. There was a Chinese feast, and
we were asked to go to it, but I did not go. For one
thing, I was extremely hungry, and I knew I could not
eat their things without being sick afterwards, and Toppy
being still *hors de combat*, I made that an excuse not
to go.

"Besides, we wanted to decorate the place for Mrs.
Bannister, in preparation for our Christmas dinner.
It did not seem an atom like Christmas, but the dinner
was very nice. The Bannisters, the Stewarts, four Church
of England Zenana Kuniongs, and two Church Missionary Society (your humble servants) made the select
party. Mildred, with Kathleen and Tom and Maud
Bannister, sat at the side table; the two latter are aged
respectively four and two. In the evening we played
clumps, and had a lot of fun, Mr. Stewart and Mr.
Bannister behaving like two schoolboys. Mr. Bannister is
a very clever man; my respect for and wonder at him
increases day by day. I really think he can do everything. He sings extremely well, and plays the violin; he
speaks Chinese almost better than any one in Fuh Kien, and
he can take the most beautiful photos, and finishes them

very well, and his general all-round capability is something astonishing. He has a patent style of managing the Chinese which is quite fascinating. In church he stalks in with a surplice on, as solemnly as any Church of England parson at home would do, and with equal solemnity you will see him march down the aisle to turn a dog out, or to shut a door in order to deaden the sound of squealing infants and pigs, as occasion may happen to require. He is equal to any and every occasion. He takes a great deal of interest in Australia, and is always asking us about it. He adds to his other accomplishments the art of doctoring, and is very good at that also. He never forgets to mention you at prayers. I am sure you will like them, they are very kind."

Topsy, being less robust than her sister, felt more keenly the privations of their new life, but faced them with the unflinching determination of faith. The following reference to a lost home-comfort is half amusing, half pathetic:—

"Really, it is wonderful the way the Lord can give one power to get over the minor disagreeables of life. Imagine us eating rice and milk for breakfast, and thoroughly enjoying it! Of course we had other things, such as eggs and bread, but we had tea instead of coffee. Now, if there is one thing on this earth that used to make me feel ill, it was tea for breakfast. I have got not to mind it at all. With every trial He makes a way to escape."

Conformity to Chinese manners required the missionaries to swallow many disagreeable things. "Mr. Stewart says," writes Topsy, "that the best way to eat, when you have something nasty, is to count 'thirteen times one, &c., &c., and you get so interested that you forget the taste of the stuff you are eating.' The recipe for eating slugs is to put the slug into your mouth and say 'Amen!'"

Topsy discourses to her mother on various subjects, and in an erratic style:—

"Now that we have settled down there will be no more exciting adventures to relate. We do nothing but Chinese from morning light till dewy eve, so there is nothing to tell you in the news line. I know some characters, and know the numerals up to ten; and we read in the 'Romanised' and 'Character' every day, and write with a brush and Indian ink in little paper books. [The 'Romanised Text' is Chinese, written in English characters, of which more anon. The 'Character,' of course, is the Chinese writing, which is extremely difficult for the learner.] The lark here is something like our lark at home; he does not get up very early. We don't start breakfast till nearly 8.30, which means no Chinese till 9.30; then we go on till dinner time, and in the afternoon, from about 2.30 till 4, we get turned out for a walk. Such jolly hills to walk on; lovely red berries like holly grow there. There are not any flowers up here just now. I did a text—'Emmanuel'—in bamboo leaves and red leaves and berries for decoration, and there was an admiring crowd of spectators all the time. Tienzai, the cook, was much interested, and wanted to know what it was, so Mr. Bannister told him, and he went off and got his Romanised New Testament and showed me the word there, and was so pleased with himself for finding it. He made icing for a Christmas cake, and copied down exactly as I had made it—'Emmanuel'—on the top of the icing, and brought it in to show us all."

The Stewarts' house was furnished with scrupulous plainness, in order to avoid giving the Chinese the idea that missionaries lived in luxury. Both the girls were resolved to follow this good example.

"All one needs is to make home comfortable, and texts are about the best decoration I know of—just things that look nice without being expensive. Table things, one uses just the same as at home, and bedroom things, the enamel things they have for travelling with. For beds, they use those which are made here, the bottom part of which is made of cane framed in wood and resting on trestles. Of course it has four posts and a top piece for the mosquito netting in the summer time. They do not cost much, about $4½ each (a dollar being reckoned at 2s. 4d. now), so that you can see whether it would be cheaper to bring one out or not. The Stewarts bought two just like ours, but much smaller, in which we slept coming up in the boat. They have mattresses made of cocoanut fibre, which is hard, but one soon forgets the hardness in blissful slumbers. My bones ached a bit at first. You had better bring a mattress for yourself, because you ought to be comfortable, but I don't want one. Every one has a *meing* made; that is, a thick business like an eider-down quilt, made of cotton-wool or something very like it. They are jolly warm things; you can put one or more on the top of the downy mattress, and that would make it very comfortable. Every one always takes a *meing* itinerating, and those who do much of it take a little folding-up canvas bed, which is placed on the top of the Chinese bed prepared for the missionary to sleep; only you have to be careful not to shake up the bed while you are making your preparations for the night, because you would stir up the live stock, and thereby cause an itinerating expedition among them which does not add to the sweetness of one's slumbers.

"This afternoon Mrs. Stewart came to pay me a visit in my little downie, and I was entertaining her with an account of Tienzai's exploits, when all of a sudden the end of the bed slipped off the stool; Nellie had been leaning against it, and bedclothes and I gracefully descended on to the floor. Mrs. Stewart, Mrs. Bannister, and 'the Duchess' looked as if the sky had fallen for about two jiffs, and then came to the rescue. We just roared laughing, and I was not hurt. It is getting much colder to-day, and Mrs. Bannister says it might snow. Every one thinks it is the funniest thing that we have never seen snow. I have a fire in my room, and every one comes and pays me a visit. They do such a queer way here with doctors; every house pays them a certain amount a year, and they come and see everybody all round once a week whether they are sick or not. The doctor here belongs to the American Mission; they fished him in to see me—Mr. Bannister did; although I objected strongly, and he said I was not to have anything but milk and stuff like that to eat. I am all right to-day, so I had some pheasant for dinner and some delicious cake, because I thought he was not coming again, but he did; he turned up this afternoon, and amongst other things asked me what I had had to eat? so I said, milk. 'Anything else?' Arrowroot. 'Anything else?' Coffee. 'Anything else?' So I had to confess to the pheasant and cake, whereat he was wroth, and lectured Mrs. Bannister, and so I am not to have any-

thing to-morrow except milk; 'ain't it sickening?' and I
am so hungry. You need not think there is anything
worse than I told you, and I am not going to die yet.
The worst part is that I have wasted two days' at Chinese,
and can't eat enough. My kitty is very good; he sits on
my bed and chews my hands till they are one mass of
scratches, but he is very good company.

"The loads have come, and they are being weighed
over at the Stewarts', and so I have got to wait till they
have finished to know if they have any letters for us, and
if not, it means another month to wait.

"Col. iii. 13-17 has been the greatest blessing to me
all day. There are such lessons of forbearance to learn,
and it is so hard; in fact, it is quite impossible to do it
without the bond of love. The love that one wants for
daily use is a Divine gift, and is not something to be
tacked on. Only a real love will stand the wear and tear
it is put to. Love, the bond of perfectness. Don't you
notice how he talks of kindness, humbleness, meekness,
forbearing, forgiving, as if they were separate things, and
love, the *bond* of perfectness—uniting them all in one—
joining together the fragments of a truly Christian character. I think of it as a sort of mortar. What do you
think?"

"*December* 31, 1893.—The last day of the old year—I
hope the new one will find you here and us together next
New Year's eve. We want you very much, dear old missus,
and I am sure you want us. It is rather a nuisance not
knowing what is going on at home. We pray all the time
that the Lord will set you free to come, and He hears. I
know in His own time it will be all right. I am better

now; but there have been cases where people did not take care of themselves when they were suffering from dysentery, and then it got chronic; so they had to give up and go home. I have had about ten lectures from various people; it is really most embarrassing the way they talk. We get buffalo milk here, and it is very good. I do not know how we would get along without milk. At present I am living on it with rice-water. We know one of the N. W. workers who was troubled with dysentery, and Mr. Stewart advised him to sell all his earthly possessions and buy a cow.

"You need not get in the least agitated, dear Petsy. They have all to be so careful here, because it is such a place for chills; that is why they go for me so persistently.

"Mr. Bannister came back last night from a country trip examining schools. He got a pretty bad chill, and stayed in bed to-day. The dear old head of the Mission will have to be very careful; he does not seem a bit strong, and he will have a terrible lot of work to do when Mr. Bannister goes down. Will you tell Mrs. Collier that they are so pleased with the things for the Christmas tree? The tree is going to be set up just before the Chinese New Year, as they have enough festivities on Christmas Day; besides the things have not come, and they have not enough of their own to make it look nice.

"Tienzai, the cook, takes great interest in our progress in Chinese, and has taught me some new words; he is quite a grand Sing Sang (teacher). I want to get a view of the compound from the hill above, when they let me go out. I am going to do it on the lid of a box Mr. Bannister gave me for the purpose; it is nice and smooth, and I am going to send it to you to decorate your little self with, and give you an idea of the place we are living in, and perhaps it will interest others too.

"I hope Mr. Martin will build us a decent warm house at Ning Taik, the more native the better. Miss Goldie has brought out three stoves with her; she got a special grant for them. Stoves are the best things to have because they do not use much wood; I don't mean cooking stoves, but those little ones for rooms."

"*January* 4.—I have been sick-nursing all the afternoon; one of the girls has influenza, and I have been down reading to her; hospital knowledge came in a little useful too.

"We are going to have the Christmas tree next Monday night. Chinese dress is so comfortable, I don't know how I shall ever care to go back to the old style, it is so light and loose; one can pile on any amount of clothes, and then there are no gloves or hats to bother about for going out in, except in the summer-time, when they all wear pith helmets—girls and all. They say we must order ours from Hongkong, but I think I will get a Chinese hat, that is, a very large straw one, made a good deal thicker than ordinary, and drooping down all round in the most graceful way; trimming is quite superfluous, they have Chinese artistic work on the top, and that does instead." ·

"*January* 5.—We are half-expecting letters to-morrow; it is no use getting excited about it, because it only makes it all the worse to bear when they don't come.

"One feels so utterly useless here the first year; there are oceans to be done, but without the language it is simply impossible to do anything. I think the first year must be the most trying time; after that, when one can work in real earnest it will be grand, at present one is learning patience by the yard. I feel as if I never knew what it was to be a Christian at home, something of the feeling Mr. Grubb had when he said he was going to *begin* to read the Bible. At home one was simply rushed to death, but here one learns how to get along with nothing to do. It is a fortnight to-morrow since I looked at Chinese, but to-morrow I am going to start to read a bit by myself, and on Monday with my Sing Sang, if I can creep out without getting promptly sat upon.

"I think I will write to Mrs. Collier to-night to thank her for the things and tell her about the tree—it may have the effect of stirring them up to make more things for next year. We could have done with more, though it did not look bad. If you want to know what sort of things—just anything noisy, like whistles or trumpets, bows and arrows, or anything that boys like, as balls, &c.; and no end of admiration for the comforters and mittens, they all like them; in fact, anything that English children play with.

"I know He sent us, but oh! how I long for home only my dear old Missus can guess. I can think of it all and see it with my eyes shut, and sometimes almost hear the tread on the gravel outside, and the click of the gate, and turn of the well-known key in the back door, yet without one feeling of regret that I shall never see it again; for even if we ever go back to Australia, I shall not care to see 'The Willows' in other hands. But it is not well to look forward, for who knows where we shall all be in seven years, when furlough time comes?"

CHAPTER VI

THE NATIVE CHRISTIAN CONFERENCE

A great gathering of Christians—The Irish missionary—A wild
beast story—Tea parties—Fervent greetings—Letter-writing
under difficulties—A poor man's contribution—A crowded
church—The singing not melodious—Dining in public—
Requests for teachers—Demoniacal possession—The baptisms
—Surroundings of the Mission station—Idol temples—Visiting
in Ku Cheng—Need of helpers.

THE great event of the year at the Ku Cheng Station is
the *Gia Hoi*, or annual conference of native Christians
and catechists, as well as missionaries. More than 500
native Christian men, besides a proportionate number of
women, assembled at one time in the Ku Cheng church,
and of these 150 partook of the Holy Communion, and
at the annual baptism 87 new converts were admitted.
The conference is a very pleasant season for the missionaries, being their annual season for meeting one another,
and enjoying social intercourse. But we must let the
girls tell the story in their own way.

Nellie writes :—

"*Sunday, February* 4.—Just come home from church ;
quite a crowd of us went over to-day. Last evening
Mr. C. (an Irish missionary), made his appearance on the
scene. He is a splendid worker ; and his wife is a dear
good woman. His pigtail is one of which he is rather

proud, as he grew it himself, and having fair hair it is rather un-Chinese. He is a very funny man, tells things in such a comical way, and is thoroughly Irish in his irrepressible spirits. Even last night, when he had been travelling hard, he sat down and entertained us with accounts of his travels and experience. He said that when Mr. Starr arrived up there the poor man was nearly frozen, and Gien Ong (the man whom Mr. Phillips in his letters speaks of as 'Beseech Grace') looked like a polar bear with two pair of socks on his *hands* to keep them from being entirely frozen, and he gave Mr. C. an account of what one of the mountains looked like as they passed it—a most wonderful thing. The whole side of the mountain is overgrown with bamboos, and these had been covered with snow till they became top-heavy and leaned right over to the ground, where the tops got frozen on, and the whole mass cased in ice. Mr. C. could scarcely believe it, but when he passed the place himself a day later, he found that it was really so, and he says that it was a most curious sight. Coming down, he said, he saw the first four-footed wild beast he has seen in China. Not a tiger. He had wanted so much all his days to see a tiger; but this was an animal like a fox, and looked rather like a big dog in the distance. Almost as soon as he saw it, it flew at a huge fat pig which was trying to crawl up some stone steps, and so disconcerted the poor pig—the 'cratur'—that it rolled from the eminence, over and over, and the fox with it, till they reached the top of the bank, and then they fell together from a height of about fifteen feet. The poor fox fell underneath, and Mr. C. said the last he saw of him he had managed to crawl out, looking very flat indeed, from under the pig, and was sneaking away in the distance. Choruses of 'Oh! Oh!' from all of us, and then Miss Lucy Stewart said, 'Was it light?' (wanting to know, I suppose, how he could see). 'Oh! no,' said Mr. C. briskly; 'the pig was not at all light, I should imagine, judging from the appearance of the fox.'

"There have been a series of tea-parties here this week; everybody asks everybody else to tea. We went to the Bannisters' old house on Thursday night. It is now temporarily occupied by six of the lady missionaries from outlying districts. All the six were there, and in addition Emmie Stevens, Annie Gordon, Toppy, and I. Ada Nisbitt would have come, as it was an *Australian* tea-party, only she has been ill, and was in bed. After tea we sang hymns, &c.

"About nine o'clock we betook ourselves home, and there was a fearful scene in the hall, B., the sister from Nangwa, embracing the Ku Cheng girls. I fled in order to escape before she attacked me, and when I got across the garden and opened the door and went in, Mr. Stewart was playing his cornet; and when he saw me appearing on the scene, he dropped his cornet and inquired where Toppy was. I said, 'She is saying good-night to B.' A moment after she appeared with her hair all coming down her back, most dishevelled-looking. Mr. Stewart laughed heartily, and said, 'This is what happens when we say good-night to B.'

"It is a wearisome business to get through writing to people when you feel you *ought* to do it. Now even to-night, with nothing particular on, I come down to the front room prepared to write letters, and there that old Mr. C. sits, and talks and talks by the yard, till I wish him further. He has stopped at last, and is seated on the other side of the little table, studying an English newspaper about two months old, occasionally reading extracts to the distraction of my nerves. Mr. Stewart has just finished prayers with the Chinese servants and teachers, and he is seated by the fire deep in the perusal of the 'King's Business.' He also occasionally gives us an extract, and altogether it is lively."

But Miss Nellie enjoyed Mr. C.'s conversation, and especially his stories. Here is a sample :—A native church was to be built, and a meeting was held to consider ways and means. Some, who were too poor to give money, contributed shoes or other articles of their own manufacture. One poor man, who owned a hen, promised the price of all the eggs he might get that year. On the Sunday when the subscriptions were called in, he stood up in the congregation and stated that his hen, not having had sufficient notice, had only laid five eggs, the price of which he handed in, and the balance would follow in due course !

"*Monday, February* 12.—Yesterday was the Sunday of the *Gia Hoi*. It was a roasting day. It is so funny how the day commences as lovely and fresh as possible— just a balmy day, like some of our spring days—and then it gets perfectly boiling in the middle of the day. Millie and Kathleen went to church for the first time here ; they don't understand anything, and are fearfully stared at in their English dress, but are not to have Chinese things till their English ones are worn out, which won't be very long. But on this Sunday all went who could, if only to

see the sight, which Mr. Stewart says may never be seen
again in Ku Cheng, of *all* the Christians of the whole district gathered in that church.   We started off—there was
quite a crowd of us in the ferry boats—and reached the
church, when we found we had to go in through the men's
tiang dong.   However, we faced the ordeal, and walked
through the midst of them in single file, with Mrs. Stewart
at our head, and the two little girls, about whom many
remarks were made.

" You enter the church through a door leading into the
women's part, and only the clergyman comes in through
that door besides the women ; but you can see through the
opening of the dividing partition between that part and
the body of the church, right down the aisle ; and such
a sight as it was !   The church was literally crammed as
full as it would hold ; and the noise that they were
making was something shocking—that is, it was shocking
to any one accustomed to the peaceful quietness of a civilised congregation before the service.   But I very much
doubt if God prefers the hearts of some of those civilised
congregations to the hearts of these simple people, who
have had no advantages at all, and who at first can't see
why there should be any difference between their noisy
idol worship and a reverent worship of God.

" The first hymn was given out, and Miss Stevens
struck up on the organ, and the choir, I daresay, sang
as well as they do at any other time ; but on this occasion, though only six yards away, I could not hear them
at all.   The noise was truly appalling.   Everybody sang
loudly, most of them in a little tune of their own, and
those that did not sing any tune chose a note—some a

very high one, and the others a very low one, and yelled on it after the most approved Chinese fashion. One old lady near me literally *squeaked*, like a guinea-pig, all the time; and as for the organ, nobody knows where it was. I tried to keep a straight face by not looking up from my book, but it was hard work.

" When the hymn was over, Mr. Stewart came down to the chancel rails and said to me, ' Just go and tell them that they needn't play the next hymn.' So I had to go past my old lady with the guinea-pig voice, and speak over the top of the partition to Annie Gordon, and tell her to tell Miss Stevens not to play. When the next hymn came Mr. Stewart gave it out, and then started it about three notes too high. It certainly went better than the first one—much better; but it is a good thing the Chinese can sing high notes, for we all had to stop when we got to the top note of the piano.

"There were 150 communicants, and you may imagine that we were rather late in getting home again. It was about 2.30 when we sat down to dinner, and the congregation that did not stay for Communion, and had eaten their dinner, came over to watch us have ours. There were about fifteen noses glued to each of the windows; it was mere curiosity, most of them having seen foreigners before, but not this particular crowd of foreigners in this particular house.

"There are two very interesting things which were brought up at the men's meeting of the *Gia Hoi* which I must tell you. About eighty miles away across the river there is a village where there has never been a missionary (not that this is anything peculiar),

E

but there were three men—tailors—from that place at this *Gia Hoi*, and they had come all that way to ask for a catechist to be sent to teach them. When Mr. Stewart asked how they knew of the 'doctrine,' they told him how they had gone on business once to a village seventeen miles distant from their village, and the nearest one to them where there are Christians, and in the street they met the catechist, who spoke to them of Jesus, and they were very interested, and took in what he said, and in a day or two went back and told the people in their village. In that place there are now between twenty and thirty Christians, but they know so little. They plead so for a catechist. They are to have one, I am glad to say. Of the five needy places brought up at the conference—all wanting a catechist—only *two* can be supplied at present, and this village is to be one. In my youthful innocence I asked, 'Could one of the Kuniongs go? Did they not ask for one?' I was told they would not have the presumption to ask for a Kuniong. Kuniongs are much too scarce; and they have to take charge, not of *one* village, but *many* villages, and generally try to manage a sort of women's school as well. No wonder they look tired, and have fever and ague and things. Oh! if only a few more would come. They are so badly wanted.

"There was another very touching story. Two or three men had come a very long journey for the same purpose —to ask for a teacher. They had heard the Jesus doctrine from some Christian who had been travelling through their part of the world, but none of them could read, so Mr. Stewart, just to try them, asked how they could manage to worship God if they could not read.

'Oh!' they said, 'this Christian had taught them a few hymns, and when they held worship they sang these, and then all prayed aloud to God in turn.' 'And do you think He heard you?' 'Oh yes,' they said, 'we think He heard us.' But they are so sadly ignorant; and yet really Christians at heart, and so earnest and true about it all, and so eager to be taught.

" Yet one more. This was another man who had come to ask for a teacher. When he was asked how he first knew about the doctrine, he said his brother had some time ago been very ill—not a cold or anything of that sort—but possessed by a devil. This he stated in the same quiet matter-of-fact way in which you would say some one had the toothache. He was possessed by a devil and foamed at the mouth, and did the most frightful things; not mad, the man said. The Chinese have two quite different ways of expressing the two ideas. Nothing they could do was any good, till at last a Christian came from a village a long way off, and hearing of this devil-possessed man, said that God could cure him if they would obey Him. So all the idols were run out, and the Christian Chinaman prayed to his Lord; and the devil left that man, and he became quite well, and ever since that time he and all his family, with some others in the village, have believed in Jesus. All this was stated simply and plainly, as if he thought there was nothing incredible in it at all. I believe that that simple unquestioning faith is what God honours. We are too clever for God. We like to show Him how to do things."

About the same date Nellie writes to a friend :—"The *Gia Hoi* is over. Last night was the wind-up. Every

one who could went over to church. All the accepted
candidates for baptism were baptized. There were eighty-
seven of them; about a dozen women and two or three
babies. It was a most impressive sight—all those men
waiting there quietly in the church, and the women in the
top part of the building. The church is in the shape of a
cross. We all sat round as near as we could to see. I
had a very good place, just behind the gate. First Sing
Mi Senang read the service, and then one of the catechists
read John iii. (which rejoiced my heart, as I could understand it), and then the baptisms began.

"A catechist, with an awfully strong face, but 'saved'
stamped in every line of it, stood against the post of the
partition, with his back against it, and read the names out
one by one from a long paper in his hand. Sing Mi stood
on the other side, and Mr. Stewart stood at the font
baptizing. It was a most wonderful sight. The dear old
thing's face just shone with the light of heaven as he
went over the words, the same words again and again,
yet they never sounded like a formula, for he prayed it so
earnestly each time. As each one was baptized he went
up to the communion rails and knelt there for a few
moments in prayer. Mr. Stewart said to them as they
moved, 'Go and pray to God to help you to keep the
vow.' One old lady, aged eighty-seven, was assisted up
by some of the younger Bible-women. She is a true old
Christian. Poor old soul; I don't suppose she will have
much longer here, but is it not a good thing to think of
the bright home waiting for her? Another was an old
man, about seventy-five or seventy-six, and he with his
three little sons were received into the visible Church at

the same time. Mr. Stewart's remarks to us in English
were very *apropos*. He does not in the least mind
explaining as he goes along in English, not an ounce of
anything approaching to levity, but in all earnestness,
just feeling that he would like others to be as interested
in the people as he is himself.

"This compound is on a hill, and is quite surrounded
by other hills; and though, at first, I missed the trees
very much, now I am getting to quite like these great
mountains, they are so rugged and steep, and the lights
and shades on them, especially in the mornings and
evenings, are simply beautiful. I should like you to see
the picture that is in my mind's eye now, which we see
every time we go to the city or to church. The river,
which is very wide but not deep, flows along outside the
wall of the city—which rises to a good height—and
there are steps leading from the river's edge to the
arched stone gateways; and standing on the raised stone
platform in front of the gateway, you look down and
across the river, and truly the view is beautiful. Far
away there is a great high mountain with a tall pagoda on
the very top, and nearer there are others—all so quaint-
looking. Then, close by, there is a heathen temple
painted red, under the shadow of a thick banyan tree,
which spreads ever so far. The temple is painted red
and looks very picturesque; and the houses in the village
on the other side are also rather picturesque—very nice
to look at, but rather unclean inside. Above the village
the mountains begin to rise, and you can see the roofs of
our houses peeping over the side of one of the nearest
hills. On Saturday afternoon several of us went for a

walk to see a great temple about three miles from here. You never saw such things as they are—the idols, I mean. It is wonderful how they can worship such things; and do you know there is a frightful weird look about some of them—something about their eyes that makes one quite believe what St. Paul says about idol worship, that they are sacrificing to devils. It makes me feel quite queer to see these things, and I cannot bear to look at them. Many of the Chinese, especially among the literary men, do not believe in them a bit, but the priests, or whatever you like to call them, play on the uneducated poor classes, and they are awfully superstitious. To-night is the Feast of Lanterns, and as I am writing I can hear a great performance going on in the city; bells being clanged, and crackers and guns being fired off, and a great noise of tongues. Toppy and I have just been outside to see if we can see anything. If it were a clear night perhaps we could see a good deal, but as it is rather misty we can only see that there are lots of lights, and the city pagoda is lit up, and there is a fearful noise. To-day we went with the Stewarts to dine at one of the American houses, and though we went through a very quiet part of the city there were a good many people out in the streets. The children shriek after us, 'Foreigners, foreigners.' If we were in European dress we should of course attract much more notice. They always observe on you as you go past, and the remark invariably made about me is, 'Very tall;' the Chinese women are all so very little. Yesterday I went with one of the ladies here to visit in a village close to the river. When we got to it the first thing we came to was a pond, which about a dozen men were draining. It was nearly empty, but at the bottom there was about two feet of fearfully muddy water, and in it you could see some fish jumping about. I looked at them with horror, and asked one of the men if they were good to eat, and he said 'Yes, very good;' and a lot more that I did not understand. They could eat any mortal thing, and the more disgusting the better. Then we walked on towards the houses; the paths are very narrow, scarcely room for one person, and raised two or three feet above the level of the paddy fields and ponds, into which you might easily slip if you were not pretty careful. When the women in one of the houses caught sight of us, they came to the doors and called to us from a long distance, loudly and excitedly, to come to their house. We went to those who called us first, and were asked in with great politeness, and a few other ladies followed from the other houses. We walked in and sat down among the pigs, hens, and children—at least, I don't really mean *among* them, for we had nice bamboo chairs to sit on, but these domestic animals came in and walked around all the time. The women all sat round and took in what Miss Gordon and the native Bible-woman said to them. They were very interested, but it seems so strange to these women to think there is a God who cares for them, that they can't understand it at all at first. Some of them—indeed most of them—are not at all happy, they have never known what it is for any one to love them or care much about their welfare, spiritual or otherwise; and the idea that any one should care enough to want to tell them about God is quite too much for them to comprehend. While Miss Gordon was speaking I felt a violent pecking and tearing at my ankle, and on looking down to inspect that part of my person, I beheld one of the family hens trying its beak on my stocking. I hinted to it with my umbrella to move on, and I am glad to add that it therewith took its departure. It is very interesting seeing the women in their own homes. I cannot understand very much yet, of course, but I can talk a little to them, and they like that.

"There has been a huge gathering of all the Christians in the Ku Cheng district here. This is the headquarters, and annually, at the beginning of the Chinese New Year, there are these religious meetings, to which all the outside Christians come. It was all very interesting. The church at Sang Bo Dong (the name of the part of the city where the church is) was quite full. The great cry of all the Chinese clergy is 'lady missionaries;' 'we want a lady for our district.' There is no way for men to reach the women in China, and until the women are reached there is not much good in getting hold of the men, because the children are what their mothers make them. People came to Ku Cheng this time from places miles and miles away to ask for a catechist to come and teach them more of the Jesus doctrine, as they call it, but there are not enough to supply all the places that need one."

CHAPTER VII

ACTIVE WORK

THE progress which our two young missionaries made with
the language is surprising. Learning to read and learning
to speak are two very different studies. In the first, Nellie
made the more rapid progress. In January she tells her
mother she had mastered all the "characters" in the first
chapter of St. John's Gospel. It appears that missionaries
are divided in opinion as to whether it is better to begin
by learning the terribly difficult Chinese "character," or
to make use of a "Romanised" text—that is, Chinese
words written in English letters, with additional marks
to indicate the "tone." Nellie and Topsy were strong
advocates of the "Romanised," by means of which they
soon were enabled not only to read for themselves, but
to teach women to read, a thing not usually attempted.

Nellie speaks up for the "Romanised" in her usual vigorous style :—

"Now, if you get the Romanised, which every one can have (only some of these people are dead set against it), you can see *exactly* how to pronounce the character, and then somebody can tell you the English, and there you are. You never forget that, but how can you remember a hieroglyphic of which you can't remember the sound, and never knew the meaning? My teacher waxes eloquent on the subject. He says it is not of the slightest use to read on and on and on till you nearly turn into an automaton. (He did not say exactly these words, Chinese teachers are a wee scrap like automatons themselves.) He wants very much to learn Romanised. Toppy has taught him a little, and when we get on a bit we will teach him some more."

In February the regular teacher took a holiday, and during his absence Nellie's studies were assisted by Tusing, a boy of fifteen, the orphan son of a catechist, who, with his mother, was on a visit to Mrs. Stewart from their home in Foochow. The way in which this poor woman had become a widow was peculiarly tragic. Her husband, a native catechist, was murdered by the heathen in the most barbarous manner, being literally flayed alive.

"Tusing, Chitnio's son, is reading with me every morning till Wong comes back. He is such a dear boy. He is only fifteen, but he is very thoughtful, and was confirmed last time because he was so anxious for it himself that his mother did not like to refuse him. He speaks English quite well, but I wish he would not talk it to me. He is a most enterprising youth, and his latest fancy is to be able to draw old English letters such as I did on the mantelpiece in the front room. He has asked me to get him a book to copy them from. Do you think you could get one at Mullen's or somewhere next time you are in town? A book with as many different kinds of letters as you can get; there ought to be a book of that sort, old English capitals and small letters, and one for illuminating. If you could get it and send it to me I should be so exceedingly grateful. We do so long for the messenger every ten days; your letters are always so nice."

Meanwhile, Topsy was not far behind her sister, and though prevented by weak health from studying the "character," which both felt very trying to both brain and nerves, she practised speaking to the girls of the school, and to the servants, with such diligence that as early as January we find her proposing to give lessons in "Romanised" to the watchman and the washerman of the household. Both the girls maintain that colloquial Chinese is not a difficult language to learn. You first require to master the seven "tones," and know them by the ear as you would know the notes of the scale in music; and having done that, you find the number of words to be learnt not overwhelming. Each word, of course, has different meanings, according to the "tone" in which it is spoken. The grammar is extremely simple. There is only one personal pronoun instead of twelve, as in our language, and only one tense to the verb.

Topsy thus writes in March 1894:—"I had my first class this morning; it was so nice, six dear little boys. I taught them some Gospel catechism, a text out of a series

arranged with a view of giving the whole Gospel, and
began them with Romanised. They are so quick; we got
on grandly together. I do love them so. To-morrow
I am going to have a class before church of little
heathen children; the ones to-day were from our school,
and are all the children of Christians. Nellie went to
Dong Gio on Wednesday, and has not turned up yet.
The coolie was sent up for her on Monday, but he returned without her this morning, as she has decided to
stay on with Annie Gordon, and go to a place called
Dong Kau, the extreme station of the Church Missionary
Society in this district. A house for the mission has just
been bought there, and they have been visited by Mr.
Bannister and Mr. Stewart, but never before by the Kuniongs. They are to stay there till Saturday next, and
return to Dong Gio for Sunday, as there is a Hiong Hoi,
that is, a meeting for all the Christians round that district.
Mr. Stewart is to be there, too, to lead the meeting, preach,
and have Communion service for the people. Nellie will
come back next Monday, so you won't get a letter from
her this time, but an extra long one next."

The visit to Dong Gio was Nellie's first experience in
itinerating. It was preceded, however, by a shorter
excursion, the cause of which was as follows:—A Christian girl belonging to the Mission school was about to be
forced by her parents into a marriage with a heathen. On
this account her teacher, Miss W., went to visit the parents
in the hope of dissuading them from this course, and it
became necessary for some one to take a class at a place
called Wong Dong, which Miss W. usually took on a
Monday morning. Accordingly, Nellie writes:—" On

Monday morning we started off, Lucy Stewart and I, for Wong Dong, taking our lunch wrapped up in paper. The sun came down very strong about twelve o'clock, and the heat and the motion of the chair made me feel rather sick, but I forgot all about that after we had crossed the second river and entered the village. It looks so pretty from the distance, nestled in a valley with more trees than usual on the mountains, and the river winding so picturesquely close to it. The coolies, who know the place perfectly, took us straight to the house; it was quite a large one, with the biggest *tiang-dong* (guest-room) I have seen. Our chairs were carried straight in, and we got a very hearty welcome from the women, who were not two minutes in collecting together, as soon as the news spread that the Kuniongs had come. Lucy took them into a nice large room (not too clean) opening off the *tiang-dong*, where I took the children. And did I not have a time! About twenty children were all around me, and outside of them a ring of men, but the latter were very nice and polite; they only wanted to look at the new Kuniong and hear what she had to say. I showed them pictures, Bible ones, and explained them as well as I could, and gave them some cards. We had a very nice time altogether, and when we were going away the women followed us right through the village down to the river, calling out to us to come again soon."

This excursion was immediately followed by the more important expedition to Dong Gio, a whole day's journey distant. Miss Gordon, the resident Kuniong there, required help in her work, and Nellie was delighted to render it. A warm friendship sprang up between these two, who seem to have been well suited to help one another. Nellie continues :—

"That night I packed up my traps in my native basket, and Sin Ciong, the cook, put some food up for me. They are always so pleased to do things like that; they are so childish in some ways. In the morning I departed, and a Chinese boy, named Gin Hok ('Seek happiness,') came with me. I call him a 'boy,' but he is really about twenty-four, and is married. His papa is the catechist at Hua Sang. No foreigner, especially a Kuniong, ought to travel alone in this place. The people never say much to you if you have an escort. I was very thankful to have Gin Hok. The coolies stopped in a village about a mile from Ku Cheng to get some food, and they put me down in front of the shops in a very crowded street. The 'Seeker' took up his position with a long pipe to smoke a little to one side of the chair on a bench, and I could just see his foot swinging backwards and forwards. He interviewed all the men who asked questions, and kept them from being a nuisance and crowding me; but the children came and stood quite close and talked away, and presently a woman came and began talking, and brought me some tea. She wanted to know what I would eat, if we ate rice, &c. I can't make out all they say. One very bright-looking boy, about ten or twelve, came and looked at me, and reported his impressions to the people standing near, mostly men, I think, though I could not see them. I told him I could not talk, and so he told them the Kuniong could not talk nor understand, and to let her alone. 'Cai' (let alone), is a very frequent expression with the Chinese. After that we got on very well. Part of the country is very quiet, and I walked a great part of the way, but whenever we came near a village I got into the chair again. Directly one person sees you, they set up a cry of 'Foreign woman,' and then a crowd turns out to have a look at you. I was to meet Annie Gordon at Sek Chek Du, *i.e.*, 'Seventeenth Du.' ('Sek' means 'ten,' 'chek' means 'seven,' and 'Du' a place a little larger than a village.) It certainly is rather a grand place, the houses are very nicely built, and much larger than you see in Ku Cheng. I cannot describe the beauty of the road along which we came. The road is like all the others —merely a stone path about two or at the most three feet wide. This path leads through fields on both sides with wheat and barley growing, the bright green of these fields contrasting very strongly with the dead brown of the mountains rising all round. Here and there you see clumps of trees, and through the trees you can just see the smoke rising from some of the houses in the village beyond. Then a turn in the path brings you down to the river side, and you travel along there for a while, under the shade of trees, which have not yet been cut down for firewood. I think there must be at least three little villages which you have to pass through before you reach Sek Chek Du proper, and I did not know when we *did* get to it that we had arrived at our destination, so that I was surprised as well as delighted, when we were going through a street crowded with shops and noisy people, to see a man lean eagerly forward to see who was in the chair; and then you should have seen the smile on his face as he called out to me, 'Ping ang, Kuniong, ping ang.' I cannot tell you how lovely it is to hear those words when

you have been stared at and crowded for several hours by
heathen, and then some one's face brightens as they catch
sight of you and call out the Christian greeting. Shortly
after passing through that crowded part, we came to the
less crowded part of the village, and presently came to a
good-sized native house, with a nice little garden hedged
with bamboos close beside it. I did not, of course, know
whose it was, but the coolies went straight to the door and
put my chair down, and then a man, whom I recognised
as one I had seen at our house during the Ku Cheng *Gia
Hoi*, came to the door and smiled on me affably, saying:
'Ping ang, Kuniong' (ping ang means 'peace'). He is a
most earnest Christian; he is what they call the leader of
the Gospel Band, and does a splendid work there in those
villages all round. Then the catechist appeared; he is
such a nice-looking, clean man; and then I went into the
house and beheld Annie coming out of the women's *tiang-
dong* to greet me. She had travelled down from another
place to meet me there, and had got there first. The
women were so nice, I like them so very much; they
wanted me to partake of a little native refreshment, but
I was not inclined for it. They are not offended if you
refuse nicely. The catechist came up and was talking
to us a bit. Downstairs is the men's *tiang-dong*, and
upstairs is the women's, but the catechist considers himself a privileged person. We started almost directly I
had had something to eat; the catechist, the leader of
the band, and the native doctor, who is also an earnest
Christian and a good worker, came to see us off from the
door; they are very nice. It is so delightful to see such
Christians in places where, five or six years ago, there

was not one Christian. Then we travelled all the afternoon, part of the time in very heavy rain, and nearly all
through the prettiest country, the little scenes of river
and trees and native houses, with the green fields so
neatly cultivated, being very charming. The catechist
declared it would be after dark before we got to Dong
Gio, but he was wrong for once, because we got there
before six. The chapel at Dong Gio is a very nice one,
and has a grand little belfry on the top of it; and the
catechist's house, and rooms for the Bible-women, and
also other rooms, are all in the same pile of buildings
(so to speak) as the chapel. You enter through a short
passage into the men's *tiang-dong*, and from that—on
one side—you pass through a passage, off which the catechist's rooms open, into the women's part of the chapel
—and on the other side there are stairs leading up to
the women's *tiang-dong* (over the men's), and a little
room on each side of it, in one of which Annie and I have
taken up our abode. The catechist here is the head
catechist of the Ping Nang district. His wife, the chief
lady here, is a nice quiet little soul, and they have five or
six children, two being at school, and other two running
about here, a boy and a girl, really nice little things, who
chatter to you, and don't seem a bit shy. Li-Sie-Mi,
the catechist, is away, having gone to meet Mr. Stewart
at Dong Kau, the biggest city about here, and he won't
be back till after I go, for which I am sorry, because
he is a nice man. His helper is a very bright, earnest
Christian. He was up a few minutes after we got here
to say ' Ping ang,' and find out if we had all we wanted.
He is a well-educated young man, and speaks pure Foochow

F

beautifully, without the least brogue. He is not married, nor engaged, and if they can manage it, I think Sie-Mi and the people in Ku Cheng will try and arrange a match for him with that Christian girl that I told you about, whose parents want to force her into a marriage with a heathen. It would be very nice if she could marry this fellow. The heathen man would beat her, and be cruel to her if he chose, and nobody can interfere whatever he might choose to do, but the Christians, of course, are quite different. I can't imagine Ding Sing-Sang beating his wife. Then the Bible-woman and the school teacher, with some of the Christian women, came up; they were so pleased to see us. Annie has been up here four times before, and they like her very much. We went to prayers in the chapel that night; there were not many people. Ding Sing-Sang spoke very nicely, and in his prayers asked for blessing on the Kuniongs, who had come up here to carry the Gospel to the heathen women. When prayers are over, all the men hurry out into the *tiang-dong*, and we have a little longer way to go, and take a longer time to get round, and then Annie and I have to march through this *tiang-dong* full of men to get to our stairs. You are not supposed to look at them, or to take any notice of them, but if one of their high majesties should say 'l'ing ang' to you, you should answer. Ding Sing-Sang is a polite person, but he takes no notice of the Kuniongs if there are other men there. Are they not queer people? On Thursday morning we stayed in bed till nearly eight o'clock, we were so tired after our long chair ride the day before. All the morning nearly was spent in doing a little (book) Chinese, and a great deal of entertaining of the Christian women who came to see us. In the afternoon, directly after dinner, we went visiting. Well, I think you would have laughed to see the procession. First, Li-Sie-Mi's little daughter, aged about eight or nine, led the way, waving my umbrella, which is got up in a white cover for the sun ; then an aged 'church mother,' about ninety I should think, but a most earnest Christian, went along and announced our arrival ; then Annie Gordon, followed by the Bible-woman, an exceedingly nice little woman ; then your humble servant and the school teacher, whom I think I like best, brought up the rear. We went to several houses, and were kindly received by the women, our pockets being crammed with all the different delicacies, which, happily, you are not expected to eat. They seem very eager to hear, and only in one or two cases were they indifferent. It is such a comfort to have on a Chinese cotton jacket, and a skirt made of the native red cloth, and Chinese shoes. They scarcely have an observation to make at all, but they always take notice of what you have on, and it would be intolerable if you were in English dress. In the first place, I doubt if they would receive you at all in some of the houses, as they would think you were a man. In one house there was a little boy with a fearful pain in his inside, who was crying and looking very bad. We made some inquiries, and then decided that we had some very simple medicine with us that would do him good. So the old Hoi-mu (church mother) accompanied me back to our abode, and I got the medicine and a spoon to mix it with, and went back to the house. The old lady informed every one that asked our business, that

I was going to give medicine to cure a little boy, and volunteered a good deal of information about the Kuniongs that I did not quite take in. The little chap took the stuff very well. They have the greatest faith in foreign medicines. Only one house we went into where there was not a friendly reception, and it was not so much that they were unwilling to let us in, but they did not want to listen to the doctrine. There were a lot of young girls, such nice-looking girls they were, but fear, downright fear, was written on their faces as they stared at us from a distance. The women did not seem to want to listen a bit, and though I could not understand a quarter of what they said, I *felt* the power of Satan there in that *tiang-dong*, and began praying as hard as I could. A moment or two afterwards, something was said that offended our old Hui-mu immensely, and she got up and said to us, 'Come away, Kuniong, come away, they won't listen.' But both of us felt it was only the devil, and that if we held on, he would have to give in. And sure enough the opportunity seemed better after that, and both Annie and the Bible-woman spoke, the latter very earnestly and well. On Thursday evening there is a week-night service; it was fairly attended. The next day was Good Friday. They had no service in the morning in this chapel. We rather wondered at that, and if Annie could have got hold of Ding Sing-Sang, I think she would have said something about it; but we came to the conclusion that, as Li-Sie-Mi was away, it would be better to say nothing. It does not do for the Kuniongs to rule the catechists. I think it would be a very good thing if they could sometimes. But they had a nice service in the evening, and a good many came. Ding spoke about our Lord's death, and told them about it all very well, and said how they ought to be drawn by His love to come to Him. On Saturday we went visiting almost directly after breakfast, and did not get back until dinner-time. In the afternoon the women came to us, and all the afternoon was spent in teaching them, and they do so want to learn. I do wish there could be a Kuniong spared to live here (I wish I could), and teach them, but they can't be spared. Why, I am sure I don't know. Annie has been four times at intervals of months, and stayed a day or two. This time she is going to stay a month. The faithfulness and earnestness of the native Christians is a matter for heartfelt praise. God has used them almost entirely to create the eagerness and readiness to learn about Him. I think it is just wonderful. But still there is a lot in the way of organising them a bit, and teaching them connectedly, and setting them an example of reverent behaviour in church, that a resident Kuniong could most certainly do. Annie and I had a great discussion about that, and it was such a joke, because when I was enumerating the things a Kuniong could teach them, I mentioned among others that she could teach the church mothers to blow their noses. Poor Annie collapsed in a moment, and has never quite recovered. She says she will ask Mr. Stewart if a Kuniong might be appointed for this special purpose, and recommend me for the post.

"Sunday was very nice indeed. In the morning a great number of women came, all eager to learn, and the usual crowd of children; and so to give Annie and the Bible-woman a chance to talk and to teach the women, I took the youngsters over to the school, and got the help of one of the young Christian women (little more than a girl she is, but she is married), who was in the Foochow girls' school. She spoke very nicely, but they want to be trained to teach, I think, and I kept the youngsters in order for her and supplied the subject, which, as it was Easter Sunday, was the Resurrection of Jesus. Fancy Easter Sunday! This time last year we were together. God grant that this time *next* year we may also be in this land, where the fields are so white unto harvest. The service was good too; about fifty women turned up, and their part of the building was well filled. Ding Sing-Sang preached. He is a real good lad, his whole bearing is so reverent and so nice, and he spoke simply enough too; but it seemed so strange to think that when he spoke of Moses, in some reference or other, scarcely *one* in that crowd of women would know who was meant. But there is a good time coming, we hope. Sunday afternoon, more church, and in the evening just ordinary prayers, with no women except those on the premises. On Monday morning we went visiting again, and had a very nice time; the women *are* so friendly. In the afternoon Annie and the Bible-woman taught the women—about thirty—who came to learn more. In the evening a message came from Dong Kau from Mr. Stewart. He said in it that he had been having a splendid time all through the north-west and through North Ping Nang, where the Gospel has not yet been preached at all. Dong Kau is a large village between Dong Gio and Ping Nang city—a long day's journey from Dong Gio. Mr. Stewart said he wished Annie and me to go to Dong Kau, and take the Dong

Kio Bible-woman. No foreigners, except Mr. Bannister, have ever been there. Mr. Stewart is the second who has ever been there, so you may imagine we were excited when that letter came telling us to go at once. He said he had had a very good time, and that the men all listened so quietly. There was a catechist and a Christian school teacher there, but no Christian *women* at all; and to make matters more difficult, there is no woman, heathen or otherwise, in the catechist's house, his wife being away; but Mr. Stewart had asked them, and they said it would be all right for two of us to go with the Bible-woman. It took a little time to make up our minds, but after prayer we felt that the Lord would have us go at once, especially as the Bible-woman was quite willing to accompany us. That night we were up long after the early household had retired to rest. We wrote letters to the Ku Cheng compound to tell them we had gone, and we packed our traps, and about twelve o'clock went to bed. We were up about 5.30 the next morning, and finished arranging our things. The women were in a great state of excitement at our going, and so was the native servant. He always goes with the itinerating Kuniong; he is a Christian, and such a nice man. His name is Ah Kien. We got up ourselves regardless, in the women's silver bracelets and our wigs done in Chinese style. It is always done up if you do not want to be taken for a man. And off we went, amid the Ping angs and all good wishes from the dear people. I can't tell you all about the chair journey. It was all through the most beautiful country, and all up hill. I don't think we were going down the side of a hill at all. The women in

the villages we passed through had never seen foreign
ladies before, and they crowded round us, especially in
the last one, where we were literally surrounded by an
admiring audience. The country grew more and more
lovely, and the air purer the further we went, as we were
rising all the time. At last, about half-past five o'clock,
we saw, lying in a valley watered by a river, a large
village surrounded by wooded mountains. We asked if
it was Dong Kau, and the coolies said 'Yes.' So, as we
were walking at the time, we got into our chairs and
composed ourselves, not knowing quite what sort of reception we should get, but being prepared for a good deal,
as no one there had ever seen a foreign woman before.
As we approached the village, Ah Kien changed his
position from the rear of the chairs, and ran on ahead to
guard us as much as he could, and to find the catechist's
house, as none of us had the slightest idea where it was.
Well, he stalked on and our chairs followed; a good many
people looked at them coming, but when we got close to
them the fun began. They stared as though they could
not believe their eyes, and we passed through crowds of
them in perfect silence, but that did not last long. As
soon as we had passed through the first lots and were
going after Ah Kien, who was trotting ahead as fast as
he could go, through the streets where the people had not
seen the chairs coming, we heard behind us a roar of
voices and soon the rush of feet coming after us. They
had soon concluded where we were going to, and were
running after us to see us get out. About fifty or sixty
men passed my chair, which was first, before we were
half-way to the place. But at last I saw Ah Kien go into

the space before a large native house, and concluded he had found our destination. Only a moment or two later my coolies walked with my chair into this place, and stopped at a wide doorway leading into a large *tiang-dong*, which was literally crammed with men, who had all rushed to see us as we passed through, and more were trying to cram in. There was a tremendous row, and I did not like to call out to Annie, but I knew that if she were going in there she would have to go past my chair, so I sat still and waited. In a few minutes I beheld Ah Kien and a man whose face I recognised, and who I guessed was the catechist, shouldering their way through the crowd with anxious and excited countenances. Directly he saw us, the catechist called out: 'Ping ang, Kuniong!' and then he told me to get out, and hurried past to Annie's chair. Ah Kien was so excited that he nearly seized me by the arm to assist the operation of getting out of the chair. But the yells, when they saw us walking up the steps! Ah Kien and the catechist took us into the house by another way, but there were stairs leading to that part of the house from the place where the crowd was, and when we got into the passage they were pushing their way up these stairs; but our two kind friends hurried us down the passage, through two or three rooms, and finally led us into what we think was the catechist's bedroom, and there we were left and the door locked on us. Well, we sat down on the bed and giggled, as you may imagine. But though we were so securely shut up, the crowds by no means gave up in despair, but did all they could to get in. Ding Sing-Sang and Ah Kien repaired upstairs to get our room ready for us, and

did not come back to let us out till the crowds had gone,
or only a few people were left. Then we went upstairs
to our room, which is about the size of our lavatory, with
no window, but several cracks in the mud wall. Ah Kien
told Ding Sing-Sang that we would die if we had not air,
and with that he bunged a hole in the thin part of the
wall. I had always heard that the Chinese were very
quick at inventing methods. It is as cold here as it was
two months ago at Ku Cheng, being several hundred feet
higher, so we had to get a board over the hole to keep the
breeze from blowing us inside out during the night.
That night a lot of men came, but the stairs were guarded,
and they could not get up, so they left us invitations to
go and drink tea at their houses next day. But Mr.
Stewart had directed us to stay in the house and let the
women come and see us, and our own feeling told us that.
We had no foreign things with us, and we ate our food
out of Chinese bowls with chopsticks. We had scarcely
finished breakfast when the first lot of women came.
Some were awfully frightened, but in most curiosity got
the better of fear. The Lord was so good in it all. He
brought them in *lots*, not one huge crowd all talking at
once, when it would have been quite impossible to talk to
them. They came about twenty or thirty at a time, and
filled the little room we were sitting in. Ah Kien and
the catechist were downstairs, and did their best to keep
the men down, but they could not prevent some of them
coming, and as three sides of the room are open, the men
stood outside and gazed all they wanted to. They all
asked questions; wanted to know all about everything.
Annie spoke a little, and the Bible-woman a great deal.

She is very faithful, but we noticed that none of them seemed to like being told of sin. They nearly all said they had no sins; but when they were asked if they never did such and such things, and were shown that they were sin, they did not like it a bit. Human nature is the same all over the world, and the power of Satan stronger here than anywhere in the nominally Christian countries, so that it is no wonder if he fights against the truth of the Gospel. Their own conscience seems to convict them, in most cases, that what we say about sin is perfectly right."

CHAPTER VIII

SPRING EMPLOYMENTS AND JOURNEYINGS

Dr. Gregory's care of Topsy—Nellie's instructor—His history—
Hopes for the future—Topsy as a nurse—Advice on diet—
Mr. Stewart's labours—And recreations—Daughters of the
family—Topsy and Elsie—Another journey—Tea-picking—
Friendly peasants—A missionary's dwelling—Rambles and
visits—Doctoring a baby—Plain living essential.

THE process of acclimatisation told more severely on
Topsy than on her sister. She suffered from frequent
headaches, which were greatly aggravated by the study
of the difficult Chinese "character." Dr. Gregory, of the
American Mission, exercised a most paternal supervision
over her, and quickly saw that she was better suited for
active work than for study. Accordingly he made no
difficulty about granting her earnest request that she
might be allowed to join Miss Marshall in her country
work at Sek Chek Du—about twelve miles from Ku
Cheng—in order that, by living among the country
people and hearing only Chinese spoken around her, she
might pick up the colloquial language, and postpone for
the present the literary study of Chinese. The doctor
only stipulated that she should return every few weeks
to report herself to him, and on these occasions she received not only the doctor's kind attentions, but as much
loving care from Mrs. Stewart as her own mother could

have given her. An unfounded report seems to have reached the Home Committee that Topsy was rather an invalid ; but so far was this from being the case that she was incessantly in active work after her first two months in China, and latterly, as her strength increased, her activity became extraordinary, as these letters abundantly show.

Meantime Nellie was giving a large proportion of her time to study, and gave promise of passing her first examination at an early date. Her usual instructor was Wong Senang—a Christian ; but he having to go down to Foochow in May for family reasons, she read with Mr. Stewart's teacher—Mr. Ting—who was not a Christian, but who was soon on terms of friendship with his pupil.

Nellie writes :—" On Saturday morning I began reading with Mr. Ting. I do like him very much, and must describe him to you. He is very tall for a Chinaman, and looks very dignified with his long blue cotton gown, and little coat made of darker blue stuff, and leggings to match. The sleeves of a literary man's coat must be very long, so that when he walks they hang well over the ends of his finger nails. I say 'finger nails' because they are such an important item, adding about an inch to the end of the fingers. Mr. Ting is quite a celebrated person, having about the best literary reputation in Ku Cheng, and besides that he is a great artist, and makes a lot of money by painting scrolls and fans and things. He has told me scraps of his history at different times, and patched together it is as follows :—Some time ago, about seven years I think, he first heard the Gospel preached, and thought it was very good, being then, like all the

literary men, a Confucianist. He wanted very much to
hear more, but his people all made such objection that he
did not keep on; but he wished to hear, and never forgot
about it. At last he thought he would try and get employment among the foreigners as teacher, but his wife
and every one raised such opposition that he gave in
about that; but soon after his wife grumpily told him to
go off if he wanted, and so he went out to Sa Yong to see
a friend of his who was Maude Newcombe's teacher. (I
think his persistence is so wonderful, don't you?) He
stayed there a month, going to prayers every night and
to service on Sundays; and the catechist and this friend
of his, between them, taught him a good deal, and influ-
enced him so much that, when he came back to Ku
Cheng, in spite of everything, he came to see Mr.
Bannister, who told him about Jesus, and got him clearly
to understand. That was a year ago, and since that time
he has been coming regularly to church, and at Christmas
time he became Mr. Stewart's teacher. I have liked his
face from the first, and, strangely enough, felt strongly
led to pray for him. And now he and I are great friends.
The Stewarts have a great roll of pictures which was sent
to them from Canada, and the other morning, when I was
reading in the study, Lena came in looking for a book,
and in her search she came on these pictures, and asked
me what they were. She held them up and was looking
at them, and we were talking about them, when suddenly
I noticed Mr. Ting's face simply staring at them with his
eyes and mouth wide open. So, after she had gone I
showed them to him, and there were two especially that
overcame him altogether. One was Daniel in the lions'

den; it seemed *so* funny to be telling that old story to some one who was hearing it for the *first time*. My Chinese is rather poor, but I managed to get him to understand, and his *interest* was something astonishing. The other picture was one of Shadrach, Meshach, and Abednego in the fiery furnace with the Lord Jesus, and the horrid old king looking in at the mouth of the furnace. I got Mrs. Stewart to come and tell him in better Chinese than I could muster, because I didn't know how to put the names of the people into Chinese. Then Mrs. Stewart lent him the book, which was Mr. Stewart's, to read the whole story for himself.

"I have had some such nice talks with him. I am quite sure he is a real Christian at heart, but he doesn't yet know enough to enter the Church. It seems so strange to talk to a creature of his intellect and literary attainments who is utterly ignorant of such things as steamboats and trains. I had such fun to-day telling him about the trains—'a cart that can walk by itself.' He said the Englishmen were very clever, and he didn't know how they ever found out how to make such strange things."

Nine months later (February 1895) we find the following in one of Nellie's letters:—"Oh! I have *such* a thing to tell you. Yesterday Toppy went to Sek Chek Du, and Mr. Wong has gone with her, so I have again resorted to Mr. Ting (Mr. Stewart's teacher), and I was talking to him as usual. This is the first time since the conference, and he was talking about his friend, the other Mr. Ting (from Sang Tong), who is such a splendid Christian, and with whom he attended every meeting, and was conspicuous in one of the front seats every night. The Sunday morning of the baptisms he was sitting in the row exactly behind the candidates, and on my reminding him of this he said, 'Next year I will be among them.' He has made up his mind to be baptized. Praise God! I am so glad. I had *such* a nice talk with him to-day."

Topsy improved her medical knowledge at Dr. Gregory's hospital, and was able from time to time to make herself very useful as a nurse to any of the lady missionaries who required her services. In May 1894, she writes as follows:—" On Friday poor Flora Codrington was brought in from her station very ill indeed. Poor girl, she had great trouble about the wife of the catechist there, of whom she was very fond, and the poor little thing was very ill; she had a baby, and whatever the horrid Chinese woman, who was called in to attend her, did or did not do, the poor little creature died. Flora sat up all night with the mother, and did all she could for her, but she has gone to the bright home above. Well, there was a terrible to-do. All the people—not the Christians, of course—say that the Kuniong killed her, and are in a dreadful way, and then it looked so suspicious, for the very day after Flora broke completely down. She had been not at all well for some time, and the grief at her poor little friend's death and everything finished her."

Miss Codrington was nursed through her illness by Topsy, who also made use of her professional experience to give her mother sage advice on the subject of diet in China. In answer to a question on this subject, she says:—" Oatmeal you can get, but don't want; at least,

I don't. Do you know this, that China is a funny place, and the things that it has are far better than imported things. Now every morning, instead of porridge, we have a great plateful of plain boiled rice, with buffalo milk and sugar, and it is just tipping! I could not possibly do without my rice in the morning now! It is not a quarter as heating as porridge, and it tastes much nicer. Now, the wheaten meal touches a point on which I feel deeply. You can get heaps of wheat here as cheap as anything. On the other hand, if you buy flour in Foochow it is very expensive—first, its own cost, and then the cost of carting it up, and it is such heavy stuff. But Mr. Bannister is a wonderful man; I do admire him very much. He got a grinding machine out from England, and bought his wheat for next to nothing, and made one of the men grind it up. So there he had his own little mill on the place; and I propose to adopt the same plan when we are settled at Ning Taik."

Mr. Stewart's time was much occupied, in the cool months, with travelling about over his vast district; and whether at home or abroad, he was doing, as the girls both declare, "the work of six."

" Mr. Stewart came back last week looking very well after his trip all round; he had a lovely time, and says that on the borders of this province, beyond Ping Nang city, there are thousands of people who have never heard of Christ. Is it not dreadful? And he says that they are such nice, kind people too, speaking a terrible brogue which he could not understand, but which you could learn easily enough, he thinks. He has a frightful lot

to do, having all the Church Missionary Society and
Church of England Zenana Mission accounts to keep,
and everybody refers to him, and all sorts of people
come after him at all times of the day, so at last he had
to take refuge in the Bannisters' house (now unused), and
there he sat all day and most of the night in Mr. Bannister's old study doing this work. Even then, in the
midst of some intricate calculation, in will come one of
the gentlemen who assist in running the establishment,
to request the Sing-Sang to come and look at the well,
or the pump, or something. On Sunday the poor man
looked a perfect wreck, but he turned up at church,
though he had stayed in bed for breakfast."

He was not above taking a little occasional recreation
at the invitation of the girls. A set of croquet, made by
a native workman, gave a good deal of innocent amusement. Nellie writes:—"I never finished telling you
about yesterday. After the prayer-meeting we sallied
outside, at least I and the children, and played croquet.
Presently, when all the people had gone, Mr. Stewart
came to play, and we had rather a nice game till it began
to get dark, and then, you never saw such a thing;
every time that man moved, he caught his leg in one of
the hoops, and carried it nearly to the other end of the
place!"

The girls had found a truly happy home with the
Stewarts. "One of the very sweetest women you ever
saw," is Nellie's testimony to the missionary's wife.
And they were both, as it were, elder daughters in the
family. About this time Nellie writes:—"I have nearly
killed myself this mail sitting up writing letters. Yester-

day morning (Sunday) I did not wake till everybody had gone down to breakfast, and I heard a little voice at the door saying, 'Father would like to know if you would like some rice put through the keyhole.' I felt inclined to sing out that 'Father needn't talk, as he is often late himself.'—In great haste, my own dearest Miss, your own loving child, NELL."

But Topsy was soon out on her travels in company with Elsie Marshall. The friendship between these two was fervent on both sides. On the one hand, Miss Marshall in her letters refers admiringly to Topsy as being "so strong" (in character, I presume) "and able to do things;" and, on the other hand, Topsy characteristically says of her friend—"She is such an insinuating little rabbit that no one can help loving her."

The following journey was undertaken some time in May 1894 :—"We started this morning, at 8 A.M., for Gang Ka, where we have just now arrived, at 1.30 P.M. It was beautiful coming along the road this morning, if one can call the narrow path a road. In some places it was so narrow that the chair filled the whole width, and just then we were sure to meet a string of men carrying tea, and great would be the exclamations in passing. We admire the way they crawl over the most awful places with the chair swinging over a paddy field a good way below. You would laugh to see the caravan going along, consisting of two chairs and four ragged coolies, a *dang-dang* (load-man), and our own coolie: it seems quite a regiment to take with one, but it can't be helped, because going out for a week we have to take so many things, and among them our beds.

"It's tea-picking season now, and nearly all the people are out doing either that or reaping. If you saw the way the tea is prepared for packing! The villages are mostly built on the edge of the fields, all now under water, and there is just a narrow path between the houses and these dirty ponds. Over the ponds are built long rafts, and on these are spread straw mats, on which the tea is laid, I suppose, to dry. We see them rubbing it in their hands. I am sure it can't be good for it to be sun-dried over those awful ponds. We passed strings of men on the way down carrying the tea sewn up in canvas bags. It's quite polite to ask every one you meet where they are going, and they all ask us where we come from, where going, what to do, how old we are, and anything else they happen to think of which may be of personal interest, but they are all such nice friendly people, I do love them so; it's just lovely going about in the country. Every one is always so glad to see us; of course, they stare and make remarks, but that can hardly be wondered at, and we are treated much better by these heathen than many so-called Christians treat them. We got in about 1.30. The Gang Ka chapel is much the same as all the others I have seen, only we don't have a room by the women's *tiang-dong*. We have a loft just under the roof, and looking out over the roofs of all the neighbours' houses. It's rather warm, but then it's very large. When we got in, of course they gave us tea, and we saw the catechist disappear upstairs with a dustpan and broom, and guessed our loft wasn't quite presentable just then, so we waited for about ten minutes and then went up. We found it fairly clean, but absolutely empty, not even a bench to sit on. Gradually the furniture began to arrive. A long bench, a chair, presently a table, with what looked like the dust of ages all round it. Of course, all the women and babies came too, but after a while we managed to get them out and got some water; one does relish a wash after a chair ride. Then our coolie fetched in some dinner for us, and that was hardly disposed of before the company began to arrive. Then some one fetched in some boards and two stools to make our bed, and then two more chairs, so that we are quite well off. The women's *tiang-dong* is just beneath our room, and Elsie has just taken all the women down there to teach them, and I am tidying up. One is afraid to move things much, or hang things on pegs, for fear of disturbing the live stock; but you can't think how nice it is being here. There is such a lot to be done—such heaps of people. It's just dreadful to think that there are hundreds here in absolute ignorance of God, and we can do so very little; but it is God's Holy Spirit that only can work, so I am glad we are weak, if it gives Him all the glory. Elsie is going out visiting with the Bible-woman. I am so tired that I can't, so will write to you a little and then lie down; only there is such a noise it's almost impossible to rest. There isn't what you would call a proper window here, but there are two holes punched in the mud wall at one side, and some of the boards are out on the side overlooking the street, so we have plenty of air, such as it is. At present it rather savours of pig; however, that's only a detail.

" We went an excursion up one of the very many hills

after some lovely pink flowers, like immense azaleas, and smelling so sweet, and passed a temple on the road, where we saw an old man kneeling down in front of the idol's table, hitting the ground with two bones on the end of a string. We stayed to watch him, and when he came out in about five minutes, we asked what he was doing. He was a very old man and rather deaf, but at last Elsie managed to make out, with the help of a tea *dang dang* who was passing, and stopped to join the conversation, that he was praying to the gods for his sons, who had turned out very badly, and had gone to Foochow as thieves (that seems to be a sort of trade here); so she told him the idols couldn't hear, and talked to him about God who could. He seemed very pleased, and as we walked along the same road he talked a great deal, and then asked us to come to his house for tea. As we got into his village—rather a large one across the stream—such lots of people came out and asked us in, so we went and had a grand time. They listened so well, and some women promised to come to-day. We didn't get back till 6 P.M., and found the women coming out to look for us.

"The following morning visitors came in crowds from an early hour. It was eleven before we got upstairs, and then only for a few minutes, because a patient arrived on the scene to be doctored, *i.e.*, a baby that had fallen down and scratched itself, and what with dirt and flies was pretty bad. However, we fixed it up, greatly to every one's admiration. We asked for water to wash it with, and one small boy went and got us a large tub; another brought a bucket of water; another a large bowl of hot water; all this was for a sore the size of half-a-crown on the baby's face; really it was so funny we couldn't help laughing. However, I hope it will get better; they have such faith in our medicines. I do think people ought to know something about it out here.

"One feels here that one must try and live as much as possible the life of one whose citizenship is in heaven, and not here. The Chinese Christians are very poor, it is the same here as it was in the days when Jesus Himself was on earth, 'the common people heard Him gladly.' 'Not many wise, not many noble;' and you feel that there must be nothing in your house, or in your style of living, that makes them think you are very rich. The Stewarts' house is almost mean in its utter simplicity —nothing but what one really wants."

CHAPTER IX

TOPSY'S SEASIDE HOLIDAY

Hot weather—Sharp Peak described—Boat voyage thither—Village
visiting on the way—Robbed in the night—A short cut—
Rumours of the war—Twenty-first birthday—Longings for
work—War alarms—Dreaming of invasion—The Submarine
Cable.

JULY and August being holiday months, owing to the
impossibility of working in the intense heat that then pre-
vails, it was settled that Topsy should join Dr. Gregory's
family and other members of the American Mission at
the seaside sanatorium of Sharp Peak, at the mouth
of the river Min, below Foochow. She describes the
place as follows :—

"Sharp Peak is nearly a day's journey down the river
from Foochow. It is a rocky island about three miles
round, just at the mouth of the Min, where it flows into
the sea. We see the steamers coming in and going out.
One of the tea steamers left for home the other day.
The three missions, two American and one English, have
houses here, and besides that there is the telegraph and
cable house for Foochow and right up inland to Pekin,
and those are all the foreign habitations on the island.
It is bare rock, except for a few terraces of cultivation
in the more sheltered parts of the island. The people
mostly go in for the fishing trade, and every morning

quite a little fleet of sampans goes out, with their dirty little brown sails up, but they look so pretty. I am stopping with some of the Americans, the doctor who has the hospital at Ku Chêng that I told you about, and the nurse who is my particular chum. They are such nice people. Before we came here I heard a good deal about the luxurious houses the missionaries had at this Peak, but the luxury is a thing of the past, if it was ever there at all. The houses are long, and two rooms deep, with a veranda along the front, and divided with wooden partitions into sets of two suites. Every sound can be heard right through, especially the babies squalling. Each inmate brings his own chair, table, &c., and whatever he wants—and picnics. The great attraction for the country folks is of course the sea. Even six months has shown me that one needs a change from the odours of the cities, and the doctors try and get us all out of the country for at least one month. On the way down to Sharp Peak there are crowds and crowds of villages, and so another girl and I made an expedition in a little native boat, instead of coming down in the house-boat, and did some of the villages on the way. We hired the boat, just a little sampan with a family on board, consisting of two men and a boy to manage the boat, and a woman, either the captain's wife or his daughter; and also a pigeon, who was bathed every morning, and lived on hard peas and seeds, and whose share of the boat room was under one of the boards, where it cooed contentedly most of the time. They couldn't make out what we wanted to do, but at last arrived at an understanding of the fact, and then in-

formed all the other sampans along the river that this was
a preaching boat. They always call out and ask, 'Where
are you going?' and our boatmen didn't at all like
being in the dark on the subject. We paddled about,
and stopped at about ten villages, where we were received
very nicely. At night we anchored with all the other
sampans, generally a whole lot of little ones attached by
ropes to one big one, and then we went on the big one
and talked to the people, and at night every one sat on
the front of the boat, and we talked and sang and had
a very good time. It was so nice, it helped to make up
for not being able to do anything for two whole months.
If there is anything I have left out, I will tell you when
I get back to Ku Cheng and have a look at your letter."

The journey to Sharp Peak is more fully described
in another letter. Having first gone down to Foochow,
where she spent a week, Topsy was to proceed by boat
to the mouth of the river, accompanied by Miss Marshall,
and these zealous young ladies resolved to do a little
visiting among the river villages on the way.

"When we started and our things were fixed up on
board, we sat down on two little bamboo stools and
contemplated the situation. We were on the way we
knew not whither, but to some place which the Lord
had prepared, we knew, because we had asked Him to.
Just as we had finished our prayer-meeting, we came
near a large village right on the banks of the river; the
men suggested going in there, and we said 'Stop' at
the same moment. So in we went. A few people
washing clothes stopped to look at us as we landed,
but said nothing; then two or three men hurried up,

and immediately one took us under his guidance and
led the way to the village, all smiles and affability, and
then the crowds came. Women and children crowded
in till the *tiang-dong* was simply packed, and they listened
with all their ears, and were so quiet, and asked to be told
about it again, and said the words were 'very good, and it
was very good altogether.' One girl's mother—I suppose
she was her mother—said she would like her very much
to go to school and learn to read and be taught, and there
were two specially nice women and two or three men who
were very intelligent. We went to two houses in that
village, and then it was time to leave, so they escorted us
down to the boat and stood there for ever so long, as we
slowly left them in the distance. These dear country
people are utterly lovable after a week in Foochow; we
even enjoyed the smells, and there was something so nice
in being in their very midst again. I think there is not
such a peace in the world as comes from taking the knowledge of life to these poor dead souls, for whom Christ
died; and as for talking about the self-denial and discom-
fort, my experience is that God is never our debtor, and
we would jump round this little boat, we are so overflowing with joy, only there is not room for one thing, and
besides it would shock the boatmen.

"Since then we have sustained several severe losses.
We went peaceably to sleep and woke about 3 A.M. with the
rocking of the boat, the lamp threatening to swing away
altogether. We wondered what was up, so I looked round
and discovered that my clothes were gone. We looked
further and found more things had departed. A thief
had come and relieved us of our belongings—most neces-

sary articles of attire—stockings, and my skirt, a sponge
bag, a cup, and a few other things. It is a very sad
world! There was no hope of discovering the man, the
whole place being crowded with them, so we put the rest
of our belongings into our pillow-cases, and went to sleep
again. 'Take joyfully the spoiling of your goods.'

"You know Sharp Peak is an island of rock, with a few
pine trees on it at the mouth of the river Min. The three
sanatoriums and the telegraph house are the only habitations, except for a little fishing village down at the landing.
The only walks are narrow paths cut round the sides of the
hills out of the rocks. As you turn round the points from
where the American house stands, you see on the opposite
hill the Church Missionary Society house, looking just
about one hundred yards away, if you could walk straight
there, but the hill is very steep, and below is a beach of
high sand hillocks, and then a tough climb the other side,
so no one ever goes that way, but follows the path around
the hill for about half-an-hour. Now I never believe in
going a long way round when there is a short way, so I
made up my mind to crawl down that hill across the sand
and get to the Church Missionary Society house that way;
they told me not to attempt it, but that only added a little
more desire to do it. So yesterday I went and did it in a
quarter of an hour, and back in twenty minutes, which
was '*a have*' for the folks who said I could not do it; so
you see I have not improved much in that respect, but I
hate being tied down to doing things in ordinary ways; it
is much nicer to invent a way for yourself.

"Fancy, in three days now your baby will be no longer
an infant in the eye of the law. It seems so funny being

away from home where no one knows. I study every morning now, it is so nice, I just love learning Chinese. I am reading Matthew now and translating into English, and then going through John with the English Bible, translating back into Chinese; it is such good practice. I suppose you have heard rumours about the war between China and Japan about Corea; no one seems to know what is really going to happen, but all down the river here, from the Pagoda anchorage, they have the military sampans out. You would have a fit if you saw them, and they say there are torpedoes down the river, but we don't believe that, as it has not come from the Consulate. Some one said there were two or three Japanese war boats outside, but it is not likely. You need not be in the least alarmed, dear Petsy; it would be rather fun, but for the loss of life. The Chinese are not likely to fight. 'Wars and rumours of wars. . . . Lift up your heads, for your redemption draweth nigh.'

" So near in God's love, and yet so far away. How I long to rest my head on your shoulder just for one minute. Is it very weak-minded? I have said nothing about its being my birthday. Although they are all so kind, and I love them very much, still I preferred to enter on my twenty-first year alone. I got letters from Ku Cheng, and Elsie sent me a very pretty watch strap, and the baby Stewarts made me a bag. It was so nice of them to remember. Dearest, I don't understand about the house, but it is well. He says, we know not now, but some day shall; and all we know here is that no one can separate us from the love of Christ—no, not tribulation, nor any of those outside blasts. He abideth ever, and we in Him.

"I can't write my letters to suit the public. If I can't write just as I feel inclined to, then nothing will go at all. I write every now and then to most of the folks, but your letters are for you, and not for the *Argus*.

"Next term Elsie and I have a scheme, yet quite immature, that we shall go and live at Gang-Ka, as that is such a good centre, and have a sort of station class. I would teach Romanised to the women, and take my teacher and study. We would have our loft done up. It is not settled yet, and can't be till we get back, but we are both longing to do it; there is so much better an opportunity out in the country of picking up the language and getting to know the people.

"*31st July.*—I took my book on the hillside to-day and lay and watched the sea and meditated. Oh! my dear mother, when are you coming? My birthday verse is— 'Jesus became poor that ye, through His poverty, might be rich.' And if we follow Him and become poor, not only in money and worldly advantage, but in the dearest links of life, that many may come to know the riches of God, surely that is our reward. 'Greater love hath no man than this, that a man lay down his life for his friends.'

"*2nd and 3rd August.*—Just the ordinary course of events. I like this, but I want to get back to the country among my beloved people. I hope our scheme will work.

"I suppose you have heard great stories about the Japs. Well, of course there are ever so many different tales, but I think it is true that war is declared. The American Consul wrote down here and sent a flag, and said they were fighting off Formosa and Corea. He said that the Chinese at Foochow believe that the United

States are in league with Japan, which is not true, but they have taken the non-combatants, merchants, &c., and others who are living in the ports under the protection of the Consulate; and he told them here not to fly the flag unless an attack was made on Foochow, which is not at all likely. In any case, dear, there is not any need for anxiety on our account, because the foreign gunboats would come down, and they would never touch us. It would involve too much. The doctor said if war really came there would be a field hospital needed, and he would go and take us two as nurses. Would not that be nice? So we got out all his instruments and cleaned them up, and looked round to see what there was, but I don't believe we shall want them after all. We heard the Chinese were going to stop the river up with torpedoes and make the anchorage for the boats at Sharp Peak, but so far the steamers have all been going in, so I suppose that is a fairy tale. We hear them practising their guns up at the forts. I hope they will be able to use them when the time comes, if it does; but all say they have no chance at all against the Japs. Numbers of rich Chinese have left Foochow and gone up country, according to the latest accounts, to hang on to their money, which they take about in cakes of gold.

"The other night some of the folks dreamt the Japs were coming. Miss Casterton heard them firing away outside, and the doctor said he heard the windows being opened and the Japs coming in, and woke up to hear a loud crash, caused by the mud plaster coming down off the veranda roof. Thus ended the Japs' invasion.

"I hope you are not allowing yourself to be troubled

by either the plague at Hongkong or the war business. We hear hardly anything about the first, except that the mortality is very great among the natives, and a few Europeans have died. The last news of the war that we can believe is that the Japs have taken Formosa; Chinese loss stated at five thousand. The gunboats are cruising about and protecting the entrance. A German boat was boarded the other day. The river is torpedoed up to the anchorage, and the Chinese are in a great state of excitement all round, but nothing has happened definitely. They burned down the native Customs with oil one day last week. We are quite safe, and having a good time. At the time of the trouble with the French there were a good many missionaries down here, and nothing happened to them at all; so don't be worrying yourself. I know you will not; but still you will like to know that there is no necessity to feel anxious at all. You will probably see greatly exaggerated reports. The men at the Telegraph House told the doctor that all the code messages had been stopped, and only plain English is allowed through the offices.

"We went down to the cable-house the other morning to see the cables work. It was so interesting. I could have sent you a message for fifty dollars in about half-an-hour. While we were there a message came in from New York that had only taken a few hours, and we saw the place where the cables come up out of the ground. If the *Menmuir* comes in I will go down, as you say, and see them. The friends here will go too, and we will go in the house-boat. It takes about two or three hours to go to the anchorage from here."

CHAPTER X

NELLIE'S MIDSUMMER HOLIDAY

Difficulty of sleeping—Packing-up—Children and chair-coolies—The summer residence—Keeping house—Native names—Superstition and cruelty—Arrival of the Stewarts—Sunday at Hua Sang—Mountain picnic—The catechist's hospitality—Visiting—Letters from home—Agitation about the war—Village homes.

NELLIE'S holiday was spent at Hua Sang, a village perched among the mountains that overlook the valley in which Ku Cheng is situated, and looking down upon that city from a height of about 1500 feet. Being thus some 2500 feet above sea-level, Hua Sang is well suited to be a summer resort, but, as the sad event proved, this comparatively lovely place was not a safe retreat for our missionaries when deadly enemies were plotting against them. In the following extracts Nellie gives an account of her holiday :—

"The Kuniongs from 'The Olives,' Miss Weller, Annie Gordon, and Ada Nisbitt, took their departure for Hua Sang on the Tuesday. I felt very bad all that day, and it was as much as I could do to crawl home, so I kept out of people's way, because I dislike being told I look ill, and have black rings round my eyes, &c. That night and the next two were very trying—fearfully hot, and lots of skeeters. Our one chance when going to bed is to leave the windows wide open, and I must say that then I can sleep, though some people can't. But these nights were

H

particularly trying, because, to add to the other evils, a Chinese theatre was being acted at the Lo-Dia's (magistrate) in the city; but though it was across the river at his house, you would have thought it was under the hedge outside the window. Every sound could be distinctly heard—the pipes, drums, singing and screeching were something frightful. But though that kept me awake for a long time, at last I fell asleep, and dreamt that Sin Ciong was banging the gong downstairs furiously for me to get up and come down to breakfast. At last, getting tired of it, I woke up, saying in agonised accents, 'Oh, shut up! do shut up!' and Frances Johnson said from the other bed, 'What's the matter?' Then we found out that it was *only* four o'clock in the morning, and it was the final performance, the killing of the devils, that had wakened me. You *never* in all your days heard such a demoniacal din. We shut the windows then and went back to bed, and to sleep, for they shut up shortly after that.

"I could not go a chair journey on Friday as I was too sick, so it was put off till Saturday, and we had to get packed up and ready to start very early next morning, so as to get the worst of the trip over in the cool of the day. It *was* a job. First I had to sort out what I wanted for Hua Sang; then all the remainder of Toppy's and my woollen things had to be sunned, brought in and cooled, and packed away in the big tin trunks with paper and camphor. With a racking head on me I managed most of it, but even then there were things that I could not get in, and they had to be made into a bundle to go to Toppy in Foochow, to be put away in our tin-lined cases.

"And that reminds me to ask you to save up all the

little tin-boxes you can lay your hands on. You want a
tin box for your papers, and if your needles and pins and
hairpins aren't kept in a tin box they turn rusty in a
single night. Mildred and Kathleen were up at 3.30 on
Saturday morning, but I didn't stir till 4.15, when I got
up and dressed and finished getting my things together,
and by that time Mr. Stewart had come over, and was
hard at work downstairs. Then he came and called me,
and I wasn't dressed, and had to tell him so, and then he
laughed at me and went away, and then we had to fly
around like anything and go down to breakfast at five
o'clock, and poor Frances Johnson had to get up and
struggle into her things, and Sin Ciong came upstairs to
get the boxes, and she had to take refuge, with very little
on, in the bathroom. Then, after we had finished breakfast downstairs, I carried her up some tea, which she
demolished; she was dressed then, and expecting another
invasion of the men for the rest of our things. Then I
went and said good-bye to Mrs. Stewart, and then we
started, Mr. Stewart coming with us as far as the boys'
school, just outside the compound gate. We got into our
chairs, the three children in one and I in the other, and
Frances came rushing down at the last moment to say
good-bye to us all. Then Mr. Stewart stood on a little
hill and shouted directions after us. We had a very nice
trip up; it was quite cool till about ten o'clock, and then
not so bad, as we had got a little higher. In one place
we came to a beautiful little mountain stream coming
down among the bamboos and rocks. We were very
hot, but I didn't dare to drink any of it, or let the children, because it is so unsafe to drink water here unless

you are perfectly certain where it comes from. The coolies made great objections to carrying the three children in the chair, and one old scamp did his best to get me to let the children's chair go last, where, of course, I couldn't see it, and he told me various good reasons why this would be the better course of action; but I simply stuck to my point, *Niegiang gien seng geang* ('the children's chair is to go in front'), and I reiterated this in spite of all he said. He argued fearfully about it, but in the end I got my way. The stairs up the mountain are truly appalling. They are called *liangs*. The last one especially was very terrible. We reached it just about the hottest time of the morning, and they requested me to get out and walk, which I did, not thinking it was very far, but I nearly expired on that *liang*—it was terrible—and when I got to the top I sank expiring into my chair. The coolies were sympathetic, but inexorable.

"However, they carried me the rest of the way. I felt rather nervous, because Kathleen, who had also walked up the *liang*, rushed on ahead, crying out that she could see houses, and when my chair started she was nowhere to be seen. But she was all right. I saw her presently, when the houses came into view, poking about looking at things. The Church Missionary Society House is the first you come to. '*Church Missionary Society House*' looks grand written down, but 'mud and wood shanty' would be a better name for it. There is a veranda all along the front, with shutters to keep out the afternoon sun, and two fair-sized rooms opening off it, and behind it three little ones and one new room added this year at the back for the children to play in.

I only waited to see that Sa Mi, the Stewarts' house coolie, was there to look after things—he is an exceedingly good honest boy—and then, with the children, turned the corner of the house and went down the flight of rough steps leading to the Kuniongs' precincts. They were very pleased to see us, and there we sat and drank cold water with syrup in it, and related our adventures and looked at their house. You go straight in from the little open piece of ground in front into a nice-sized room which is their reception room. Folding doors, always kept wide open, divide it from the next room, where they have their meals, and that is the whole width of the house. The bed-rooms, six in number, open off the other rooms, and each one has in it a little comfortable bed, table, chest of drawers, and a bamboo chair.

"Well, since our arrival on that Saturday I have been doing Mamma up here, with two men and three children to manage. I get on all right, though I thought I mightn't at first. On Sunday we had a very quiet day— the children and I—and in the afternoon Ada and Annie came up, and we sang hymns for a good while and then went for a walk. Monday and Tuesday pretty much as usual. I have been painting a wooden frame for Toppy's birthday. I have put on it, 'Jesus became poor that ye, through His poverty, might be rich.' Is it not a wonderful, wonderful verse? When I look at it, it just thrills through me. The little girls are quite happy watching me paint, and I have to tell them stories. They have a perfect passion for being told stories. There is one great trouble here, and that is about the water. There is a spring near the village, but the people won't let us have any water from it; they prevent our men drawing it, and simply won't let us have any. Of course, they want money; you can't blame them; they are nearly all heathen. If we were to appeal to the Lo-Dia (magistrate) we could get it, because they have no right to prevent us, but no one does that (none of us, I mean) unless there is absolutely no other way. Then there is another man here who has a large well, and last year the Bannisters and the Kuniongs both together only paid three dollars for the use of it, but this year the wretched creature won't let us have any unless we give him six dollars, which is simply ridiculous. The Kuniongs' cook and my two retainers are in a terrible stew, and I have written a letter every day to Mr. Stewart about it. His last instructions, received by the milkman this morning —(we get buffalo milk from Ku Cheng; it is very nice; a rich white)—were to give him what he asks. But it is fun. You ought to hear me airing my Chinese—still decidedly limited—on these two men. One of them is named Lek-Muoi, which means 'sixth little sister.' He is a great broad-shouldered strapping creature, and to be calling him Lek-Muoi seems the height of absurdity. The reason of this peculiarly inappropriate title is this— that when a little boy is born the parents wish to keep him from evil as much as possible, so they frequently give the boys some absurd name like that, so that the evil spirits will be deceived, and won't try to hurt the youngster, or worse than that, take him away. They think the spirits don't like girls, so very often they are called 'Muoi,' which means little sister. One of the Kuniongs' men is called Mo Miang, which means 'no name,' and another man who comes sometimes—a nice man he is, too—is called 'stupid old woman.' Aren't they queer people? Can you imagine any one in their senses worshipping spirits which they think are so cruel and horrid? There was one man near Ku Cheng who had several girls one after another, and no boys. They threw them all away as they arrived—poor little wretches! —threw them out on the hillside to die; but when the fourth little girl arrived on the scene, this model father destroyed the poor baby in a most cruel manner, saying triumphantly to the evil spirit, which was supposed to have possessed each of these girl children, 'There, now, will you come back any more?' The black frightful superstition that possesses these poor creatures is really terrible. I have heard things that they have done—and are doing every day all round us—that simply make me sick. I can quite understand that people don't know about them, because they could not be put in print, or told at a respectable meeting. Mr. and Mrs. Stewart arrived on Friday, and on Sunday some of the Hua Sang people came to our service and had a look at the harmonium. Some of them had never seen one before, and were greatly interested and delighted at seeing it, and said I was very clever to be able to play it. I heard them telling each other that I played it with feet and hands, and that you couldn't do it with hands only. They all came and admired it.

"On Tuesday we had a great picnic at a place some four miles from here. We started about three o'clock. Of course, in Ku Cheng, nobody would dream of stirring outside the door till at least two hours after that at this

time of year; but this place is 1500 or 1600 feet higher
than Ku Cheng, which again is 1000 feet higher than
Foochow, so you can imagine there is a difference in the
atmosphere.   All the same, it was terribly hot walking,
especially up the precipices, which were nearly the whole
way.   I was with Lena most of the time, as she walked
near the chair in which the two little ones were carried.
We were getting higher and higher, and part of the walk
was really beautiful—some of them said just like an
English lane—though I don't suppose any one ever
walked through an English lane in such a state of heat
as we were in, after toiling up more than one precipice.
At last we got to the place, and on the very tip-top was
a great rock, under the shadow of which we took our seat
and had our tea; it was very nice, and we all enjoyed it
very much.   It looked so queer to see from our exalted
position the city of Ku Cheng and the river which flows
along beside it, ever so far down in a valley—we could
look right down on it.   There is a pretty high hill—I
thought it quite a mountain—in Ku Cheng, with a pagoda
on top of it, that from this great rock looked like quite a
little hill, not hiding the view of Ku Cheng from us at all.
I never saw anything so wonderful in its utter strange-
ness as that scene was.   The view towards Ku Cheng
was more open, consequently we could see the city, but
on the other side you look straight down a great valley,
where the river, at the bottom, looks like a thread winding along; and then you carry your eye straight up a
great mountain on the other side, with two or three little
clusters of houses dotted about, a short distance from
the river and each other, and then after that you can see

nothing but the tops of mountains. It is a most curious sight, tier upon tier of mountains, but you can't see anything of them except the tops, miles and miles and miles away. We were on the highest peak except one in that part, and on the very highest of all you can see a little white speck nearly at the top, which is a Buddhist monastery—so desolate it looks there. What *can* be the idea of such a life? The peak we were on is called the Mount of Olives. Isn't that a funny thing? Perhaps some centuries ago there was an olive grove there: but there isn't a sign of a tree of any sort now. We had quite a gay picnic. The ants got into the sugar and the cake that our friends the Kuniongs had provided, and we had to hook them out; but otherwise it was enjoyable. I drank three cups of tea straight off. Then, when we had decided to move on, we thought we would explore another mountain near by, but the chair coolies disappeared by another path in the direction of home, and the two little boys were left to us to take care of. When we got to the top of the second mountain we beheld the chair making off as fast as it could go, and I can tell you it was no joke to carry a huge creature like Evan Stewart on a rough little path that was both steep and pebbly. So a great shouting match began, Mr. Stewart and the two loadmen calling to the coolies, who at last saw fit to stop, but did not retrace their steps, and I had to carry Evan to them.

"How very strange the Lord's dealing about 'The Willows' is. One truly feels 'His ways are not our ways.' But there is one thing that I have been feeling very deeply just lately, that if we are indeed to be given

that *highest of all honours*—that which Paul prayed for—
to know 'the fellowship of His sufferings,' it certainly
cannot be by having everything just as we want it. We
can but pray and—having really and completely surren-
dered all—trust. Some one said yesterday that it is only
in this life that we shall have the privilege of being par-
takers in Christ's sufferings, and the priceless honour of
glorifying Him in suffering.

"We have only one more Sunday here—how the time
does go round! I must pick out a few events to tell you
about. One day last week we were invited by the Catechist's wife to a feast. Hua Sang, I think I told you, is
a terribly hard place; they don't seem to want to listen
a bit; Satan has them in real bondage, and many of the
people are really bad; and over and above all that, they
literally hate the foreigners. I think the catechist knows
some reason for this last, but the Chinese are so queer;
even to Mr. Stewart he won't disclose a single thing that
he thinks might reflect on the people. They are extremely 'close' about things, always, and all of them. So
we went to this feast. The catechist's wife, a real nice
little woman, received us, and her daughter, E-ming, was
all smiles and very nicely dressed. The second son's wife
was there, and she appeared to be the menial. E-ming
didn't do anything, but sat and talked to us, or rather to
Ada Nisbitt, while I sat and watched the rain dripping
from the edge of the roof outside the window. Presently
I saw a sort of railed veranda outside the house next to
the catechist's filling with people who wanted to have a
look at us. They only stared, and made no observations.
They had a good view through the window of the room

we were in. Two small tables had been put together in
the middle of the room, and the daughter-in-law, assisted
by our hostess and another of her small sons, put the
dishes on; or, rather, the bowls filled with all sorts of
things. When we stayed to dinner at Cie A, on our way
from Dong Gio, the hostess would not sit down to table
with Annie and me, but that was extra superfine. They
do that sometimes; but on this occasion there was a great
fuss over who should have the highest seat. At last
every one was seated to their apparent satisfaction, and
each person provided with a pair of chopsticks and a
little bowl and a china spoon with which to get the gravy
out of the bowls. This was rather a nice feast, because
E-ming and her mother know quite well what we eat, and
what we can't eat, and they never press us to take anything we don't like. For instance, one of them planted
an ugly-looking black thing, with the appearance of a
preserved slug, in my bowl, but E-ming, who was sitting
next me, grabbed it with her chopstick and put it back
into the dish, and presented me with a piece of fowl
instead. After dinner they handed round a wooden basin
of hot water, with a rather dirty-looking towel in it to
wash your fingers on. They certainly need something of
the kind; because, when chopsticks fail, you always seize
your chicken leg with your fingers.

"At first the Kuniongs did not visit much in the
village, every one being more or less used up, and need-
ing a rest in this awful heat. But now that it is near
the end of the time, and we are soon going back, the
public opinion is to be energetic and go frequently. So
one day Ada Nisbitt and I went together—the first time I

had been—and we had a very nice time. In one house quite close they invited us in, and they listened to Ada Nisbitt so nicely. One old woman seemed specially interested when Ada spoke about our Lord's death, and asked a little about it; then she said she was very stupid and couldn't learn to read, so it would be no use to her being a Christian; but of course Ada said that didn't matter if her heart was believing. Another old lady, when asked if she would believe in Jesus now, said that the doctrine was very good, and that she would believe next year. Isn't human nature alike after all? But Ada told her then that Jesus might come back again for those that love Him before next year. I can understand nearly every word that Ada says, and she speaks very well, but I can't understand very well when the people speak; even the servants talking to Mrs. Stewart I can't understand, but after a time I shall, I hope. By the time you get this I shall be teaching two classes every day. It is not right to plan ahead, but you must do so to a certain extent; and, so far as we know at present, Mr. Stewart wants me to take the class of boys (that Elsie Marshall has taught up to now) from 9 to 10 every morning in the Picture Bible. Of course I shall have to prepare carefully with my teacher each lesson; and I asked him the other day if he thought I could manage to make myself understood by the boys, and he said quite decidedly that I could.

"Yesterday Mr. Stewart had a letter from Sing Mi Sing-Sang, saying that a report is going round Ku Cheng that the Americans and English are helping the Japanese against the Chinese, and that in consequence of this everybody is very much excited, and they are going to burn down our houses for us on the 28th of this month. They are always making a fuss about something. Our servants and teachers simply laugh at it. Se Say, the Kuniongs' cook, says that the Ku Cheng people wouldn't do that, and I am sure they would not. I have had notes from time to time from Toppy, who is at the seat of war, so to speak. They seem to be getting some fun out of the prospect of an invasion. Toppy will most likely tell you all about it. Of course there is nothing to fear—everybody laughs at it all.

"Now to go back to the visiting in the village. After Ada and I had been in that house of which I told you, we went on round the mountain to the village, and going along the main street, which is about a yard wide, we were hailed from a window over our heads with cries of 'Kuniong,' 'Kuniong.' So we looked round, and this was a young woman into whose house they had been before, and she wanted us to come again. She had come to this other house from which she hailed us to talk to some friend of hers, but on seeing us called to us, and then hurried after us to escort us to her house. It is such a queer feeling to step from the slippery stones of the high road over some high threshold into the passage that leads into the dark rooms beyond—no light or air. And the odours! Well, in this house, in the first room we came to, there were two women—one an old one—sitting near the window (the guest-room always is ventilated). She looked at us with a good deal of interest as we came in, and got up to get us seats. She was pulling out long fibres from a sort of grass that you get here, from which

they make the coarse cloth that all the poor women wear.
The other one was sitting at the side of a large wooden
frame, on which they make the matting that we put on
our floors at home.   Our friend who had escorted us
immediately seated herself on the form in front of the
frame, and then she and the other one commenced to
work.   Ada talked to the old woman, who, I really think,
would like to believe; but the power against us was very
strong in that house.   I believe strongly in Eph. vi. 12
('the rulers of the darkness of this world') since coming
to China; but still more in the great power of Jesus, who
has promised to be with us 'all the days.'   Some men
came in after a time, and then the girl who had escorted
us began talking to them, and it was very difficult to get
them to listen after that.

"In the background we saw a most wretched object in
the shape of a daughter-in-law—I mean one of those
wretched creatures who are engaged when babies, and
who come to live in their future husband's house.   I
never saw anything so wretched as she was—never.   You
wouldn't believe that people with hearts could allow a girl
as ill as she looked to work and go about.   Her face was
a sort of green colour, with an expression of utterly hope-
less misery on it; her tiny bound feet looked large when
compared with the thinness of the skin that appeared
above them through her battered clothes.   She is dying,
I am sure.   They all know it, too, quite well, and say that
they are going to wait till she dies, and then get another
girl for the man.   Isn't it dreadful?"

CHAPTER XI

THE MANDARIN'S FAMILY

Resuming work—A teacher's difficulties—Distinguished visitors—
The Mandarin language — Fashionable dresses — A flattering
invitation—Nothing to wear—An admiring crowd—The Mandarin's wives and daughters—Inspecting the house—Refreshments—Etiquette—Objections to pork—Christmas cards and
texts.

THE beginning of September saw our missionaries again
in Ku Cheng, and resuming their usual work. Again
Nellie is our historian :—

"Is it not wonderful to think that by the end of next
week it will be a year since we left Melbourne ? Really,
I can scarcely believe it. Time has gone round so quickly,
in one way, and it makes you feel that the end of all
things must be near—only a few years at the most.

"My little boys are as nice as ever, but two of them are
such funny little things. I am afraid they do not listen
much to what goes on. They have a portion of what we
call the 'Picture Bible' to do for every day, and just now
they are doing the Old Testament. I carefully prepare
the questions that I ask them—that is, the leading ones;
little ordinary ones I can think of as I go along, so I know
by the way the others answer that they can understand
all right. They all answer well except one boy, who, I am
afraid, does not listen, because when I go round to him,

telling him perhaps all about Moses leading the people out of Egypt, then I suddenly ask him the question—'Who led the people out of Egypt?' He puts on a puzzled expression, and after a moment's reflection answers, 'Tok-sack' (Joseph), and when I say 'No,' then he tries 'A-back-lak-hang' (Abraham). I told Mr. Stewart this, and he laughed and said that the other day one of the men over there went through a long list of names in answer to a question Mr. Stewart had asked him, all sorts of names, ending up with Mo-que (the devil). But more and more it seems to me that the great work of the missionaries is to be teaching the Christians. The other day we were thinking about how Jesus Himself spent such a lot of time in specially preparing the Twelve, though, of course, at the same time itinerating and preaching the Gospel to the crowds who came.

"On Sunday we had a great excitement, the first time such a wonderful thing has happened. Miss Casterton had been over to lunch, and Toppy went back to the American compound with her, and poor Mrs. Stewart had been obliged to retire to bed with a frightful sick head-ache, so that I was alone in my glory when the door opened, and the two Kuniongs appeared with three of the Lo-Dia's [Mandarin's] womenkind from Ku Cheng city, dressed up like anything, with several retainers, and a swarm of rabble in the shape of dirty children coming after them to see what was to be seen. Mr. Stewart was there, and I heard him calling me, and this was to observe that I was to do the honours; and then he ordered the tea, after which he took himself off. The rabble having been shut out, we all sat down. There was the Lo-Dia's wife, his eldest son's wife, his daughter, and another woman, who, I suppose, was another son's wife. You never beheld such grandees. Two of them sat there for some time, and then, with some of their retainers, departed, while a man, who appeared to be a sort of footman, remained behind to look after the third lady (the eldest son's wife), who was the one I saw most of. They could not speak colloquial, their language being Mandarin, but they understood a little, and the conversation was chiefly carried on through an *amah* from the school below, who was at one time in a Lo-Dia's establishment, and so could speak a good deal of Mandarin. It was great fun. I showed the lady my big scrap-album, in which she seemed to take a certain amount of interest, and when she had looked at it she handed it to the daughter (her sister-in-law, a girl of fourteen); and, looking at me rather superciliously, said, in a most affected way, 'Cing ho!' (very good!) However, I was flattered to think she would condescend to address me in the colloquial at all. She was such a nice-looking young woman—not more than twenty-two or three. She was quite pretty when she smiled, but her face in repose had such a fearfully blank look. Poor creatures! they have little opportunities of knowing anything outside their tiny little circle. She was beautifully dressed in a pale blue figured silk jacket, with broad pieces bordering the wide sleeves of a beautiful shade of pink, embroidered in deeper colours and gold. Her petticoat was of some thin black material, with figured gold ribbon trimming, and where it divided you could see her pants of the most elegant stuff in a very bright shade of pink. Her little boy was very elegantly attired, and

I

was carried by a stout maid. They drank some tea, but when we carried round the gingerbread the grand lady would not touch it. They sat on till pretty late, and then took their departure.

"Mr. Stewart says the reason they came over is because the Lo-Dia is away, and they are having a spree in his absence. If so, they evidently intend to make the most of the free time, because to-day we were again cast into a state of excitement by the arrival of a '*tikè*,' that is, a letter with the Lo-Dia's name on it, inviting us to-morrow to drink tea at the Yamen.

"*Later.*—I remember, when I last wrote to you, the mail went down just before we had the privilege of dining at the Mandarin's house, so before I go any further I will tell you about that. The whole compound was in a state of excitement about our being invited, for I can tell you it is not every one who gets invited to the Mandarin's. We did not know exactly what to do about our clothes, because, as our work is almost entirely among the poorer classes, we have very simply-made garments of chiefly blue cotton; but in the summer we have white muslin, which we brought with us, made into jackets, trimmed with blue, and red cotton skirts, with braid on them. But this would not do for society in Foochow; if you were to go dressed like that to any of their houses you would most likely never be asked again. We did not know exactly what to do, but at last, acting on the advice of Mr. Stewart's teacher, who is a Ku Cheng literary man, we decided to go in our white jackets, as he said they would know we were foreigners, and so not up to their customs. Our hair was magnificent to behold, done in Chinese fashion with flowers

and pins. The teacher saw to the answers to the invitation being sent, they had to go early in the morning, and
the only characters that appeared on their great red card
were the Christian names of those who were accepting the
invitation. This is almost the only time a woman needs
to use her Christian name. Our surname is Sung, but
that does not appear at all, as it is bad manners for a
lady to put her name on a thing like that. We managed
to get ourselves up at last, and accompanied by Mrs.
Stewart's two little girls, who were in English dress, we
departed in chairs for the Mandarin's house, the Yamen.
Everybody who met us seemed to know where we were
going, and if they did not know, they asked us if we were
not going to a feast at the Lo-Dia's. Our chairs were taken
through a sort of court that led off the street, to a great
doorway which we went through, and then up several steps
to what, I suppose, you might call a reception-hall, where
there was a crowd of men, some of them retainers, and
the rest a dirty crowd come to have a look at what was
going on. We were taken possession of by a major-domo
gentleman, with a long pig-tail and a smiling countenance,
and he conducted us to a room where our hostesses were
sitting waiting for us. They were very polite, and rising
and putting their hands into their sleeves, they bowed and
smiled quite nicely, and then begged us to take a seat,
which we were not slow to do. In the middle of the
room there was a round table with cups of tea all round
it, and cakes in the centre, and as we took our seats to
partake of this refreshment, we could see the ladies well.
It is not manners to touch your tea till the Tai Tai invites
you to do so, and takes some herself. The Tai Tai is the

Mandarin's eldest wife. She was such a nice-looking woman, and very handsomely dressed; the embroidery on their skirts and jackets is something wonderful to behold. The second wife is a much younger woman—such a bright, quick, talkative person. I liked her very much. She seemed so pleased and excited at having us there. The eldest son's wife looks like a girl of nineteen, and I thought she was quite pretty; she had such graceful ways. The Mandarin's daughters are about four in number, and the two elder ones were, I thought, rather uninteresting; very handsomely dressed, but nothing striking about them; but three of the younger children—two girls and a boy—I took a great fancy to, they were such bright little things. When we had drunk our tea, we were escorted over the Yamen by the major-domo, but there is very little to describe about it—a great, rambling, draughty, not over-clean Chinese house. The ladies did not accompany us, but were on the look-out for our return to their part of the house. The first room we came to there was the eldest daughter's bedroom, where there was a most magnificent red bed, built into the wall after the fashion of Chinese beds, and decorated profusely with gilded wood. They don't have bed-clothes all over the bed as we do, but only a quilt—in this case a costly coloured silk one—rolled up long-ways, and put against the wall. Turning round from the door, I saw the Tai Tai and the eldest son's wife appearing at another door, and when they saw me they began making signs and calling to us to come over, which I immediately did. They led us through two or three rooms into one rather larger than the others, where they invited us to sit on the edge of the bed and converse. The old Tai

Tai took up her position next to me, and taking my hand, patted it affectionately. Through the door into the next room I could perceive a young man lying on a bed with all the apparatus for opium smoking beside him. Just fancy a man, young and strong, having no better employment than to smoke opium in the day-time. But that is a Chinaman's idea of happiness. One of our men the other day, when he was asked what he thought made heaven a happy place, answered that it was because there would be nothing to do. The man who answered like that is not, as you may imagine, a very energetic person, and, of course, it is their nature not to want to work if they can help themselves; so that when you see the catechists, as many of them do, walking miles all over the country to preach in out-of-the-way places, carrying the Gospel to those who have never heard it, you know there must be some very strong impulse which moves them; stronger than love of money, certainly, as they really get very little—less than they would make in trade. But I must finish about the feast. After sitting in the bedroom for some little time, we were conducted to the feast. A round table was set all round with a little dish and spoon and a pair of chopsticks to each person. The very middle was left empty, but all round it was a ring of little dishes on stands, holding fruit and funny sweet things of all sorts. We took a long while to sit down, but as soon as every one was convinced that they were not usurping the seat of honour, they got settled. The Tai Tai was the only one of our hostesses who sat down with us; all the rest were surreptitiously beholding us through a crack in the door. The dishes were brought in one by one and placed in the middle of the table, and then the Tai Tai would raise her chopsticks, and look at us all round, inviting us to eat; and then every one had to stick their chopsticks into the dish and take what they could get. I was sitting next but one to the old lady, so she had a good range of my little dish and spoon, into which she frequently popped choice morsels. The food was really very nice, all except the pork; and I really must draw the line at pork, not so much from its appearance in the dish, as on account of the pigs themselves, as they march about and clean up the streets. All the vegetables in the dishes were very nice, for, of course, these people live much better than the poorer Chinese; they are in some ways quite different. We took some old Christmas cards with us, on which we had got the Chinese teacher to write texts in classical characters (which is what they read), and they seemed so pleased to get them. Of course, they live a very secluded sort of life, and scarcely ever see any strangers at all, and certainly not foreigners. If you know anybody who has lots of Christmas cards that they don't want, I should be very glad if you could get some, and then if you would make them into a parcel, there would most likely be an opportunity to send it. The Chinese love them, and with the texts in character written on them, or pasted on the back, they are a good way of teaching the people texts. None of the mandarins are Christians—it is not allowed by Chinese law—but it would not prevent their women from becoming Christians, and if they were, they would teach their children."

CHAPTER XII

TOPSY'S AUTUMN WORK

The question of dress—Village visiting—Unhappy wives—Itinerating and doctoring—The bondage of fashion—Country walks—Gathering flowers—Value of medicines.

THE opinions of missionaries in China appear to be divided on the question of the desirability or otherwise of adopting the native dress. At the ports where Europeans are constantly seen there may not be, perhaps, any necessity for doing this, and there may even be very strong reasons why it should not be done. But in the interior, where the sight of a foreigner is a rarity, exciting intense curiosity, and even, in some cases, terror, the rule would appear to be different. At all events, these letters abundantly show that such work as that done by the ladies of the Ku Cheng district would have been impossible had they not conformed as much as possible to the customs of the country in the matter of dress as well as in other ways. There is no limit to the absurdity of Chinese ideas about foreigners, and if our ladies had gone among the villages in English attire, the inevitable result would have been that women and children would have been scared out of their way, and the men would have mobbed them.

In this chapter Topsy tells of her autumn work :—
" Back again in Ku Cheng ; it was ever so nice to begin to

work properly. It's much cooler now, so I have been out visiting several times with a Bible-woman. Yesterday in the city, and to-day I went to a village about six miles off, through paddy fields and along the stream. It's quite a big village, where the people are very anxious to be taught, and want to have a church of their own. At present they have a house, which they rent themselves, and to this house we went first. There was great excitement on our arrival, and a man was told off to go and sweep the place upstairs, which done, we all adjourned thither, and the place was presently crammed to overflowing with men, women, and children. We talked to them about the lost sheep, and how the Shepherd took such trouble to go and find it, and then said that Jesus had done so much to come and find us, and they listened and answered so nicely. Sometimes when the women talk about heaven, they say one of the happy things will be that there will be no more marriage there. Poor things, their lives are made so miserable by marriage that it's not much wonder they look forward to a time when there will be none. One of the girls in our school has just had the last arrangements finally settled, and the Kuniong in charge says she has quite altered, and become quiet and sad. If you only saw the homes! It is very little better than slavery, cooking rice and minding their babies—and there are such crowds of babies; that's one thing that makes it so hard to teach the women—they have always a baby to hold, and just at the most important part it begins to scream. One has to be very patient and long-suffering, but one need never be discouraged, though the work is great and the workers are very few."

Later she writes:—"As you see by the date of this, I am out itinerating again with my little chum Elsie Marshall. We are having splendid times. This house was formerly rented for the catechist and doctor, but they have both moved on elsewhere, and so we have it all to ourselves. It is purely native, very big and empty, and rather desolate; but there is so much to do we have no time to think of that. Every morning first thing I hold a clinic for two hours or more in a little room off the lower *tiang-dong* or guest-room, while Elsie talks to them outside as they wait. Legs, arms, heads, with all manner of sores, malaria, and weakness, are the chief complaints; our medicines have a wonderful effect on them. To-day we were going to a village, when we met an old man who told us of a sick baby in a village close by. He said—'Last week there were two foreign women in Lang-Leng who had a hospital and cured people.' It was rather amusing, as we happened to be the two; we informed the old gentleman on the subject, and he made us a deep bow. We went to see the baby, and found it simply suffering from excessive dirt, with sores as the result; prescribed immediate application of warm water, which I super-intended, and then gave some ointment. The country folk are as simple as children, and their faith in us is supreme. We have women in swarms all day, especially in the afternoon. Yesterday the *tiang-dong* was full the whole afternoon from two till six, nearly all dressed in silks and embroidered garments. They seem to think quite as much of dress as even our Collins Street beauties. Very often these heathen women strike one as not being so very different from us in many ways. There is the

same bondage to afternoon tea, appearances, and fashion.
I was informed I couldn't have a high collar on my
Chinese jacket, because it wasn't the fashion; and to
them it's quite as important as the same thing at home.
I went shopping the other day with the old *huoi-mu*
('church-mother,' the title given to all the old ladies in
the church), the object of this expedition being to provide
myself with another pair of *ko* (native trousers) for
country wear. We went to see another *huoi-mu*, who
was to make them for me, and found her in a neighbour's
shop-front making shoes. Of course our arrival was the
cause for a crowd to collect, consisting of men, women,
and babies, and the details of the *ko*-making were all
gone into in a loud tone of voice, with suggestions from
the others, who were all interested!

"These villages are all numbered, this one being called
Sek Chek Du ('17th village'). We don't stay in one
place all the time, but go out for long days to villages six
or seven miles off. It's such a rest getting out in the
country for a long walk through the fields, and up and
down the hills, that are so steep in some places, but all
have stone steps cut in them. It is so quiet and peaceful
as we tramp along, every now and then meeting rice *dang
dangs* (carriers), who generally stare and invariably say:
'Where are you going, Kuniong?' Occasionally we rest
after a long climb in one of the rest-houses that are
always built at the top of the steps, with some other
equally weary traveller. A text we often give them is:
'Come unto Me, all ye that labour and are heavy laden,
and I will give you rest. Take My yoke . . . ye shall
find rest unto your souls.' The Chinese translation uses

the word for a heavy load borne on the shoulders called a *dang*. It is the usual way loads are carried here, just the same as you see them at home, with the baskets on each end of a stick balanced on their shoulders. It is wonderful how their hearts do open, and how glad they are to hear; it quite repays one for the exertion of going.

"Well, I began to tell you about Sek Chek Du and all the other 'Du' round it. All these villages are built in a great valley in the midst of rice fields surrounded by mountains—the endless mountains, one never sees beyond them; the higher the climb the more mountains there seem to be further on. It reminds one of the 'Blessings of the Almighty, who has blessed even unto the utmost bound of the everlasting hills.'

"Now the rice crop is being gathered in, and the ground is being turned up for a fresh sowing, so look out for malaria. As I stood at the door last night watching the sunset 'go into the mountains,' as the natives say, I could see a bluish mist rise up from the ground. They say seven feet up it's all right, so we always sleep upstairs in every place we visit. The trees are turning such glorious colours. We nearly always bring home bunches of red leaves, ferns, and beautiful white flowers like orange blossom, to decorate with. The people think it's so funny, and laugh at the idea of bringing 'grass-chair' into the house, and now and again some of the children bring us things, and their choice shows us they have no idea what we do it for. They bring any old bit of grass or weed, and ask if we like it. Of course we take it, and say 'yes.' I have to go down to Ku Cheng to-morrow, as they told me to stay only a fortnight, and I have been

three weeks. They don't think it's good to be too long
at first in a native house, especially as I'm not supposed
to be strong. I go down the river in a passenger boat.
They are just ordinary open boats like canoes; it's the
first time we have tried it, so I don't know what it will be
like. Now I must go and get some more medicines ready
for Elsie, as she won't have time when I have gone. We
have grand clinics. It brings numbers in that would
never come any other way, and she talks to them outside,
and they come in turns to be doctored. We sell heaps of
quinine at five cash five grains, which comes to about one
farthing a dose; but then one must remember all a cash
is to a Chinaman. Five cash buys a lot here for them;
but they put on the prices pretty considerably for us, as
they have an idea that the foreigners have an unlimited
supply of cash, which is so true, especially of the missionaries. At Lang-Leng, the last village where we stopped,
we got ever so many people in by our medicines. One
man was attracted by the report of the foreign medicine.
When he came in we saw at once he was different from
most of the crowd, and noticed that they paid him a good
deal of attention. He came to say that his little boy had
a pain in his back, as he expressed it, but it turned out to
be a rather nasty sore. We told him to come next day,
and in the meantime found out that he was a literary
man, one of the class that are so opposed to Christianity.
They both came next morning, such a dear little boy, and
the man was very nice, and listened to all that was said;
he came every night to prayers, and we have since heard
that he does so every night now. The little boy was
nearly all right when we left, and they were so grateful.

His wife was such a nice woman, quite refined and very
intelligent. She came to see us the morning we left, and
they sent 'greetings' to the Kuniongs by the catechist,
who was here yesterday on his way into Ku Cheng.

"You mustn't judge all the Chinese by the specimens
you see in Melbourne, although here you see that sort
too, of course. Please excuse the tear in the paper;
Du-la, my dear little wee pup, was fighting, and made my
hand wriggle."

CHAPTER XIII

THE BISHOP AT DONG GIO

First alarm about Vegetarians—The Bishop expected—Nellie goes to Dong Gio—Coolies and servants—Mishap to the tea— Benighted on the road—A friendly welcome—Death of a "Church-brother"—Preparing for the Bishop—His arrival— Evening service—Sunday—The confirmation—Troublesome children—Interview with the Bishop—A native squirrel.

IT was in October 1894 that the first alarm about the so-called "Vegetarians" was heard. From the first the native Christians seem to have taken a more serious view of the matter than the missionaries. Several of them came to Mr. Stewart in great alarm to tell him of the doings and designs of these enemies of the Government and of Christians.

Nellie writes:—"Their tale was that there was a man (a heathen) who had some quarrel with the Vegetarian Society up there at A-deng-bang, where it is very strong, and that, in great wrath, the Vegetarians had surrounded this man's house and threatened to kill him. The man, in a fright, went to the Christian school teacher and asked his advice. Now this gentleman is one who leaves much to be desired, and only that Mr. Stewart does not like to make too many changes all at once, I think he would not have been allowed to remain as long as he has done; but anyway, he was there, and what do you think he advised?

He gave this heathen man the scroll with the ten com-
mandments on it, which was hanging up in the school,
and told him to hang it up in his own house, as the
Vegetarians would not dare to touch him then. Wasn't
it an awful thing? He did this, and when the Vegetarians
broke into his house, he showed them the scroll and said
they were not to touch him, or else the Church would be
down on them. This put them in a terrible rage, and
they said that they would not have anything like that,
they weren't frightened of the Christians; and with that
they went off, some 300 of them, and attacked a Christian's shop, and destroyed all his things. One young
man, who was to give evidence on this, was in a state
of terror, because the Vegetarians threatened that if he
dared to give evidence against them, they would kill him.
The Mandarin sent out runners to inquire into the business, and the young man did not give evidence about it.
I think one cannot blame him; it was not a matter of
principle. He was one of the eighty baptized at the *Gia-
Hoi* when we first came up here: do you remember?
Then it all seemed to have quieted down, we had a lot of
prayer about it, and all seemed quite right. But Satan
cannot afford to let the Gospel spread as it is doing,
praise God! without opposition, and the Vegetarians are
the most wicked and the strongest sect of any here;
and they are strong all over the province—like a secret
society spread all through the place.

"One night last week I heard the Stewarts' coolie
coming very softly upstairs, and he called Mr. Stewart
up, if you please, to go off at that hour of the night to
the Mandarin. Mr. Stewart said he couldn't do anything

till next day. A few minutes after up came Sami again; this time accompanied half-way up by four or five men, all of them being in an anxious state of mind. All that day the Vegetarians had been having a gay time at A-deng-bang, cutting down the Christian's harvest; 300 of them, armed with sticks, had gone and reaped his fields, and, of course, that means terrible loss to the poor creature; then they were going to burn his house, and had really been going on awfully. At breakfast time the next morning the deputation was still there, but Mr. Stewart said it was very curious that when there were four catechists just then in A-deng-bang, not one of them should have come or sent to him, and that these Christians should have come on their own account. He accordingly dismissed the deputation, saying he would do nothing till he knew about it from one of those in authority. Well, about ten o'clock who should appear but four women, the wives of the four catechists in A-deng-bang, with the story that these four unfortunate men had been caught and shut into the chapel, which was to be burned that night. There was Mrs. Sen Ging the doctor's wife, the A-deng-bang catechist's wife, the Gospel Band's wife, and another one, all in terror about their poor husbands. Mr. Stewart was interviewed, but didn't like to go to the Lo-Dia (magistrate) till he heard something reliable.

"About 12.30 I was upstairs, and out of my window I beheld the 'Gospel Band' himself stalking round, and he called out to me to know where the Sing-Sang was. The poor Sing-Sang was, I expect, having a rest; however, he had to come down and see him. Of course, the story about their being shut into the chapel wasn't true, but all the same, it is a very serious thing. In the afternoon, Mr. Stewart started off in a chair to see the Lo-Dia, accompanied by Tye Ing (the 'Gospel Band'), with the result that the soldiers were sent up there; but since then we have heard that the Vegetarians didn't care an atom, and simply ran at the soldiers with sticks, and drove them all from the place. It is very serious, for if they gain their point there, they will think that they can do anything they like to the Christians everywhere. I believe there is great agitation in some of these places. There is a placard posted all over the place in Dong Gio, to the effect that no one is to touch the Christians. The Christian women were talking about it, and they said the devil is very powerful, but afterwards came to the conclusion that God was more so.

"The Bishop got to Foochow at the beginning of last week, and after his business there, of examining and ordaining men, he would leave for Ku Cheng, which, according to letters received, he did last Tuesday, and would get to Sui-Kau on Friday night, and was expected in Ku Cheng on Saturday night. My trip to Dong Gio had been put off, so that I could be there with Annie when the Bishop visits the place; so I departed on Friday morning, and know nothing of what has happened in Ku Cheng since. I left about 9.20 on Friday morning, and from the beginning the coolies growled, and said we couldn't get there that night, but I smiled cheerfully and said we would. I had my lunch in my chair, and a great idea, which was Mr. Stewart's patent invention—to wit, a bottle of tea and milk mixed, which I was to get the

K

'Sixth Little Sister' to heat up when we arrived at the
Sek Chek Du bridge in the middle of the day, where the
coolies always stop for dinner.   The Sixth Little Sister
(I think I told you) is Mr. Stewart's load-man; the words
are the exact translation of his name, but are not at all
applicable to the great, strong creature.   I have given
him a name which I think suits him much better, and
that is 'Chimpanzee.'   He is uncommonly like one; grins
at everything in a vacant manner, and is intensely stupid,
though kind and good-natured to a degree.   We went
along all right till we came to a village some distance
from Sek Chek Du.   We got there about twelve o'clock,
and there we stuck; those horrid coolies put my chair
down in a most unsavoury place, and then went off to eat
opium; the Chimpanzee sent one of them to ask me if I
would 'siah-dan' (eat my dinner) then, but I declined
with thanks, and at the same time requested the gentlemen to hurry up.   So he said, 'Ho, ho' (which means 'All
right'), and went off, and I saw no more of them for ever
so long; the Chimpanzee, instead of hurrying them up,
departed with the load, so that when at last we did proceed onwards he was quite out of sight.   So then I
meditated on what I would do, and presently we came
to a lovely spot overlooking the river — a cool shady
place with rocks to sit on, and I got out here to eat my
dinner.   I thought of you as I was sitting there; if you
could only have seen the spectacle!   I was sitting on a
rock with a paper of sandwiches on my lap, my chair in
the background, and three of the most desperate-looking
opium-smoking villains you ever beheld for company.   How
is it that we can and do travel alone all through the loneliest

places without the least fear, and they never touch us? I gave one of them a sandwich, but the others declined it, as they said they had had enough to eat, and only wanted to smoke. This person was seated on a rock just in front of me, and slowly eating his sandwich, said the Kuniong was very good. At last we arrived at the Sek Chek Du Bridge, and the coolies went for some refreshment, and then I saw Chimpanzee, who had arrived before me, coming to ask for the bottle, as he said he had found a place to heat it up. So I let him get it, and through the heads of the people (all men), who were crowding round the poles of my chair, I could see his beaming countenance, as he watched the bottle where he had stood it—in a large shallow pan on an open stove in which was a blazing fire. The pan had about an inch deep of boiling water in it. After a minute or two I heard cries of astonishment and wonder, not to speak of horror, 'Ai-a, Ai-a,' and the Chimpanzee, with a face that I could not imitate if I tried, came to me, accompanied by an awe-struck crowd, holding in his hand the bottle with about an inch neatly taken off the bottom, out of which the tea had all run. I could have screamed with laughter, only that there were so many people present. It was the most comical thing you ever saw. Of course I told him it didn't matter, but I could hear them saying, 'The Kuniong has nothing to eat, Ai-a! nothing to eat!' And one old chap came with his basket to give me some of its contents, but I declined. Still, it was very kind of him, wasn't it? Then I had a regular row with the coolies, wholly unaided by the Chimpanzee. They said they couldn't get to Dong Gio that night. There is now no resting-place at Sek

Chek Du, and I drew a picture of myself spending the
night alone, nobody knows where, along the road, and I
said, 'You *must* get there.' They said, 'We can't—it's
impossible!' I said, 'You must! If you won't carry the
chair, I will walk, and then when you get back to Ku
Cheng, you'll catch it!' Whether they understood this
harangue or not, I don't know. I did not understand all
they said, and several men also came and said that we
could not get to Dong Gio that night; but I said we must
start *at once*, and hurry up; so, when they found I was
determined to go on, they started, and went on very well;
but just at sunset, when we were still a long way from
Dong Gio, a traveller asked me where I was going, and I
said, 'To Dong Gio,' to which he replied, 'You won't get
there to-night.' This was cheering, but the only thing
to do was to hurry on. We went through a village just
about six o'clock, or a little after. They were shutting
up. It was dark and quiet in the dirty little streets.
The coolies' feet are absolutely noiseless, and my shoes
(Chinese ones) made scarcely any sound on the stones; it
was quite weird. Then the moon came out as we left the
village behind, and I saw a long stretch ahead before we
turned round the mountain, and then I wasn't sure that
it would be Dong Gio. Then we came to a turn in the
road, and the coolies did not know which way to take;
the Chimpanzee (who, I was relieved to find, was close
behind me) was appealed to as having been there before
with the Sing-Sang, but he had forgotten. The coolies
were very cross—they can't bear being out after dark—
and it seemed to me as though a voice said, 'Go straight
on! it's all right.' So I told them to go on, and they

seemed content to do as I said. On we went. Oh! it
was strange, with those dirty old things, the only human
beings within call, in the loneliest road you ever beheld;
but the moonlight was strong enough to keep them from
falling into the ditch, and I did not even feel nervous—
never thought about it much till afterwards. We crossed
a queer old bridge, with not a soul near it, and the sound
of the river falling over the rocks was so strange in the
deep quietness. When at last, through the great trees
which overhang the road that leads into Dong Gio, I
could see the smoke from the houses looking like a silver
mist in the moonlight, I was very glad, and it was not
many minutes before my chair was put down outside the
chapel door. There were voices in the *tiang-dong*, and
when I went in, Mrs. Sie Mi and the old fellow who
looks after the church (*huoi-bah* is his proper title) rose
with astonished countenances, saying 'Ping ang!' Ko
Kuniong (Miss Gordon) had told them, according to my
letter, that I was coming on Saturday night, and she herself had gone to Cie A with the Bible-woman. It was
my own fault, as I had said all along I would come on
Saturday, but changed my mind at the last minute, and
didn't let her know. But it was all right. They welcomed me so lovingly, and Mrs. Sie Mi and the other
women came upstairs with me, and we talked, and I told
them all the news; and when the Chimpanzee arrived, he
got me my supper, so I was all right, and then I went to
bed, but I was so tired that I didn't sleep very well.

"Next day, just at dinner-time, Annie and the Bible-
woman arrived, and were very glad to see me, as I was
to see them. Sunday I spent in bed, being exceedingly

weary, and also rather sick; but when I didn't turn up
at church the women told each other that it was because
I was shy of coming, because I am so tall! It was only
the outside women that said this, but the Bible-woman
confounded them by asking whether they thought I
would have come up here at all if I did not like being
seen.

"Annie was very tired, having been itinerating for
about a fortnight, so that the first two days we did not
do much going about, and fewer people came to see us,
all being so busy just now with the harvest. But on
Wednesday we went visiting in Dong Gio, and on Thursday we had a great day. Three miles from Dong Gio
there is a little village where there are two Christian
families, and one of these we went to visit; it was the
family of a *huoi-bah* of the Dong Gio chapel, a man who,
with his whole household, has been a Christian for some
years. This last week the good old man was taken home,
and we wanted to go and see them to show them our
sympathy, the Bible-woman especially anxious to go.
So a little after nine we started, and it took us an hour
and a half to crawl there: it was literally crawling, because the Bible-woman has small feet, and goes about as
fast as a snail. They were very glad to see us, but they
did seem to feel the loss of the old man very much. His
widow was quite pathetic, and her daughter could scarcely
keep from crying. It was very touching; but one could
not help thinking how different it was to the way the
heathen howl and scream. Their quiet grief showed the
affection they must have had for each other. She told us
a lot about it all. She spoke with a terrible brogue, but

I could understand a little, and the rest I found out afterwards. She said that he was so glad to go, the old man,
very glad because he was going to heaven, and not the
least afraid. Just a short time before he died, he called
to his wife to come and see the tall man all dressed in
white, who was standing in the room; she came, but
could not see any one, but he declared there was one
there all in white, and then he said, 'It is the Gen Cio
(Saviour Lord) come to take me to heaven,' and shortly
after that he went. We stayed to dinner with them, it
was the most dreadful stuff—really, I don't wonder the
Chinese have stomach-ache so badly, when they eat such
horrible concoctions. We drew the line at only two
things—the fat pork and the sea fish; you can't think
how loathsome these two delicacies both looked and
smelt. But being a Christian house, they don't mind the
foreign ladies eating what they please, and leaving the
rest. After dinner, we visited another house, and after
speaking to the women who came in, it was time for us
to return. Next day Annie had the women—or some of
them—who were to be confirmed on the Monday. But
it was on Saturday that we had the fun. It was arranged
that Mr. Stewart and the Bishop should have our part of
the house, and sleep in the two rooms, one each side of
our *tiang-dong*, and that we two should remove into Tie
Ming's room the other side of the chapel. So we started
early to get our things moved, and we tidied the room for
the Bishop, and decorated the table in the *tiang-dong* with
autumn leaves and red berries; and then we stayed in
the *tiang-dong*, and watched with great enjoyment the
excitement of the natives. Li Sie Mi came up, and said

that our flowers were nice, but he had some much better —because taller than ours—and so he brought them in a brass vase, and also his clock with which to decorate the table. It looked so funny when he had finished; and he also got some Chinese sweets—very nice ones, too—and fruit, which he arranged in little dishes. They brought two elegant bamboo chairs for their excellencies to sit on —a thing they never dreamt of doing for us, as we remarked to them, in fun, of course, and they were as amused as we were.

"Then they all got themselves up regardless. Sie Mi's eldest son, aged about six or seven, was resplendent with a red cord plaited into his pigtail; he is such a dear little boy—I do love him. To get over to our new quarters you have to pass through the lower *tiang-dong*, and then through a little room where the Sie Mi family have their meals, and when I was going over once with some things I saw the good man sitting there with his wife shaving his head.

"We wanted very much to see the Bishop, but not to be seen ourselves, and to that end when we moved to our new room we had the outer door open, but not a sign did we see of the procession up the main street of Dong Gio. A lot of catechists were in from all round, and these all set off, with Li Sie Mi at the head, about one o'clock to meet the Bishop, who, by the way, ought to have been in Dong Gio at one o'clock. They had a long wait, and we had almost forgotten all about them, and I was working away at Chinese translation when some one called out that the 'Gang Dok,' as they call him, was coming. And, sure enough, from our door we could see the catechists one by one going along, and then came the blue-covered native chair—Mr. Stewart's, of course—and, lastly, the Bishop, in a Foochow foreign-made chair, with a perfect crowd of admirers round it, and followed by half Dong Gio. Mr. Stewart's blue chair would have gone through without attracting the least notice beyond a remark or two, but the green cane Foochow arrangement caused a great sensation. As soon as we had seen them pass, we ran to a room in the front of the chapel, where we could see them get out. We were dying to see the Bishop; the Bible-woman came too, and as we looked out we saw the chairs being carried by, and stop outside the chapel door, and then we saw Mr. Stewart get out, but we couldn't see the Bishop. Wasn't it sad? After that we had a lot of work to do, and couldn't trouble ourselves any more about the Bishop. But it was so odd; their servant came over to ask us whether the Bishop was to have supper with us or not. In our bedroom, you know! He was a very stupid man, and I felt like telling him so. As if we hadn't moved on purpose so as not to meet him, or run across him at all—strict attention to Chinese etiquette!

"That night (Saturday) there was a service in the chapel. Such a lot of women. Oh! it is lovely to see so many willing and ready to be taught, but it is much more than one can do alone. And the men's part was crammed too. Mr. Stewart spoke, the Bishop being too tired to come at all. The passage Mr. Stewart spoke from was about Hezekiah and the Assyrians, and he told them that they must trust in God, not in the foreigners or the Lo-Dia, or any other power, for deliverance in this trouble from the Vegetarian *huoi* that is coming on the Church. They all listened with deep interest. . It is much harder for the women than the men, as they nearly all have to take care of a squealing youngster. They receive much exhortation about this at all times, but especially just at this particular time in honour of the Bishop, and they were strictly enjoined to carry the youngster out at once if it squealed.

"On Sunday morning there was, first, Sunday-school, and then came church at 10.30. The chapel was crammed, and when Mr. Stewart and the Bishop came in, every one stood up. It is against my principles, but Sie Mi, in our hearing, asked the men to do it, so we didn't like to refuse. Mr. Stewart read the whole service, and the Bishop preached from Psalm xxxii. 1, 2. It was nice to hear a sermon in English, though it was only a sentence at a time. Mr. Stewart interpreted beautifully; he was in great trepidation about it before, but he needn't have been. I am sure the Lord helped him. We had rather a picnic with some of the women and their babies, but on the whole—considering that there were about ninety women—they behaved well. In the afternoon there was another service, and also in the evening—Mr. Stewart spoke at the first service, and Sie Mi at the second. There is not much to tell about it, except that after the afternoon service there came an old curiosity who was once a fortune-teller and is now a Christian school-teacher, and his great anxiety is to get a Kuniong up at his place, which is somewhere in the wilds of Ping Nang. It was most amusing to see the way he gesticulated all the time he was talking to Mr. Stewart about it, and the parson and curate of this place, who are honoured by the presence of two Kuniongs in their house, smiled and seemed much amused. The more one sees of Li Sie Mi, the more one observes what a nice way he has with the people, and how the Lord does use him. He has just been to Foochow to be examined by the Bishop, and this year—in a few weeks now—he is to be ordained. I am so glad, for he is such a nice old thing. His face literally glows when he is preaching to the people.

"This morning (Monday, 22nd October) the confirmation service was held in the church. There were thirteen women—all sitting in the front row of the women's part. I sat at the back with Mrs. Sie Mi. There were three rows of men, prepared by Sie Mi and examined by Mr. Stewart. One woman, a nice-looking young woman, from some distant place, was confirmed at the same time with her husband and her mother. She has two of the very naughtiest and most spoilt youngsters that I have ever seen, and that is saying a good deal. She got a tremendous exhorting about them, that they must not carry on in church, and she was quite desirous herself that they should not bring disgrace on the women in general by howling or otherwise. But it was very difficult, for her relations were themselves being confirmed, and who was to mind the children, for they shriek and yell if any one else looks at them? So, as it couldn't be helped, she had to keep them, but the Bible-woman sat just behind her to take the younger one out if it yelled. They were both pretty good the first part of the service, but presently began to get lively, and twice I saw the Bishop look severely round in our direction, and Annie and I were both feeling rather

nervous, when all of a sudden the baby began to yell.
Horrors! It was promptly seized by the Bible-woman
and taken out, where we could hear it fairly bursting with
rage—you would have thought it was being murdered in
cold blood. Then the boy began, young scamp; he drew
several awful looks down on him, and at last his father
managed to get him to go out. But ten minutes later, to
my horror, I beheld him returning with a tall branchy
piece of sugar-cane plant in his hand which he brandished
aloft. He came in, and walked round to the end of the
Communion rails near us, just inside of which Mr. Stewart
was standing, but did not see what was coming, till the
youngster was brandishing his palm right on the rails.
Then, if looks could have slain him, he would have
expired; but Mr. Stewart could not move him himself;
he requested the old lady nearest him to put the boy
out; but as she did not move, I seized him in such a
way as to prevent him smiting me with his sugar-cane,
and dragged him out somehow, and shut the door, but the
latter precaution was of little use, as they are in and out
all the time. However, he did not molest us again. The
women were thirteen in number, and they went up and
knelt down so reverently, and then the Bishop went round,
laying his hands on their heads, and Sie Mi walked round
on the outside, holding up the Chinese prayer-book, open
at the place where the Bishop's words are, and, after the
words were spoken over each one, everybody responded,
'Sing-sing-su-nguong' (true heart that which desires).
The Bishop is pretty old, but looks older than he is, and
is very feeble; his hair and beard are quite white, and he
wore a black cap. The Chinese respect the ancient very

much, and you could see that he was commanding the
greatest respect and reverence. He looked so nice in his
surplice thing with the full sleeves, and I could see them
taking note of his array too. He spoke on the second
half of his text of the day before. When it was over—
about twelve o'clock—we had a rest and then our dinner,
after which a message came up to us from the Bishop to
say that he wished to see us, and was waiting in the
chapel with Mr. Stewart. We had not expected this,
and were exceedingly frightened; but there being no
help for it, we went and sat—in an awful draught—in
the women's corner of the chapel with the Bishop and
Mr. Stewart for about half-an-hour, while Annie told the
old gentleman about her work. He was very nice to me
too, and asked me how I was getting on with the language.
Mr. Stewart answered up, and said that I had passed my
first exam. on half-a-year's study, to which the old gentleman replied that it was a very difficult language, that
he has been forty years in China, and does not yet consider that he knows it. He shows, however, a great
interest in the ladies' work, and asked a lot of questions,
and was extremely pleased that there were so many
women, which shows that he noticed them in church on
Sunday, which I was positive he hadn't. I never saw
him looking, but Annie said that he not only counted the
heads, as far as he could, but spotted us, in spite of our
Chinese clothes. The women—most of them—stayed till
next day, and, after some conversation with them, that
afternoon we went out for some fresh air on the hill near
Dong Gio. We were sitting on a bank there, when we
became aware of a great rustling going on in the branches

of the trees near. There are lots of trees on this mountain, and they are looking so pretty now in their autumn tints. We went closer to find out what this was, and presently discovered that it was caused by the funniest little animal you ever saw. It could sit up like a squirrel, and hold nuts and berries in its little front feet, but its tail was not bushy, though it seemed to assist him in his acrobatic performances. He had a striped velvety coat, and you can't imagine how quick he could run down to the very tip of the boughs and get a berry, and then tear back again. We sat quite a long time watching him, and when we got back it was time for supper."

CHAPTER XIV

NELLIE'S DECEMBER WORK

The sisters together—Sunday classes—Intercourse with peasants—
Visiting—Return by river, boat hire—Difficulty with boatman
—A lively dispute—A chilly voyage—Obliging fellow-passen-
gers—Mr. Stewart and Dr. Taylor — Hospital needs — The
Christmas-box—Ill-fated pets—Very busy—Enervating climate
—Christmas-tree at Sek Chek Du—Children on the chair
journey—Chinese curiosity—Christmas Convention—A dis-
turbed night — Sunday services — Return to Ku Cheng—
Christmas feast—New Year's presents—Friends and letters.

" December 16, 1894.—This is the day last year that we
got to Ku Cheng. Such a lot, in a way, has happened since
then, and yet we are only at the beginning of our work.
Now I must try and tell you what has been going on
since I last wrote. Elsie Marshall being away from Sek
Chek Du, I arranged to go for a week to be with Toppy.
Not that she is either sick or could be lonely with the
Chinese that are there, but I thought it would be nice,
and I did not like to be away for longer than a week, as
Mrs. Stewart has my class to teach, in addition to all her
other work, when I am not here. So on the Saturday I
started. Annie Gordon was also going to Dong Gio, and
as my destination was half-way to hers, we arranged to
go together, so that she could have her dinner with us.
Annie, of course, had her chair and load (two coolies),
but I only had a load, as I proposed to walk, and both of

us walked the whole way to Sek Chek Du, twelve miles, and got there about 12.30, which gave Annie lots of time for her dinner, and she got off in good time after it. It was very cold in that house after such a long walk, and I think it must be that one gets chills here much more readily than at home; but on Sunday, though tired, I felt all right, but I spent Monday in bed, feeling very bad indeed; and I afterwards had a note from Annie, saying she also had been ill, but she was bad on Saturday night, while I took longer to develop—perhaps because there is more of me.

"On Sunday we had a very nice time with the women. There were also a few dozen little boys, and we had one large class, while Toppy took another of these gentlemen in the morning, and then some women came whom Toppy interviewed, and I had *all* the little boys in a back apartment. After dinner we had more women—quite a lot—and they listened so nicely while the Sing-Sang-niong (doctor's wife) told them about the lost sheep, and read the 10th John, and Toppy talked to them, and afterwards I did. When they departed to cook their suppers, Toppy and I went for a promenade through some fields to a mountain at the back of the village, and then home through more fields. The men there hoeing up their plantations are so different from the trades-people in the streets; these quiet old Hodges talk to you in such a nice friendly way, and don't seem a bit afraid that you will eat them. Of course, in Sek Chek Du they are pretty well used to foreigners. Coming back we met an old woman who has been sometimes to the house; she was standing on the narrow little path reaching across

the ditch to gather the beans on a fence overgrown with
beans that surrounds the garden belonging to her place.
She could not reach them very well, so we stopped to
help her, and picked quite a lot for her.   Poor old lady;
it was rather slow work for her; but her basket was
pretty soon full.   We also improved the occasion by
telling her of the gospel of Christ.   She said she had very
little time to come to church, but the doctrine is very
good, and she would like to believe in Jesus.   In the
evening we had prayers with the family in that exceedingly airy and cool *tiang-dong*.   Such places for draught
you never saw.   Monday, as I said before, I spent in bed,
the results of my exertions two days before.   It takes a
lot to keep me in bed in a Chinese house; it is only the
third whole day I have spent in bed since we came.   God
has been very good.   I have a great deal to thank Him
for, being so strong; such numbers of the Kuniongs are
not at all strong, and often have to be in bed.   Twice my
being in bed has been the result of over-exertion, and the
first time was the chill I got when we landed in Foochow.
All Tuesday we were busy getting things ready for the
women that are coming, and on Wednesday we were
about the streets going into the houses to see people.   A
young man came with his mother to ask us to his house,
but we could not go then, so they said they would send
for us to go in the afternoon and see the women in the
house, and accordingly we went and talked to the women.
It was very nice.   You have to listen to all they have to
say, all their questions, and all they want to know, so
many things about our foreign country and our ways of
doing things, and then you can get in a word every now

and then.   We stayed as long as we could, and then had
to go to another house in the street near the river.   In
the morning Toppy went off after breakfast to Lang-Lens.
I made her go in a chair, otherwise I think she would have
wanted to walk, but I thought it was too far for her to
walk.   She did not expect to get back till the day after,
but she turned up that evening at tea time, to my great
surprise, and I expect she has explained the cause to you.
On Friday we went to a village called I-bo.   It was a good
long walk, about three miles, and we went by ourselves, so
that we were not quite so grand as usual.   Toppy had been
once before to the house of the woman we wanted to see,
and after a good long promenade through the streets of
the village we got to her house; there were a lot of other
women who came in, and we had quite a nice time talking
to them; such a lot of them were there.   As we were
walking back a woman with a nice little girl, about twelve
or thirteen years old, came tearing along and shouting to
us to stop; she did not want anything in particular, only
to ask us a few questions.   Her husband was there, an
old man who said he often came to worship, but I don't
know if it was true or not.   The time in the house flew
by very rapidly; there were so many things to be prepared for the coming festivity.   On Saturday morning I
was to depart, so on the Friday evening I asked the
doctor if he would kindly see about a boat for me to go
down in, as I did not feel equal to the exertion of another
long walk, and did not want to go in a chair.   So the
good man immediately went off to arrange the business,
and told the boat-owner that I wanted to *hire* the boat.
Now this just shows the idea that some of them have of

us; they think we are rolling in money, and that we are come here to duke it round in a lordly style. So the sooner this idea gets out of their heads the better. When I heard that he had hired the whole boat for me I found that two or three other people had heard of it too, and that every one was going down in my boat. They always do that coming and going to Foochow. If a foreigner is paying for the boat the boat-owner never charges for any Chinese who may go in it. But it is a bad precedent to set at Sek Chek Du, and I was in quite a way about it. I could not think what to do, as they said I must have the boat now that it was engaged; but we explained matters to the doctor, telling him that it was not so much for the money, but that we want to be as much like themselves as possible. However, in the morning, though I was packed up by eight o'clock and ready to start, no boatmen appeared, and so I waited till 10.30, when I got desperate, and asked one of the men to go and get me a chair from the street. However, he came back and said there was no chair, but that he had seen another boat, in which he had taken my passage, and so, my baskets being ready, he seized them to carry them down to the place. Toppy and I arrived a few moments later, and found that there was some difficulty in getting the boat-owner to look at things from our point of view, and he was rather objecting. But you would have thought there was a regular fight going on. The boat nearest to us was empty, except that in one end of it I perceived my baskets, and one passenger was endeavouring to take his seat. So I, being directed to do so, went and spread my rug in the bottom of this boat, and sat down to survey

the scene.   The boats near by were being laden with tea
and other things in baskets, while their owners were just
calmly doing what they had to do, and occasionally
putting in a word to the people on the landing; but the
owner of my boat was in an apparently awful state of
mind, with a 'nothing-would-appease-me' kind of look
about him and on his face.   The doctor, who badly
wanted a shave, was talking to him like a father, only to
bring down another burst of indignation, and then some
one else would interfere.   This one was Gin Ong, Mr.
Phillips' man.   Then 'Fringey,' our teacher, would
interfere and give his opinion; but he soon gave it up,
and came and calmly disposed of himself and his belongings in the boat as if it were all settled, and as if
there was not a most awful row going on!   Then I cast
my eye further on, and beheld Gin Hok in bare feet, with
a bright blue stuff jacket on—a most picturesque figure
standing on a stone forming the corner of the bank overlooking the landing; and he also from time to time gave
expression to his feelings.   But the one who did most
of that, and, apparently, with least effect, was the church-
father, who, from some distance away, held forth cease-
lessly in loud and strident tones, looking as though he
would willingly eat some one; but no one seemed to be
listening to him, and this fact was so apparent to the
casual observer that Fringey turned round and remarked,
with his usual grin, that the 'church-father spoke very
many words, but nobody was listening or benefiting by
them.'   The young man known as a church-brother was
also very much there.   He is rather in the tragedy style
—very heavy tragedy! (You notice this specially if he

happens to be in the room over your head.) He waved
one arm frantically, and advanced one foot a step, with
the expression of all the heroes on his face; while the
other arm was somewhere inside his clothes, the sleeve
that it ought to have been in hanging loose, after the
style of the Crimean veteran, by his side. The passenger,
meantime, about whom all the fuss was, sat stolidly in the
boat, and, like Goma of old, surveyed the little birds up
there, and anything else she could see, with apparent
indifference. At last the doctor, in desperation, after
nearly bursting with laughter more than once, turned
round and said: 'All right! Then the Kuniong will not
go at all in your boat; we will get her a chair, and the
men will walk, and you will not have any passengers at
all,' being all the time well aware that there were not
any chairs. But the boat-owner did not know it, and so
when he heard this intimation he pretty quickly came
round, and presently got into the boat, and we moved
away from the shore. It was beginning to rain, and as
Toppy had no umbrella I told her she would have to share
that of the doctor. I don't know whether she did or not,
but think it unlikely. In the boat there is only room for
one abreast, and you dare not move for fear of capsizing.
Gin Ong was nearest the end; then me, squatting on my
rug; and then Fringey on his big *meing* rolled up into a
high cushion, on which the boatman would not let him
sit, as it was too tall, and caused the boat to heel over,
rather sad after all his trouble in rolling it up; and then
the passenger. They were all very nice to me—I might
have been a queen. I cannot describe to you what it
was like going down. The scenery was interesting and

beautiful in parts; but the wind—lawks! it was cold.
I have never felt anything to come up to it; it nearly cut
us in two. At a place about a mile from Ku Cheng the
three gentlemen got out and walked to warm themselves,
and left me with the two boatmen. I never asked any
of them to do anything for me, but when the boat reached
the landing at the first gate of the city, I asked the boatman if he knew any one who would *dang* my baskets up
to the compound, and he said he had asked the passenger
to do it, and he had said he would; so all I had to do
was to wait his arrival. Presently I looked up towards
the crowded street at the top of the landing, and saw the
three gentlemen, of whom the one I called 'the passenger'
came forward and shouldered my baskets, Gin Ong having
taken possession of my rug and rain-cloak, and put them
into the ropes of the baskets, and so we started. In
another half-hour we had crossed the stream and got up
the hill, Gin Ong and I talking nearly the whole way. I
was glad to get into the house, and I daresay Gin Ong
was not sorry. We started in that jolly-boat at eleven
o'clock, and did not reach the compound till 3.30, and
all that time had nothing to put inside of us, and had
to sit in that awful wind. Gin Ong asked me more
than once if my stomach was empty, but when I asked
him how he felt he answered not very cheerfully, 'Only
pretty well!' Mr. Stewart had been away in the country
examining schools, and he arrived in the course of the
evening. He says there is such a wonderful improvement in the day schools, and that the children understand so much better what they are doing, and really
seem to be converted, and answer questions wonderfully.

Almost the same minute with Mr. Stewart came Dr. Taylor from another direction—Sui Kau. He came to stay a day or two on his way to Nang Wa, to see if he can do something towards helping them to carry on the hospital which has been opened up there. He is now the only doctor in the whole Fuh Kien mission, and when his furlough comes early next year, there will be actually not one. It is not quite right, I think. That hospital was allowed by the Mandarins because they thought a doctor was coming, and now that one has not come, they think that Mr. Collins was telling them a lot of crams about it. They don't understand that a doctor was promised to Fuh Kien and then sent elsewhere.

"Thank you, dearest, darling mother, for the box so lovingly got ready. Thank Kate, too, *ever* so much. I will give Miss Gordon the parcel. It has not come yet, and we don't even know when it will; but can try and see if it is there. It will, I know, give a good deal of pleasure. I will write to Mrs. Collier. If you knew what it means writing letters you would not wonder we write so few. I have been trying for days to write this, and now it is eleven o'clock the night before the messenger goes, and I am writing against time, which I don't at all like when I am writing to you. I do wish we could have one of Rose Craddock's kittens; Toppy's pup is lost; I don't think she will ever try to have any more pets. Now I must shut up. We must leave all in God's good hands, knowing that He 'holds the Key,' and that all He does is best; though it might not be what we would choose now, it would be, could we but see the end.—Your own loving NELL."

"I finished my last letter to you about 12.30 the night before the mail left, and there has been one continued rush ever since, so that I truly do not know how to get along. You see there is not anybody to help in Bible teaching in the schools now but me, Miss Stewart and Elsie Marshall and Annie Gordon being away in their different districts, and where Elsie goes, there will also Toppy. Ada has gone away, and Miss Weller has the girls' school, so there is nobody but me. But I am so well and lively, I can do lots, though I cannot *hold out* as long in this climate as I could at home—I mean, if you are working, and it gets past your dinner time at home, you don't seem to mind much, but here I get a faint and sick feeling at once, but am all right again as soon as I get something to eat. I have found that when going about in chairs, it is very unpleasant eating in the chairs, but if you don't you are sure and certain to have a head-ache, and a headache here is no joke, as I have found. Last Saturday was the end of the Convention at Sek Chek Du and the day for the Christmas tree, for which such preparations were made. I and the little girls were invited, so on Saturday morning we got ready to start ; the children were in such a state of excitement they must have been up about, I should think, six o'clock. It had been uncertain whether they could go, as we had failed to get coolies in the city at the usual place. But early in the morning one of the men went over and got four coolies and a loadman to carry the children's load ; and so we had breakfast about 7.30, and then came the bother. The coolies did not arrive, and then what were we to do. I by myself would simply have walked off to

Sek Chek Du, but the children could not, of course, do that. So this went on, waiting about, sending messages, and all the experience that only people can know if they have gone through the agonies of waiting for coolies who don't turn up, and when a long day's work is before them, and must be begun early. At last we went off, and at the ferry we met our noble coolies, so I scolded them well, and in addition I fear the Stewarts' coolie (who went with us), swore at them volubly. It was ten o'clock when at last we really got off, the children in their chair and I in another one. The children's chair is made for two to sit inside, facing each other. They don't get in from the end as we do, but from the side, and then a curtain is let down, so that you cannot see who is inside the chair; otherwise it is an ordinary native chair with its painted blue cover. It is very amusing going through the crowded streets at the end of the city wall. The coolies howled and shouted, of course, to make room for our chairs, and then heads were turned to see who was coming. They only just cast a glance at me—quite a common sight there, a Kuniong in native dress in a native chair; but that other chair all closed up like that! I could not help being amused at the evident interest displayed. Of course the general opinion was that it was a Chinese girl going with me, and you never can see into a Chinese lady's outdoor conveyance by any chance. Outside the streets the first person I saw, going up the flight of steps leading to the great bridge just in front of us, was Li-Sie-Mi, munching some dainty morsel which he had probably just bought at some cook-stall in the street. I wondered if he would turn before he got to the top, and watched to see. And sure enough he did, and at the sight of the chairs (which can be easily recognised by our people who know us well) he half stopped. 'Who's this coming?' was the expression on his face, and then, when he caught sight of me, 'Sung Kuniong, Ping ang!' he said. 'Ping ang,' said I, and then still being at a good distance he trotted on over the bridge, when his curiosity could be restrained no longer, and he stopped and waited for us to catch him up, trying to look as though he was not; but he smiled brightly enough at me when we got up, and then said, 'Kuniong, who is in that chair? Is it a Chinese woman?' 'No,' I said, 'it is the *Du Sing Sang Niong's* two little girls.' And then he trotted along with Si Mi at the back of my chair, I believe for no other reason than to see the children get out of their chairs at the boat. However, he had the pleasure of seeing them before that, because, as soon as we were clear of the streets, I got them out, and we walked along the road down to the ferry. It is not that he had not seen them dozens of times, but never before in the country. We were rather late in getting in. I sent my chair back half-way and walked the other six miles. When we were within half-a-mile of the Sek Chek Du bridge, I got the children to get into their chair and stop there. So that when we got on the bridge, instead of having a howling mob after us, all they saw was an ordinary-looking Kuniong walking after her chair, and accompanied by her servant, as proper as could be. Was it not a good thing that I did not bring my chair on? If they had only known. Si Mi said to me, as we were coming into the 'street,' 'Kuniong, they don't

know who is in that chair, or they would be very
excited; they think it is your chair.' We thought it
was tremendously cute. We had a very nice time
there altogether. The Christmas tree was a great suc-
cess, but I dare say Toppy will tell you all about it. I
made one contribution which was greatly admired, viz.,
a 'gak-giang' (little sleeveless jacket), for the doctor's
baby. It was made of Toppy's sleeves of her red serge
dress, and lined with a little piece of fur taken off the
green coat, which is now, I think I told you, a green coat
no longer, but a green Chinese jacket. God has answered
prayer about the convention at Sek Chek Du, and about
the doctor and his wife, most graciously. Several of the
women had real blessing; both Elsie and Toppy said
they could see it. The two ladies whom I went to see at
Wong Tung, and whom I met as I was coming down in
the boat the previous Saturday, were much blessed. One
of them is such a dear old lady, and wanted to be talking
to the outside people who came in about the doctrine.
It was quite like a convention at home, on a small scale;
the people who were getting blessing wanted to bring
others in and get them blessed too. After the tree was
all over, we were very glad to get to bed, but I am
grieved to say that where I was there was no rest for
the weary. Toppy slept with Elsie in her little half-way
house, which is, however, a good way from where the
women were located, this happy spot being just next to
Toppy's room, where Millie, Cassie, and I slept in a very
large bed. The two small persons enjoyed the whole
thing, but being very sleepy they were soon in the land
of nod. Not so their large friend, just alongside, for

next door these women kept up such a racket of conversation that it was impossible for me to go to sleep. However, as Christmas comes but once a year, I stood it very cheerfully till about twelve o'clock, when one dear old lady, following the example of Paul and Silas, began to sing and give praise in the not too melodious strains of a Chinese hymn, at the top pitch of her voice. This was more than I could put up with, as for one thing I was afraid she would awake the children, so I called out—'Huoi-mu O!' not loud enough, however, for there was no cessation of the hymn-singing next door, but there was of the talking, and in a minute one of the women answered in the funny brogue that they speak, using a word that always amuses us very much (it is not a dictionary word at all), the word they use for 'call.' So I replied, using the same word, 'It was I who called, and I think it would be better if the hui-mu would wait till to-morrow morning to finish that hymn.' So there was an immediate chorus, 'That is just what we think,' and a round robin was sent to the old lady to request her to finish next morning, which she quite peacefully complied with. Sunday morning was rather far advanced when the children began to move, and I had been awake about twenty minutes and had a strong notion that it was late, but was all the same in no hurry to get up, being rather weary. Then the children began, 'I say, Nennie, isn't it awfully early?' The wooden shutters were closed and the room pitch dark, which made them think it was so very early. 'Not so very,' I said, 'I should think it is about half-past eight.' 'Oh! hadn't we better get up?' was the chorus; but, however, we did not get up for some

time after that. Sunday was a very happy day ; we had
plenty to do, for there were lots of women, and Toppy
and Elsie were busy with them the whole morning and
afternoon.   The latter meeting was most encouraging,
except that the doctor, who was invited to address the
meeting, was rather longer than he ought to have been.
They don't seem to be able to take in the idea of a short
bright service, but wind themselves up indefinitely.   I
did policeman at one end of the place, and, as I write,
the whole scene rises up before me : I am standing near
a dusty table, a short way from the stairs which lead to
the upper *tiang-dong*. The whole of the side, against
which the dusty table is placed, is open to the elements,
and from the edge when you have climbed up, you can
see down into the weather-well.   But just now all
available space is occupied by a few children who were
allowed in on special conditions, their service being
over ; the rest of the *tiang-dong* is packed with women,
all those of the Reading huoi being of course present,
and several from Sek Chek Du itself.   On the side
furthest from me are the two Kuniongs, the black-haired
one nursing the doctor's son, a young Turk of about four
years old, and a golden-haired one casting looks of mute
entreaty at some of the women, who show signs of conversing on topics of general interest.   The afternoon sun
streamed through the open side and lit up the whole
scene—the tall skinny doctor, in his long blue coat and
crimson silk *gak-giang*, holding forth at the top of the
room ; I, as I have said, doing policeman in the background.   It was necessary, too, I can tell you, for every
moment there was a raid on the stairs, and a tribe of

little **boys would come up** wanting to get in, but of course we could **not** allow that ; there would be **no** peace at all. **We were** specially anxious **about** this **service,** or else we **would have** arranged that one of us should take the boys **in a class by** themselves; **if we were** there always, **we** could manage things differently.

"**In the** evening **we all sat** together in a circle, the **twelve** women **and ourselves,** with the doctor's wife and **one other woman, and sang hymns ;** and then I had the pleasure—**I really mean that**—of 'addressing the meeting.' **I had not known what** subject **I** should take, **and felt as though my Chinese was** really too poor to be **able to do it properly ; but then I felt** immediately that **my message was given me from Dan. xii.** 3, 'They that **be teachers shall shine as the** brightness of the firmament, **and they that turn many to righteousness,** as the stars **for ever and ever '**—and **certainly God** not only took **away my awful shyness, but made the women** understand most splendidly. **Is not He good ?**

> "'The King of Love my Shepherd is,
> His goodness never faileth, never !'

"The next **morning we were in a great** way to get **home, and started about eleven o'clock** in the boat ; it was most **dreadful, even worse than the** time before that I **told you of—I mean having to wait** about and fight with **the people. There** were **Elsie, Toppy, the** children and I, **in one boat,** and our luggage and *meings* went in the other **one. It was** really **awful; the** excitement of the **last two days** had worn us out; the heat was rather great **for the time of year; and we had too many** clothes on !

At last the effect of weariness and the sun on the water
resulted in my being sick on the river, a disgrace to any
person! I will suit my boat and travelling to circumstances another time. When we at last neared Ku Cheng
(not till nearly two o'clock), Elsie and I got out and
walked the rest of the way. I felt all right as soon as I
was out of the boat. It was Christmas Eve. We did not
do much that evening, but we put up a few berries and
ferns in the rooms in honour of Christmas. The next
morning the first thing was the carol singing, about two
in the morning, by the school girls, and they really can
sing remarkably well. 'Hark the herald angels sing'
came first, and then some other carols. After breakfast
we all strolled off to church, where now I always play the
organ. We had a nice bright service, the girls and boys
doing most of the singing, but there were many women
there too. Mr. Sing Mi did the preaching, and it was
very good. When we came back the first thing was a
feast at the girls' school, to which we were all invited,
and to which we all went. There were awful things to
eat—slugs, and so forth. Mr. Stewart came down to say
grace and start us, and then we all ate to our hearts' content. After the feast we had a short rest, and then all
went down to the Christmas tree in the big room of the
Foundlings' Home. It was very nice. Oh! the delight
of those boys over the comforters and mittens which they
received! After that we went down to the boys' school
to fire off crackers; at least I did not fire many crackers,
but the boys did. In the evening we had a little tea-
party of our own. Those are the things I care least
about; and we were all so tired that I don't think

anybody was sorry to go to bed. Mr. Stewart went off
first thing next morning round his districts examining
schools.

"Just received your letter, dated 6th November. We
are looking forward with the greatest excitement to the
arrival of the box. It has not yet come, but we expect
it this week; thank you ever and ever so much. The
boots that we have heard so much about will be in our
possession in about a week. We are just dying to see
them. Do you think it would be a good idea to send
Mrs. Collier a list of the sort of things that are nice to
give away? I don't like to do it; it seems like cadging,
which I can't bear.

"*New Year's Day.*—The box came this morning. Hip,
hip, hooray! First of all I must wish you a bright and
happy New Year—whatever may betide. He knows it
all, and He has gone all the way Himself first, and He
makes the rough places smooth, and the crooked places
straight. I must tell you about this morning. Toppy
was to have gone back to-day, but I persuaded her not
to go, as the box *might* come to-day, and I could not *bear*
to have to wait till she came back here to open it, and
yet I could not open it without her, so she waited. The
children were in great excitement. We have been hoping
it would come for about four days, and at last the
children came in great excitement this morning to say
that they could see three boxes coming up the hill, and
the middle one was black. Oh! the way we ran downstairs, and were at the compound gate before the men
got up the hill. We had a terrific time getting it opened
and finding all the things out. You say that you enjoyed

packing it, but it was nothing to our enjoyment in getting the things out. The beads, the dolls, the bags, and all the woollen things are simply charming. Kate's parcel of a pink jacket and bootees was lying there, but the ticket on it had come off. When Mrs. Stewart came in she began admiring it almost at once. Afterwards we found the ticket, and were so amused to find that the very things she had admired so much were for her own baby. She was delighted with them. The hoods are the very things for riding in cold weather in chairs or boats. My dearest Petsy, you cannot think how much we prize them. Mrs. Stewart liked them very much too; we showed them to her. Mrs. Millard gave her a grey woollen one, but she thinks ours are nicer, and so do we. The sleeves are an excellent idea, and as for the boots, they are simply grand. Toppy must take hers to Sek Chek Du for sitting reading in that cold hole of hers. The pin-cushions were greatly appreciated. How kind the Colliers are. I will write to Mrs. Collier and to some of the other people next time. I am literally racing now, as the man will be here in about five minutes for the letters."

CHAPTER XV

JANUARY EXPERIENCES IN COUNTRY WORK

Topsy in charge of a dispensary—Case of life and death—A poor dwelling—A casualty case—Digression on the language—The patient improving—A station class—An unhappy wife—A brutal husband—Mr. Stewart's pleasant surprise—Another demoniac case—Nellie's hopeful pupil—Change of air—Winter cold at Hua Sang—Topsy's flying visit.

THE practical efficiency of both our missionary girls had wonderfully increased in the course of a year. This is well shown in Topsy's case by the following account, written from Sek Chek Du in January 1895 :—

"The doctor, Sui-Ging, has gone to Foochow for all the catechists' money and other business. He started this morning and left me his patients to doctor; but I didn't expect many because of the rain, the Chinese having a rooted objection to going out in the rain. Presently, however, a man came in downstairs, and after some conversation, I heard a demand made all round for the Sung Kuniong, in answer to which I appeared on the scene. There I met a man who, with many gesticulations, told me a long story of a man whose head had been hit and had been bleeding. I didn't like to go out then because I was just expecting the regular patients, and so told him to come after dinner and fetch me; but in a little while another man appeared, and then I began to see that the case was more serious than I had first thought. The first man spoke so fast and indistinctly that I couldn't make out very much from him. So I said I would go at once, and went to get ready and get some medicines, after which we started, the man leading the way, and I vainly endeavouring to keep out of the water, which was running in streams all over the pathway. I call it a pathway for want of a better word. Then came the *huoi-in*, who thinks the Kuniong can never manage without his assistance. He is such a nice boy, and even his deep-rooted objection to water in any form could not keep him back this morning. The place was in a village about half-a-mile away, and it was sopping wet everywhere. My friend went in front carrying my basket most politely, and so we got to the place. The house was a trifle dirtier than even most that I have seen—evidently the people are poor—the front *tiang-dong* being very small, and containing only one very old form and some baskets; while standing at the door was a tiny little child, nursing a tinier baby. A woman came out and asked me to come into the back *tiang-dong*, which is in all Chinese houses a continuation of the front *tiang*, with a partition between, the front side being decorated with scrolls or family portraits, and usually containing a table with the ancestral tablets. From this hall a room opened off, into which she first went, and I followed, but so dark was it that I could see absolutely nothing; so she got a light, or an apology for one—just a little round iron saucer standing on two legs, and filled with oil and two long pieces of wick, like strings of vermicelli, lying in the oil and sticking a little over on one side with the ends lighted. You

may imagine there wasn't an over-abundance of light
about that sort of thing. Of course, a whole lot of people
tried to crowd into the room to see what could be seen;
but I got some of them to go out, and then went to the
bedside to try and take in the state of my patient. Truly
an object for pity and love, and I did so long that Jesus
Himself were there as in the olden times. But I know He
was with us in the room, and His power is not diminished.
If it wasn't for knowing that He was there, I couldn't
have been there myself. The man was lying on one of
those dreadful sheepskins—dreadful, I say, because of
the state they are always in—and covered, all but his
head, with a blue *meing* (quilt or cover). His whole face
and head, and all the top part of the bed, was thick with
blood, and just below on the floor was a great pool of
blood, and the pieces of rag with which they had evidently
been trying to stop the flow of blood. I could see nothing
at all of the wound on his head, for it was well plastered
over with some horrible native medicine, a bowl of which
was on a box at the head of the bed, and which looked to
me like coal dust. I shouldn't like to make a guess at
how long it took me to get the top dirt off, and get to the
place of the wound. It will take some time to get the
hair all free from that dreadful stuff, and of course they
won't cut it. But to-morrow, when I go, I must take my
lantern, to be able to see what I am doing. The poor
thing seems so weak, and for a long time was almost
unconscious, but after a little his lips moved, and I gave
him tea out of a spoon, which every one seemed to think
was a funny thing to do, and the poor man himself couldn't
quite make it out. But afterwards he seemed to like it,

and would make funny little sounds with his lips every
time he wanted some. He never once opened his eyes
the whole time, and had no strength to move. They say
he has been like this for eleven days, and has eaten
nothing for some time. I couldn't get from any one
exactly how long he had been without food; they all
seem hazy on that point. I think it's best to try and get
them to let him into the hospital in Ku Cheng, but they
may not be willing to take the trouble, and certainly
won't unless the rain stops. And this poor man is only
one in thousands. It's not that the cut on his head is so
bad—in the hospitals at home one sees ever so much
worse—but it's the surroundings and the awful dirt that
make the difficulty of a cure. It certainly is true that
prevention is better than cure in this land, and easier,
too, I should say. I brought a man back with me for
some stuff for the patient, and told him to come for me
if the bleeding started again, and not on any account
to touch his head, which I had done up in most truly
'casualty' style. They always call doing things up like
that, making a '*ban*' of them, and use the same word
speaking of doing up a *parcel*. It's rather funny to say
you do up a person's head or leg in a parcel, isn't it?
But it is a funny language altogether. Sometimes there
are ever so many words for one thing, and then again, as
in that case, there is great poverty of expression. Don't
you agree with me? I hope no one will ever be discouraged at the difficulty of the language, for there is no
need. In its construction it is much simpler than any
I have ever heard anything of, and the Lord helps one
wonderfully. Of course, the character is a bother to

*

learn in some ways, and if one is at all weak it's trying;
but then one can go slowly with the reading and learn to
talk from the people. It's 9.35 now, dearest, and I am
so tired, so I must go to bed. I was thinking of you
coming home this morning, and the thought suggested
hot water and dry stockings. Were you there with me
then, dearest? So I did it most obediently. Wasn't
that good? You will scarcely believe it.

"I didn't write at all last night, because the Sing-Sang
Niong (doctor's wife) came up to sit with me, and didn't go
away till so late that I was too tired to sit up any longer,
so to-night I must tell you of two days. I was to go to
Dong Gio to-day, having half promised to do so, but my
'professional duties,' as the doctor calls them (he is always
making fun of my doctoring), kept me till 1.30. The
man's head is better, and he talked a little yesterday, and
the others also are getting along. I was too tired to do
anything but lie down when I got back, and so spent the
afternoon studying instead of going to Dong Gio. To-day
Nellie and the children came back from Dong Gio and
had dinner here in true picnic style, after which they
went on to Ku Cheng and I went to see my patient
with the head, whom I found much better and objecting
to have his head washed, which is a good sign as regards
returning health. The last two days he made no objections at all. Yesterday, after I had fixed him up, I got
all the people outside the door and talked to them about
the 'Jesus doctrine' as well as I could. I think he must
have heard and taken it in a bit, because when I went in
just before going he said, '*Kuniong cing tiang ngtrai*'
(Kuniong very much loves me), so I said there was one

that loved him still more, even enough to die for him, and then, quite of his own accord, he said he was coming to church when his head was better."

It is an amusing circumstance that this supposed wounded man turned out to be a woman! Topsy's imperfect acquaintance with the language, as well as the imperfect light of the sick room, caused this mistake at first. In subsequent letters the patient will be mentioned under her true designation.

Some experiences of another Kuniong, in one of the remoter parts of Ku Cheng district, are given by Nellie about this time.

"They have had rather stirring times at Sa Yong since the summer. First they had that awful fire that I told you about; and just lately they have had two disturbances, and as both of them illustrate the queer ways the Chinese can do things, I think I will tell you about them. Miss Codrington had been having a station class, or rather a series of them. To form a station class, you get from twelve to sixteen or seventeen young women and feed them for three months, getting them either to live in the house with you or renting one next door. They make nothing by it, so as to offer as little *outside* attraction as possible, so that those that come, will come, as far as we can tell, solely for the purpose of being taught the doctrine. They may bring one baby—no more—and they just get their rice, and their chairs paid in and home again. Mrs. Stewart says it shows how God *has* worked here in opening the way for missionaries to work, because a few years ago you could not get *any* *women at all* to come and live like that, or any way approaching to it, for love or money. The suspicion and dread of foreigners has decreased so much. It means a most unusual amount of trust, when the Chinese men will allow their young wives to come and live in the Kuniongs' house for three consecutive months; but the fact that they do it, shows God's power over the 'unruly wills of men,' does it not? But Chinese are so funny, and it is so impossible for foreigners ever to get to know all their queer customs that we have to be very careful, and no woman is ever taken unless with the recommendation of the catechist, who is asked to find out about her. Sing Mi and Sie Mi are both very decided on this point, and, as a fact, no one ever dreams of doing anything of this kind without first consulting the Chinese parson. But a little while ago a girl, who had only been married a few months, asked Miss Codrington if she might come into her station class, and seemed so earnest, and just longing to learn. Of course, Flora was very anxious to have her, and made many inquiries about her, by which she found out that she was not living in her husband's home, but with her parents, who seemed very nice and friendly, and said she might go. To make a long story short, at last the girl was installed at Sa Yong, and was very bright and eager to learn. But one fine day a man, who said he was her husband, came and claimed her; but as there had been no previous business with the husband, Flora did not like to give the girl up to any one but the parents, who had given the girl to her. So she refused to let the girl go with this man. He was her husband all right, but Flora could not be sure that it would be right to give her up to him without the permission of the parents. So

then there was a row. The man went off and joined the
Vegetarians, and threatened to bring a crowd of them and
storm the place, and carry the girl off. Flora did not
know what to do. Of course they committed it all to
God, and they felt, after praying about it, that the best
way would be to communicate with the parents if it could
be done, as these Vegetarians were trying to prevent anything of the sort. For two or three days they were in a
very uncertain state, not knowing what would happen
next, and then the husband proved his authority, got an
agreement from her parents, and appeared in state at the
Kuniong's house again, and demanded his wife. Of
course, this time she had to be given up. She protested
and cried, but the man was inexorable. They had brought
a chair, and into this she was put bag and baggage, and
taken away with her husband and an escort of Vegetarians.
At a small village some little way from the Kuniong's
place they stopped, and she tried to escape, but they then
got ropes and tied her into the chair by her wrists and
ankles. A man we know met the procession after they
had left that village, and saw her tied in as I have told
you. She lived in her husband's house for some short
time, and then the brute sold her to an opium shopkeeper,
who is himself sunk in the vice of opium smoking. One
could make a good story out of it. The pathetic part of
it—the poor child's grief at leaving the Kuniong, almost
the first person she had ever known who showed her any
kindness; her keen disappointment at being now hindered
from learning anything about the Saviour Christ, whom
she was just beginning to learn to love—all this would
touch any one's heart; but when you think of that girl—

a living soul—being sold into the hands of those brutal
opium smokers, it just makes one sick to think of it.

"On Sunday a strange young man read the Second
Lesson, and I wondered who he was. So at dinner I
asked Mr. Stewart if he knew him, and he said 'No;' he
supposed he was one of the students going through from
Foochow. So I thought no more about it till two nights
ago, when Mr. Stewart began to tell us about a boy he
had met in a curious way years and years ago, at a little
place miles away from here in the western district. Mr.
Stewart was visiting a school at a rather large village, and
he was told that to get to the next place he would have to
go through a tiny little village where they told him there
was one lad who worshipped God. His people were all
against him, but still he stuck to the doctrine, and seemed
to know a good deal about it. So, of course, Mr. Stewart
was very anxious to see the boy, and on his arrival in the
village he was disappointed to find that he had gone with
his father's dinner to a place among the hills where that
person was working. So he had to go without seeing
him; but some way further on he met a lad answering to
the description that had been given, and stopped him to
find out if he really was the same. The boy's eyes brightened, and his delight at meeting the foreign missionary,
and the way he answered all the questions Mr. Stewart
asked him, was remarkable, showing him to be not at all
an ordinary young person. Mr. Stewart was delighted
with him, and wanted very much to get him for the boys'
school, but he could not get him, as the opposition was too
strong; but after the Stewarts went home the boy must
have, in God's good providence, overcome the opposition

to his being a Christian, for he got to the boys' school, and afterwards to the Foochow College—in training for a catechist—the same warm-hearted lad as ever. And last Sunday he read the Second Lesson at Ku Cheng, and last Monday made himself known to Mr. Stewart, of whose delight you may judge. Was it not lovely?"

In the course of the month of January Nellie made a little expedition to visit the wife of a native Christian, who was said to be afflicted in a manner not uncommon in China—to be possessed, that is, by an evil spirit. We give the conclusion of her story:—"The next thing I remember was a bridge, close to the village, composed of one plank thrown across the stream about six or eight feet wide. The catechist, probably owing to short-sightedness, seemed to be in a state of trepidation about crossing the bridge. So as we came up we beheld him, crab-like, crossing it sideways, feeling the way along with his umbrella. Such an object as he looked! When he had gone over he stopped and called out to a woman who was there to come and help the Kuniongs over, but almost as he said the words we had marched across the thing as coolly as possible, drawing forth an exclamation of astonishment from the catechist over these wonderful Kuniongs! The village being a wee little place, we soon got to the house, where we were given some tea, and requested to take a seat. Kui Ko was very glad to see us, and took us to see his wife, whose recovery from possession is another wonderful instance of God's power. The catechist had been to the house the Sunday before, and prayed with her—or rather for her—and the devil left her on the spot. They tell this with perfect calmness; you can't get

any startling particulars or any theatrical descriptions of
it out of them at all. They simply believe that in answer
to prayer made by a child of God the thing is done. They
do not doubt that God will cast out devils, and, though
deeply thankful, and much impressed by His goodness
when He does it for them, they look on devil-possession
as the most ordinary of occurrences. She was weak, but
quite in possession of her senses, and apparently understanding what had been done for her. She is quite young,
not more than twenty-four, and is a nice little thing. She
seemed shy, and, of course, is ignorant, but seemed pleased
to be talked to, and answered a few simple questions
about God and the Lord Jesus quite correctly. She says
she knows now that she must show how glad she is that
the Lord has delivered her body and soul, and how grateful by showing other people and teaching them the little
she knows herself."

Nellie gives some interesting experiences of about the
same date:—"I think I told you a good deal about the
week succeeding the return of the Stewarts from Hua
Sang, and now I am freezing myself in the same place,
and am so cold that I can hardly hold my pen, but I
must try and give you a lucid explanation of all that has
been happening. They came back looking much better
after having some decent nights' rest. The weather in
Ku Cheng was very hot, unusually so for the time of
year, and every one was looking more or less done up.
I felt rather seedy, and when I am run down, of course,
the first thing I do is to get a sore throat. It was very
sore all Saturday, and on Sunday it was no better; but
all the same, as it was such a lovely day, I went over to

the church and had my women's Sunday-school. A great
number of women came, and among them a new woman
from a place not far from Ku Cheng, but to which I
haven't been. This woman was not very intelligent, but
she was quite new to the place, had never been to church
before, and knew nothing. My work on Sundays is to get
everybody arranged in their classes and see that they are
being taught, and when that is done I teach any one who
is 'over,' as it were, and I had this woman that day. I
asked her if she knew who Jesus was? 'Don't know,'
was the answer; 'you teach me, Kuniong, then I'll know.'
So I taught her that Jesus was the Son of God. 'Where
is His home?' 'Don't know.' 'It is in heaven, a beautiful place, where those who love Jesus will go some day.'
Then I began again, and asked her who Jesus was, with
exactly the same answers to all my questions—'Don't
know; but you teach me, Kuniong, then I'll know.' So
then I stopped a minute and prayed, and then I turned
to, with a great determination that that woman should be
able to answer at least three questions before I had done
with her. And so she did. She could tell me after a
moment's reflection who Jesus was, where His house is,
why He died on the cross, and why we cannot go to
heaven as we are, and what will cleanse our hearts, so
that we may be fit to be in God's presence. So that was
a triumph, wasn't it? I do hope she will come regularly,
poor woman, as she seemed quite ready to hear all I
had to say. They are so utterly devoid of anything like
reasoning power, poor creatures. Down-trodden and
neglected for so many generations, how can they be
anything else? It is a wonder that they have any brains

at all. You will see by this one illustration I have given how far they are from beginning to learn anything of the Bible. Those who have been coming a long time know only a very little, and forget so easily.

"At the service I sat beside Mrs. Sen Ging, Toppy's 'missus.' She says the La Kuniong (little Kuniong, as they call Toppy most inappropriately), 'very much loves her,' which is true. But if they like any one a great deal they invariably say, 'He or she loves me very much.'

"At home you would scarcely ever think of having a change to other scenes unless you were very bad, but here, close to Ku Cheng, within four hours' chair ride, there is this great mountain, Hua Sang, and the houses standing there empty all the year round, so that if any one feels ill the trip here is as short as to any of the places we are continually going to on our work, and the air is so pure and good that a week's rest completely sets one up, at no further expense than the dollar which the coolies charge for carrying your chair, and perhaps 200 cash (about ninepence) which you give a man to carry your baskets.

"The thermometer, if we had one here, would have gone down to nothing by this time. It has got colder and colder ever since we came. The swaying bamboos, no longer upright and feathery, are all bent in a curve over to the ground, weighed down by the icicles at the end of each slender leaf; in fact, each separate one has a little coat of ice on it, with a large glittering icicle from the tip. The stems are all white with ice, and the pines glisten with the same glittering apparel. Our fingers and noses are not white at all, but a brilliant scarlet, and we think we would rather have summer. We can't see the village at all, much less the mountain view in the distance, because of the great thick white clouds which roll up the valley without intermission.   For fun I ventured out in the mud to have a closer view of the bamboo nearest to our house, and made the discovery of the cause of his poor stem being bent down in such a cruel way.   Then I got hold of the leaves at the very end of the stem, which only a day or two before had been waving in the air high above our heads.   They are fourteen or fifteen feet high the shortest of them.   I shook it up and down, and the icicles all jingled so nicely, but not one fell off; they were frozen on too hard for that.   You may imagine I was quite glad I had brought my warm clothes.   Every stitch I possessed was on my back, and Lena, who had not thought she would need them, has now the most fearful cold.   During the day we get on all right; but the nights—oh, you never felt anything so cold.   It was really awful.   On Saturday we hardly expected Toppy to come, as it was raining so hard; but in the afternoon, when we were all collected in the back room near our one fire, Annie Gordon suddenly spied A-Kien coming through the mist and pouring rain down the side of the hill to our house.   This little house was built for summer weather, and in that season is a very nice place, but in the temperature we are now having it is rather too airy for comfort.   For instance, the room where I sleep, at the back of the house, is built of mud walls, and there are decided chinks in the walls, through which you may view the landscape.   There are two windows, the frames of which don't fit, so that a good breeze can come through them.   Fortunately for us, the rain has not been accompanied by high winds, otherwise I think we should have died. The only fireplace is in this room, and with a fire there all day we manage to get along very comfortably.

"On seeing A-Kien arrive, we all rushed to inquire if the Kuniong was coming, and were told that she was, and we saw that along with A-Kien had come a man carrying her load. We were astonished, but returned to our fire to await her arrival. She was not long in making her appearance, more like a drowned rat than anything. Her rain cloak was dripping and she was wet up to her knees, having walked the greater part of the way, the latter, of course, being no one's fault but her own. We got her dry things and put her by the fire with some tea, and then conversed affably. Sunday and Monday passed in the same way, 'pouring cats and dogs' the whole time; but I did not care—I have done a lot of Chinese. The Acts of the Apostles is very difficult in Chinese. I have been all through the New Testament as far as translation goes; but the character takes longer to learn, and I am only just finishing Acts now. Of course I am not doing by any means full work at the character. The Stewarts are not very keen about knowing heaps of character; and, another thing, it affects my head in the hot weather if I do much of it.

"Topsy would not consent to stay here any longer than Tuesday, and the cold was really so great that, knowing how much she feels it, I did not bother her to stay on. I think the couple of days' rest would do her good in the end; but she is very keen about going on for her first examination, and wants to go back and work."

CHAPTER XVI

THE FEBRUARY CONFERENCE AGAIN

A general reunion—Improvement in church music—Demand for Kuniongs—Good news of an inquirer—Topsy's visits in town —New Year excitements — Debtors and creditors — In the country again—Teaching the women—Heart longings—Scholars and teachers—The language not difficult—Visit to a grand house—Courtesy of the host—How old are you?—Feminine vanities.

THE month of February 1895 brought back the New Year festivities, and for the Christian the important Annual Conference, and the season of baptisms. The latter numbered over sixty for the Ku Cheng district alone. In the previous year, when the number was eighty-seven, the two districts of Ku Cheng and Ping Nang had been combined. Nellie's letters of this month refer chiefly to the conference.

"*February* 6, 1895.—Not one moment had I to write since last Friday, nearly a week, and there is heaps to tell you this time. It is Cie Huoi round once more. The fun began by the women arriving on Friday afternoon to see us. I mean the Bible-women and teachers from the country. Elsie and Toppy proceeded to the church to pay a visit of greeting, and in the meantime several of the women were over here. The Dong Gio catechist and Mong Cho, the Dong Gio school teacher, were among the first I recognised, and we felt quite like old friends, as, of course, we are, though this time last year I did not know them.   There was a ladies' station committee meeting later on the same afternoon.   All the Kuniongs collected in the Stewarts' front room to discuss any fresh business in hand, and to make any new resolutions and plans that might be thought advisable.   At the beginning of the meeting a book was handed to me, with the remark that as I was the 'tail,' I had better keep it.   I did not know what this meant, but I subsequently discovered that the one who has last passed a language examination has to act as secretary to the station committee.   So I had to take notes of all the things that were passed as resolutions, and write them afterwards in a book which is kept for recording meetings of the Ku Cheng station committee. You would be lost in wonder and admiration to see how well and systematically the work is carried on.   One or two of the people here are unusually clever and gifted. Mrs. Stewart, of course, heads this list—not one here can hold a candle to her in any way—and she is by far the best Chinese speaker we have.   At least, I ought not to say 'by far,' for several others also speak well.   Miss Codrington and Miss Maud Newcombe are also in that list, and now that Hessie Newcombe has just arrived, she will also be in it.

"On Saturday evening there was a packed meeting at the church.   All the women had got in, and all the men too, so the church was full, as full as it could hold.   But one thing was rather sad, and that was the weather.   It had been so lovely and bright just the two or three days before the thing began, but on Saturday it rained all day and night without stopping. In spite of this we went over to church quite a large party, with lanterns and rain-cloaks and umbrellas and boots. I am organist, and as I had a vivid recollection of last year's performance in the big meeting, with so many voices, when Mr. Stewart stopped the playing of the organ because it was not with the people, but about a mile ahead and putting every one out, I just asked him whether he would like me to play the hymns or not, and he said he would. I was rather afraid to try, so he told me to try how I got on, and if it was not all right then we would not have any playing afterwards. So I played and we succeeded beautifully, the congregation and I arriving at the end of every line *quite* together. I think much the best way is to listen to their singing and accompany *them*, of course keeping time, as they always *do* very well."

Here Miss Nellie adapts herself to the real principles of Chinese music, which knows nothing of tune and less than nothing of harmony, but recognises time and rhythm.

"In the afternoon they all came across to our com-pound, and a praise and testimony meeting was held in the Babies' House. And one girl was so much blessed that afternoon that she went and took off her bracelets and the stuff that she had in her hair and cast them aside, saying how much dress had been a temptation to her, but that now she was going to be out-and-out for Christ. The evening meeting was almost the nicest of all. All the Kuniongs went, and Li Sie Mi had arrived from Dong Gio, and they put him in the seat of honour, and his happy old face was just shining as he spoke out his message. He *is* the nicest old thing. It was great fun in

the afternoon when he began to expostulate with Mrs.
Stewart, and said to her that now all the Kuniongs and
Sing Sang Niong (the pastor's wife) had been arranging
and talking about things for several days, but what was
the practical result?   Who has been chosen to go to Ping
Nang? (as much as to say you have not done much if you
have not got another Kuniong or two to go to Ping Nang).
The answer to that question is the same as formerly, *i.e.,*
No one. And why? Because there *is not* any one to send.
Where then are the *Sung-Kuniongs-two-piece* (the two
Misses Saunders) going to? 'It is not yet settled.' There
is an answer to everything if you can only just happen to
think of it at the right time." [The question, indeed, was
one which caused some division of opinion among the
missionary band.]

The following is from Topsy, describing some visits in
the city made by her at conference time :—" So they all
came, and we had a very nice time in the house of the
church-mother. She is such a nice woman. She is
coming in here before long to the women's school as soon
as it starts, and then I suppose we shall still be able to
go to her house to speak, because her daughter-in-law is
very much interested. She has a nice little boy too, who
can read quite nicely, and answers well. He was in our
day-school in Long Gaek last year. It strikes me that,
perhaps, you don't know from my saying that we had a
very nice time, exactly what that is. Well, I must try
and tell you. You would have been amused to see the
procession up from the school-house to the house of the
church-mother—this crowd of women, some of them
young, and lots of children, following the church-mother

and me, as we went along through the dirty narrow streets. When we got to the house—such a clean little one compared with many of them—we all crammed in, and after being given tea to drink sat down, and I spoke a little, and then turned Mi-Gi on. She is a gentle girl, about twenty-two, married, but I don't know where her husband is, and she lives in the Babies' House, and is employed there to teach the babes. She is a true little Christian, and speaks very nicely to the women. Of course, they keep on stopping us to ask questions, but I am getting to know much better now how to manage them, and we had a really nice time with them, they seemed so ready to listen. Afterwards, I got three of them to learn a text. The way to do that is to have some texts pasted or written on the backs of old Christmas cards, and when you teach the text you present the women that have learned it with a card each, which pleases them immensely. All the cards you sent in the box have texts on their backs now, and they are being used up gradually, and they are extremely useful. And that reminds me that I wrote to Mrs. Collier and didn't thank her for the bundle of cards. Wasn't it she who sent one? I know Kate got the other from Miss Dairs, or somebody. I also give them now as rewards to the women at the church; anybody who comes three Sunday mornings running will get a card! When we had concluded this meeting, we went to a house which belongs to a relation of Mi-Gi; she is a heathen, poor girl, and lives in a crowded busy street—the main street of Long Gaek. She seemed very pleased to see Mi-Gi; they really are very affectionate, poor things. We all went in and sat down in a sort of hall, behind the *tiang-dong*. A crowd pretty soon collected, and Mi-Gi spoke to them very nicely. An old mad lady created a diversion in the middle of the proceedings, by going to sleep and snoring horribly—such an old comic she was; and then she revived, and seemed anxious to do my hair for me, but I declined with thanks! Milly drew a lot of attention, as she always does—any English child does—they think their fair skins so *very* nice, and, of course, their clothes, too, are remarkable. We were tired when we got back after the long day.

"On Tuesday, I went out by myself in the afternoon to the city; at least, I went so far as Mrs. Fringey's house by myself, and felt quite proud that I could find it without any one to guide me there. Then she and I and her woman went visiting. The idea is only to look up women who have not been to church for a Sunday or so, and we went and visited two women: and then, as we were going to the house of a third, we heard behind us a woman's voice calling out from the front door of a large house in one of the principal streets, calling to us to come in and speak there, which we did. There were five women in there—quite a superior house, and we talked to them for some time. In the middle of it all, a man walked in with two baskets full of fowls, saying that some one had told him they wanted fowls there. So one of our hostesses got up and produced a little weighing thing and some rope to tie the fowls' legs while she hung them on a pole on which they weigh them. She did the whole thing, arguing all the time at the top of her voice about the doctrine. The fowl man had gone, and we were still there talking when I saw the master of the house lounge in from the

street into the room where we were sitting. He is a
literary swell. He did not see me at first; but when he
turned his face from scrutinising Mrs. Fringey, who was
opposite the door, he saw me, and I was surprised to see
that his face quite brightened as he said, 'Oh! it's the
Kuniong,' and he was quite polite to me. We had a great
conversation, but I could not understand all he said, for,
when he got agitated, he spoke so fast. He was asking me,
too, about the war: they are very much frightened that China
is going to be cut up. Oh! how it will change the place if
it is; but God will do what is best for us all, I know.

"I forget if we have told you about the customs they
have at New Year time. The greatest business is getting
the money affairs settled up. Men are out collecting all
day amongst their debtors, the women stopping at home
keeping accounts, and having a general spring cleaning.
By the wonderful means of irrigating used here, a stream
of water is diverted off from the river, and runs past each
little village, generally down one side of the main street,
if you can dignify the muddy tracks with such a title.
This little stream is used for everything—washing clothes,
vegetables, &c.—and at evening time the water for the
house is drawn in buckets. The 'spring cleaning' is a
great event, all the tubs and buckets, and everything that
can be carried, being taken down to the bank and piled
up there, and then the women scrub away at them with
bunches of coarse grass, and have a very jolly time, judging by the sounds. The houses are all swept—walls,
ceilings, and all—with bamboo brooms. On the last night
of the old year I think very few go to bed.

"The great object of all the debtors is to get into hiding

until sunrise on the 1st, when all claim over them ceases; so you may imagine the hiding and hunting that goes on. There is always a great deal of idol-worship, too, as they have to be propitiated with rice, so as to be in a good temper for the next year. Then most marriages are made at New Year, and continually we heard the wedding trumpets blowing, and saw the procession going along, the little bride—perhaps only a tiny child—being taken to her future husband's house in a magnificent red chair, with banners waving, and men blowing awful things that sound exactly like Scotch bagpipes. So you see it's a pretty lively time."

After the conference, Topsy returned to her country life at Sek Chek Du, where evidently she was winning the hearts of the people.

"You would be amused at the way they all take care of us. Sin Ging said to me to-day, 'Kuniong, are there any things you want made to cook foreign food in that Gin Hok could make for you? because, if you tell me, I will make the tins, because you can't eat rice like us, and we don't want you to get ill and go home.' Wasn't it awfully kind? I showed him your portrait one day, and he said you were 'a very old man,' which was a great compliment. They always use the word 'man' indiscriminately for men or women. There is also a distinctive word for either sex, but it's only used when either is specially indicated. And he hopes you will very soon come. I shall be so glad when you come and see all these dear people. I do love them so; my heart is quite wrapped up in them. It was so good of God to send us. If you could only come, dearest, there is such an ache for you in my heart.

"To-day (Sunday) eight women came from one house that we went to yesterday, so that we had about nineteen or twenty in all. About six brought their dinners, and stayed all day. The dear woman whose head I cured was one. Truly God was good about that woman. I did feel so bad about her head, it was such a serious cut; but it's perfectly well now, only a scar left to tell the tale. She is a dear woman. I do love her. One of the church-mothers has gone with Elsie, and one has gone to a village near to open a day-school for women; I am to go and keep an eye on it. One day this week they want me to go for a service, and are going to send two men to bring the baby organ up. They do love the organ so, and every Sunday afternoon it is a treat when we play it for them and sing. There are two such nice girls from Miss Bushell's girls' school in Foochow, living quite close, who are going to take a class here every Sunday. Sudden interruption—I hear a call of 'Sung Kuniong,' and going out find an old church-brother on his way from Ku Cheng through to a village near, come in to say, 'How do you do?' Ping-ang ('invite peace') is what they say.

"*Monday.*—I went out this afternoon, not having a church-mother to escort me, and going up the street a little way I got a very nice girl to come out with me. We went to a house quite close by, to do up a woman's leg; that place I am sure God means to bless; the woman invited herself to the reading *huoi* that we had at Christmas time, and seemed most anxious to make friends, and since then I have been several times to her home; she seems such a nice old person.

"It seems we can have the woman's school much sooner

than we first hoped, and so perhaps after all I will give up the hope of having my examination. The women are the first importance; I can't take the time from them. God didn't send me here to pass examinations, when there are such oceans to be done; and Elsie can't have those women at Sek Chek Du unless I take them, she has so much itinerating work to do. Of course, some people would say I was very wrong to be taking a three months' school like that, instead of studying, but God is giving it to me, and the Stewarts approve. They always tell me that when I do get through my examinations, I shall be younger than any of the others were at starting. So I must be content to go slowly. Mrs. Stewart says that if I hadn't given up studying last year, she is certain I should have been sent home. Would you have liked that, dearest? We have all laid down our lives for China, and the next thing is, how to keep them and prevent the devil from driving us to extremes; if he can't stop one coming, he will surely try and stop one working.

"To-day, as there is nothing specially Chinese to do, there is more room for aches than at Sek Chek Du, where I have no time for them. There is an ache to go to Sek Chek Du, and an ache for Hua Sang, and an ache to stop here; and larger than usual, the never-ending desire, beyond an ache, to have you. And yet, above all, is the peace of God that passeth all understanding; and there is another longing too, dear Petsy, and that is to put aside this burden of the flesh, and go into the calmness of the *Long Life*—'With long life will I satisfy them.'

"To-day was splendid. Last night there was a dreadful thunderstorm, and we woke up and both thought that the rain would prevent any one coming. But the day broke fine, and the women came—nineteen or twenty in the morning, and twenty-one in the afternoon. Some that are now beginning to profit by last term's teachings we got to help the other women. The woman, whom, for want of knowing her name, we always call 'the nice woman,' is getting on so well, and she can read fairly well, and knows the Lord's Prayer, and is reading the Picture Bible, and is so earnest. The next-door woman, that was so hard when we first came, is softening wonderfully, and there is a funny old one that almost lives here, just like a rag bag. She looks like an old Irish washerwoman, and has such wicked black eyes and no teeth. She always shuts one eye when she talks to you. We didn't like her at all at first, but she is getting quite nice now. We do love them all so much, and I think they love us too, for they always seem pleased to come and talk with us. I had my class for the first time on Friday, and six women came, but two went away almost at the beginning, and one about the middle, and that left me three—the nice woman and two others—all of whom seemed to have made up their minds to learn. We have a very nice church-mother with us now, and she teaches them in between times.

"There was a rule made at the station committee in Ku Cheng, at conference time, that if the Kuniongs like to ask a woman (a Christian, of course) to come and live with them, they might do so, because this would help to train the women in the most practical way for teaching heathen women and preaching to them in the villages. It is really the way the Lord trained His disciples, having them always with Him, and I believe He will bless that arrangement to have the women one by one with a Kuni-ong, always to go out with and help us. The advantage to us, too, is immense, because it's always so much better to have a native to explain one's presence in a place, and tell them what we want and what sort of people we are.

"To-day was a truly lovely day; surely the prayers brought down a blessing. I had twelve women in this afternoon to read. They are getting on so nicely, one helping the other; it's not much like an orderly school; I did indeed get them to sit round two tables, all facing the right way, but that was a big enough conquest, and Hattie Tolley, who is staying here now, took the children away. I had one church-mother to help me, and we began with prayer, and then each took a table, and at the end I questioned them to see what they knew, and it was wonderful how much they remembered. They all sat up straight, and looked so like students when I came and sat down and told them to shut up their books, and they all said, 'Kuniong is going to *Ko* (examine) us now,' and they quite entered into it. After that we taught them a few sentences of a prayer, and then prayed it over to-gether, and then asked any that wanted to stop and read more to sit down. One said quite indignantly, 'We've only read half-an-hour!' which wasn't true, for it was more than an hour; so I comforted her heart by saying she could stop and read some more. Then we left the church-mother to go on teaching them, and Hattie and I went to see my woman with the cut head. It's quite healed up now, and she is coming on nicely. I think two women in that house seem quite willing to learn, and I believe there will be a chance to get a weekly class in that village, as there is going to be a school there this term— a day school—and the schoolmaster is a very nice old man, so I think perhaps the Lord will make an opening in his house to teach a class of women, especially as he has said he is going to teach his wife to read. You can't think how nice it is to be able to talk with the people—not that I have by any means attained to linguistic perfection, but manage to get along, and they are so smart that they always seem to know what you want to say. Miss New- combe said if we talked Greek to the church-mothers she believes they would understand! No one need ever de- spair of the language; there are other difficulties greater than that—difficulties spiritual; the power and strength of the devil here is something to be felt. The kingdom of darkness truly is here, but praise God, the light that lit up chaos in the beginning will light China even in these 'last days.' Will you pray specially for this place—Sek Chek Du—that God's grace may conquer?

"This afternoon I took the church-mother, and we went in search of the house that Mr. Stewart's teacher told us of. He is friends with the head of that house- hold, who asked Mr. Ting to invite us to go and teach his womankind. It's quite a grand house, standing alone in paddy fields, with five front doors. As we drew near a group of women came to the door, and looked very pleased to see us, and asked us in. It was all so beautifully clean inside, with wide stone steps leading up to the *tiang-dong*, which was furnished with handsome carved chairs and little square tables in between. The table at the top was also carved, and had ornaments; great lamps hung from the ceiling, and the wood-work pillars were all painted in red and black, so it had quite a nice appearance. The people belonging to the house made quite a large crowd, and they all came round and talked and poked. Almost the first demand was to *Gong Cu*, which means, to preach, so you may be sure we went at them. Presently the head of the house appeared, the church-mother introduced me, and he bowed most profoundly, and then offered me his pipe to smoke. I returned the bow, and also the pipe, and then, after an interchange of politeness, went at them again. He stood there and listened all the while, and as every one seemed a little overawed at his presence, I had a better show, as it was quieter, even the church-mother leaving off talking, which was something wonderful for her to do. She is a most conversational little person, but very true and good at heart, which is the main thing; she always reminds me of a sparrow. Presently the host left, at which every one became lively again, but we had a very good time teaching and talking. He came back in about a quarter of an hour, carrying a tray of dainties, which he put on the table, and then placed two chairs for us. I am sure this was meant as a great honour, and then with many bows and scrapes we were invited to sit down. The tea was so nicely served, in beautiful fluted bowls of the most delicate china, and cakes and dates on pretty little plates. Everything was very nice, but you do feel awfully like a lion at the Zoo when every one comes to see it feed. They all stand round and look at one, and make remarks. These people were all very nice, and one old gentleman said that it was very gratifying to see me in Chinese dress. Of course they wanted to know how old I was, but the gentlemen were too polite to ask, and so they prompted one of the ladies to do so, which came to exactly the same thing in the end, as they all heard the answer, and all exclaimed, 'Ai-a!' (just imagine!) I have had to put on a year since Chinese New Year, because they have such a funny way of reckoning. Suppose a baby is born the last month of the year, then in the first month of New Year they reckon it two years old, although it only lived one month of the preceding year. Then they wanted some singing, so we sang 'Jesus Loves Me,' and then talked some more, and then went away. Although it was getting dark, there were several more invitations to houses to see sick people, and then we came home, and now that supper is over I am writing all to-day down for you, so that you may know in a little while the result of your prayers.

"On Wednesday afternoon the women all came over here, and the meeting was held in a large room in the Baby House. It took the turn of personal dealing now, and testimony. A good deal was said about foot-pinching, which still seems to have a strong hold over the Christian women, and also wearing quantities of ornaments. Can you wonder at this when we, who think ourselves so much higher than they, are so long in bondage to feathers and flowers? One Bible-woman got up and spoke very straight about it; she said so many wore the bandages under their stockings, and that they disliked big feet because they thought the small ones looked so much nicer, and admire the mincing walk that they are forced to adopt with the small feet. They looked to me as if they would fall down every minute, but evidently that is correct Chinese beauty. After the meeting one girl said she was going to take off her grand things, and another woman said she was going to unbind her feet; and another—a dear little thing, the wife of one of the nicest men here, and in a rather good position in the church—looked most miserable. Will you pray for these that they may be kept firm? On Thursday all the women went home."

CHAPTER XVII

ALARM AND FLIGHT FROM KU CHENG

Nightly visitors—Serious news—Morning preparations for flight—
Character of the Vegetarians—Over the city wall—Accident to
a native—Visit from the Mandarin—His testimony to the
Christians—Hua Sang not a safe retreat—Urgent necessity for
flight—The start—Trouble in crossing the wall—A hurried visit
home—A pupil's farewell—Journey to the river—Suddenly
recalled—Remarkable coincidence—Dividing forces—Home to
Ku Cheng—The Consul's summons—Farewells — Foochow—
The language and the people—A stumbling-block—Reaction
against the Vegetarians.

NELLIE to her mother, 27th March, 1895 :—"This letter
will begin with what might be termed a *spree* of the Vegetarians (or, as we call them, 'Vegetables.') We kept our
birthday with great doings. I finished writing my last
letter to you the night before last about ten o'clock, and
then, after seeing that all the various things I had to send
by the boatman to Du were safely in the hands of the
'Seeker,' I retired to roost. It was the night before the
messenger went down, and that night is for the Stewarts
a festival of doing accounts and writing letters, Mr.
Stewart's being all business ones. I don't see how one
man can continue at what he has to do without breaking
down. I heard twelve o'clock strike, and they were still
downstairs, and after that I went to sleep. The next
thing I knew was being suddenly waked up about 3.30

by a voice which I recognised as that of 'The Gospel
Band' (Li Daik-Ing Sing Sang) under my window, shouting excitedly for Mr. Stewart. He could not get to their
side of the house on account of the wall and outside stair-
case. Then he called out again, 'Sung Kuniong! Sung
Kuniong!' and just at that moment I heard the veranda
door on the other side open, and Mr. Stewart came out
and walked downstairs, so I composed myself till the
morning to hear what had brought the visitors, guessing
at once that it was something about the Vegetarians.
Well, Mr. Stewart went downstairs and unlocked the
door, and I heard voices in confabulation outside, while I
watched the light from their lamps flashing on the ceiling
of my room through the window as they went round on
hearing the door being unlocked. Then they all went
into the Chinese guest-room, which being exactly under
mine, I heard a pleasant rumble of voices going on for I
don't know how long. Afterwards Mr. Stewart told us
they had brought the most wonderful tale about an old
man who brought news to the Mandarin, no one knew
what; but he entered the Yamen, and requested the
attendant to take the letter he brought to his majesty,
which the attendant declined to do. Whereupon the old
man declared that, if he died in the attempt, he must see
the Mandarin. So he was let in, and what was in the letter
did not transpire, but orders were immediately given for
the city gates to be closed up. Mind you, this was about
nine o'clock in the evening. So the Yamen people went
round looking for wherewithal to block the gateways.
There are no gates; only arched gateways.

"There was nothing to block them with except *coffin*

boards. The coffin man's shop is near Fringey's house, and he heard the violent protestations of the owner of the shop as the people came in to take these boards—mostly great pieces of unhollowed tree trunks—and with these and huge stones they blocked the gates, and there was a tremendous row. It was about six o'clock next morning that Mrs. Stewart came into my room, expecting to find me asleep. She came up and began to talk about not wishing to frighten me, or something, and I said, 'Oh! I suppose it is the Vegetables. Is it not? I heard the Gospel Band last night, and I guessed what it was.' She then told me all the news herself, and that we had better have breakfast as soon as possible, as no one knew what would happen. We were to have had it in any case at seven o'clock, because Mr. Stewart was to have gone into the country that day. Such a morning it was! Mr. Stewart looked like a ghost, and had not been in bed all night. The report was that 3000 Vegetables were marching on Ku Cheng, and, of course, their first move would be on our houses, merely for the plunder. You may imagine the feelings of Mrs. Stewart, as she surveyed her five youngsters, and of Mr. Stewart, as he contemplated getting a party of Kuniongs and children and his wife out of the way of the Vegetables, for, of course, he is held responsible. Well, the decision was that we should all go up to Hua Sang with all speed; pack up and fly were the orders. It is half-way to Sui Kau—by a different road across the hills—and is a quiet place where no Vegetables have ever been heard of.[1] The load-men were ordered and came, but could get no

---

[1] This was the very place where the massacre took place four months later.

chairs, and so proposed to walk. It was pouring rain, and this did not add to the pleasantness of the prospect; but it could not be helped. Mr. and Mrs. Stewart were all round the compound from about **seven** o'clock **to** nine (they had no breakfast to speak of), getting the women, girls, boys, and babies all **over to** the chapel, within the **city.** The only means of entrance to the city was by a ladder **over the** wall. Everybody except ourselves and the servants **were gone by** about nine, as Mr. Stewart **dreaded sending the children in the** rain. About ten a **messenger came from the Mandarin,** bringing his card, **with a** message that, **as the** danger to us was great, he **invited us into the city to** take **refuge** there. So a message **was sent to Dr. Gregory to ask** him if we might move **for the present** into the **American** Mission, and the answer **shortly came back in the** shape of the doctor himself, to **say that we could certainly go, and** that he strongly advised it, the excitement in the city and the dread of the **Vegetables coming** being something intense. The Vegetables, I may remark, *en passant*, are not made of sugar. **They are a fearful set of men, and all** the cut-throats in **the place seem to belong to them.** They are held in great **dread by the Mandarins, on** account of their utter defiance **of all law and order. They go about with** long knives concealed under their clothes. The Stewarts have been through some extraordinary experiences, **but** they have never heard **of** anything like this. **It is** far the most serious thing that **has** ever been, and it is the first time that the city gates have ever been blocked for any reason. Thousands of dollars **have** been spent within the last few months in repairing the walls, as I have told you **in some** of my last letters.

" Well, before long we had started on our way to the city.
The Stewart family, Lena, and I left the house together,
but passing the Olives Mrs. Stewart went in for the
Kuniongs, telling me to go on. I was carrying baby, and
Lena had some parcels and rugs, and a few dozen umbrellas. So we crossed in the boat, Lena and I and the
babies. The old familiar gate of Lang Bo was closed—no
admittance. It was so queer, from the wall above several
people were admiring us. 'The foreigners are coming
into the city for safety,' they all said. Mr. Stewart
escorted us to the ladder, which was put up against the
wall almost exactly opposite our church, and, if you
please, there we had to tuck our skirts together, and
mount that ladder, and crawl over that wall as best we
could. Mr. Stewart just saw us on our way, Herbert
and Evan being carried over in two baskets slung on a
stick upon a man's shoulder, and baby being carried by
another man, and then he went to help the others. Before
long we were all in our new quarters. The Wilcocks'
house is a very large one, so we all fitted into it. The
scene of confusion on the veranda is utterly indescribable.
Owing, I think, to the Kuniongs' cook having rather lost
his head, they had nearly all their belongings brought over
to the city in boxes, baskets, or otherwise, and I never
saw anything like the state of confusion everything was
in. We brought scarcely anything. The few things I
managed to save went into two baskets, but the remainder
I simply let go, as the Stewarts did, as it was useless trying
to save more. We had our dinner about three o'clock,
and just before that Mr. Stewart had started back to our
houses, where he proposed to mount guard. But we had

scarcely finished when he came back, the reason being that as one of the Kuniongs' boxes was being dragged up the wall the rope broke, and down came this iron clamped box right on to the head of a poor fellow who was standing below helping to push it up. Mr. Stewart said the blood literally poured from his head, and when they had got him up from underneath the box the poor creature could scarcely stand, so Mr. Stewart brought him back to the doctor, who stitched him up and washed the blood off him. So then Mr. Stewart could not get back as the ladder was taken up, and they would not put it down again.

"That was Thursday. All Friday Mrs. Stewart was in bed with a frightfully bad head, brought on, I think, by nervous excitement. The rest of us just walked about, and I put in a good day's hard work at Chinese. The city gates remained blocked; there was no going either in or out except by the ladder, which was only put down at stated times. There was a guard all round the city wall. We were much amused in the morning at a procession of soldiers from the Yamen, who, with the Mandarin himself at their head, went all round the wall inside to see how things were getting on. We also had a visit from his excellency—at least Mr. Stewart had, while we only looked at him through the crack in the door. One very nice thing to notice is this, that when selecting men to form the guards the Mandarin asked particularly for *Christians:* 'They never quarrel nor use bad words, and they are so trustworthy.' This was the testimony of the heathen Mandarin when he was in need of some one to rely on to watch the walls. We were all very much pleased and praised God for His goodness, for has He not done it all? On Saturday the trouble was, if anything, increased.

"The Vegetables were still meditating a raid, and were gathered in large numbers in places not far from Ku Cheng, and our anxiety was not a little increased by hearing that Du was appointed as the rendezvous for these people. A messenger was sent flying post haste to Elsie and Toppy, to tell them to come in immediately. Another move to Hua Sang was decided on, and we were getting ready for the second time to go there when we were stopped by the sudden appearance of Lang Go (the caretaker at Hua Sang) and a Hua Sang village man, to tell us that the Vegetables were planning a raid on our houses there, should any one go up. It was evident God did not intend us to go to Hua Sang. So then there was nothing for it but for the whole lot of us to go to Foochow. We had a prayer-meeting and a council of war in the study, and then came to that conclusion. My two baskets with my few belongings were soon packed and ready, and being very tired from having had very little sleep the two previous nights, I was lying down with Nellie and Cassie for about half-an-hour, while the most awful fuss was going on outside. The temper of the people in the city towards us was very friendly—indeed, could not have been more so. The Mandarin and our people are friends, the Governor being favourable to us; so they know that it is of no use being anything but nice towards us. But that morning (Saturday) a placard was posted all about the city, with four characters on it which mean—'When the Government is stubborn, the people rebel.' The people, in fact, were very discontented at the stopping of

all trade through the shutting of the gates, and were beginning to hatch a rebellion against the Mandarin, to
force him to open the gates; and then what we feared
was a rush of the Vegetables on the city, and, *of course*, to
our houses, first thing! So we planned a hasty retreat.

"After swallowing some dinner we started. We had
secured six chairs with only two coolies each, which
meant walking most of the thirty miles to Sui Kau.
Miss Stewart arrived just as we were starting. The Sek
Chek Du Kuniongs we knew could not be in till about
four o'clock at the earliest, and though I wanted tremendously to wait for Topsy, I would not add to Mr. Stewart's
anxiety and responsibility by asking leave to stay, for I
knew he wanted me to go with the rest, though he half
relented and said I might stay if I liked. We left the
house in a long string—first, two chairs, each containing
two of the children; then me walking; and then all the
others, Mr. Stewart bringing up the rear to see us off the
premises. As we passed Dr. Gregory's house, the doctor
himself appeared on the veranda, and waved his cap and
called out, ' Good-bye.'

"Right along under the wall we came, down to the
west gate, which we found blocked, of course, and no
beseechings or offers on our part would persuade them to
open this gate, so we had to retrace our steps a short way
and climb up on to the wall, from which there was a ladder
put down. Mr. Stewart was up first, I was next, and
the others were stopped by a heap of brushwood and a
crowd, so were some minutes later getting up. But those
few minutes on the wall, looking down the ladder outside,
I shall never forget. There was a crowd of excited men

standing on the inner parapet, among the great loose
stones that were lying about, presumably to throw at
the Vegetables if they should attempt to climb the wall.
The man that owned the ladder was there, in a frightful
rage, declaring that we should not go down his ladder
unless we paid an enormous sum of money, and the noise I
never heard anything like. I was standing just behind
Mr. Stewart, who knelt down and seized the ladder to
prevent them pulling it up, which they were trying to do
with all their might. Once they nearly pushed him off
the wall. One of our boys was there, and an American
church catechist, who bawled and yelled at the men,
but not with much effect. In a moment Mr. Stewart
had got hold of the top of the ladder, and then looked
breathlessly around to see if any of us were within reach.
'Come on,' he called out to me, just behind, 'get hold of
the thing if you can!' But I couldn't, and so he swung
himself off the wall on to the ladder, and began to go
down. The men, seeing this, got more frantic than ever,
and seizing the top of the ladder, they tried to *shake
him off* with all their might. His face was white as
death, and he could scarcely articulate a word. If he
had fallen on those sharp stones below he would certainly
have been very much hurt. I was glad Mrs. Stewart
didn't see it! She, in fact, doesn't know anything about
it. Another moment and he was on the ground all
safe, but they immediately collared the ladder and drew
it up; however, there was another *very* short and clumsy
one there, which Mr. Stewart got, and with the help of
two or three of the Chinese held it up near enough for us
to be able to get down I was down first, as I was right

on the edge of the wall, and then the others followed one after another, I helping to hold the ladder and to get them down. At last we were all down and journeying along the road past the end of the city. Lucy Stewart, having had nothing to eat since breakfast time, thought she would like a little something to refresh the inner woman, and I wanted to get some things from our own house, so we two started off at full speed right round the city wall, having a good twenty minutes' walk to Sang Bo, where we had to cross the river to get up to the Mission Station. The last thing we heard from the group that we left getting their chairs fixed outside the gate was Mr. Stewart shouting to us through his hands, 'You must be very quick.' So we called back, 'All right,' and flew on. It was now about 2.30. When we got to Sang Bo we saw the boat the other side of the river, and nobody to pole it! Dreadful loss of time—what was to be done! Just at that moment who should appear on the steps but the tailor, a great friend of ours and a great character into the bargain. He said he would take us across in an empty boat that was there, and we felt sure that it was God's goodness to us again, so in we got, and the tailor pulled us across, and I asked if he would take a letter back into the city for Topsy when she should arrive, and he said he would. When we got to the other side, we simply flew up to the houses, but on the way met two of the village men, whom Lucy asked if they would carry a box for her, and they agreed, and came with us up to the house. I got the key of our house from the watchman's wife, and went up with all rapidity. Oh! how deserted and empty it all looked. I got a few things into

the 'spotted handkerchiefs' (boxes known by this name),
Mr. Stewart's Chinese Dictionary (a most valuable book),
and then caught sight of the seltzogenes, which had been
filled only two nights before. I wanted to empty them,
so that if they ever came back they would not be spoiled,
but could not, as Lucy was already calling to me, so just
seizing a few sun-hats (nearly everybody had forgotten
their sun-hats, as it was raining when we left the house), I
fled. The tailor accompanied us back, and in the boat I
wrote a hasty note to Toppy, and sent her her sun-hat by
the tailor. The last recollection I have of Sang Bo that
day, and the thing that went to my heart more than anything, was the sudden appearance along the path of one
of my darling boys, Ing Ong, going home with his father.
He had straw sandals on his little feet, in preparation for
the long trudge, and his little face had a sad look as he
gazed at us; but he smiled all the same as he said 'Good-
bye,' and then called out, 'Kuniong help us by prayer.'
After that we went back to the place where we had
left the others, and found only one chair. They had left
the two men to see after us, so we got one of them to go
to another coolie shop and get me a chair; there was *one*
there, *and that was the only chair then to be got in the city;*
so I felt that God really intended me to go.

"We reached Coi Yong at six o'clock, feeling very
tired, and my head was literally splitting. We rigged up
beds, and though it was noisy in the chapel, we managed
to get a pretty decent rest. We had breakfast next
morning about seven o'clock, and started on our twenty-
four miles from Coi Yong to Sui Kau. It was a queer
way to spend Sunday.

"I cannot tell you all about the **trip**; we just went on and on, every now and then wondering what was going on in Ku Cheng.

"We reached Sui Kau about four in the afternoon, the coolies having walked well. Our boats were hired already —a small one for the Kuniongs, and a big one for the Stewart family and me. The loads were being put on, so we went in and sat down, 'weary and worn,' but not 'sad!' In a short time everything was ready for us to set sail down river, and Mrs. Stewart was just speaking to the man about going, when one of the Kuniongs appeared to say that a very important box had not yet arrived, and could we wait for it? So, of course, we had to wait, though anxious to be off as quickly as possible. Ten minutes later a man dashed on to our boat, hot and breathless, with a letter for Mrs. Stewart, containing only these words, 'Peace is declared between the Vegetable head and the Mandarin; the city gates are open, and you can all come back.'

"The reaction of feeling was so great as nearly to give us the shakes all round, but we *did* thank God. The children were still to go on to Foochow, but the rest of us might go back; so we had some tea as a means of restoring our shattered nerves, and then began to get all the loads rearranged, and in doing so discovered that the box we had been *waiting for* was there on the boat all the time. Only for this little 'circumstance' we should have been far down the river when the man came with the letter. Is it not lovely to see how God takes care of His own? And it is another instance of answered prayer. Mr. Stewart told us afterwards how he had prayed so hard that the 'chariot wheels' might be 'made heavy,' that we might somehow be delayed, so that the man might have time to get to us. He wrote that in a letter that Mrs. Stewart got next morning, not knowing where we were, or whether the letter would reach her or not.

"That night (Sunday) we slept in the boat. Oh! it was hard—the boards, I mean—and my bones ached next morning. We didn't start very early, as it was impossible, with our tired coolies, to go more than half way. The half-way place, where we were to spend the night at an inn, was not reached till nearly half-past five. It was a wretched night. The baby screamed, and Mrs. Stewart had no sleep; none of us had much, and I was really afraid Emily Weller was going to be ill, she seemed so upset. Before we retired to rest we had more prayers for guidance, and another council of war, consequent on another letter which was brought asking us not to come back in a long string, as matters were not all that might be desired So then it was decided that three should go from there to a place two puo (six miles) away, from whence, if necessary, it would be easy to get to Sui Kau.

"Mrs. Stewart, Miss Weller, and I were to return to Ku Cheng. At last we got off, and though I was dead tired, my spirits began to revive when, from a little rising ground, we caught sight of dear Ku Cheng about 2.30 that afternoon. Oh! it was nice to get back again. Topsy met us at the boat with a smiling countenance. I *began* this letter before we left the American castle, and now I am finishing on Thursday, 4th April, about a year, as it seems to me, since the beginning of last week. The new Kuniong, Miss Wade, was in all this too. She only came up last Monday week, and her first entrance into Ku Cheng city was over the wall by a ladder. We have been careful to assure her that that is not our usual mode of entrance.

"*7th April.*—A letter from the Consul, saying that we must all be sent down to Foochow. He says, what we have been hearing from the native Christians, and what Mr. Stewart has been saying all along, that it is *not* a case of standing by Christians—as such—in a time of persecution for Christ's sake. It is not that at all; the whole thing is political entirely. These Vegetarians merely go under that name, and have those rules about not eating meat as a cloak to their real motives, which are to overthrow the present government and take the power themselves. The Chinese have such a tremendous regard for power of any sort, that if they *can* only be shown that the Vegetarian Society is greater and stronger than either the Mandarins or the Jesus Doctrine people, numbers and numbers of people will be sworn into their ranks, and the very thing they desire is to have immense numbers of people on their side, so as to act effectually against the government. A big attack on our houses for plunder might result in one or two of us being killed, but that would not retard their plans, it would only bring on a general disturbance, which is what they want. Our presence with the Christians simply draws attention to them, and renders their safety more difficult in case of real riot. The Ku Cheng Mandarin, we hear, is to be suspended for incapability. The Consul really wrote very nicely; he is a very good man. He said how sorry he was to have to disturb the work, and that if it were a case of persecution of the Christians he would advise us to stick by them, but

he feels he cannot do otherwise than recall us as matters
stand at present. On Saturday evening we all met for a
prayer-meeting, and Mr. Stewart said there was nothing
to be done but to depart for Foochow again; but this
time we should be able to pack and take our things with us.
The next morning I was over with the women as usual—
Oh! is it *really* the last time? Owing to the heavy rain
many of them did not come; but still, with the few there
were, we had a nice time. In the afternoon we had
another council of war, and the following was decided
on:—Hessie Newcombe and Lucy Stewart were to go
east to Sa Iong (to Miss Codrington), where there is no
trouble at all; and if there should be any, they can go
to Foochow by Lo Nguong, and not come through Ku
Cheng at all. The rest of us are to go to Foochow. I
had my dear little boys on Monday morning. I could
scarcely bear to let them go when the time was up. Two
more of them had returned—Co Uong and Co Hai. The
former will make a fine man; he is such a nice little
boy, and he was so delighted to be back. They looked
so happy, and smiled at us with such delight. But
God's work need not cease because He has taken us
away."

"Foochow, 11*th April* (Good Friday).—If peace with
Japan is declared we shall go back, as then the soldiers
can return to guard Ku Cheng from the Vegetables. I
don't believe I told you that it was the withdrawal of the
soldiers from the country districts that brought Vegetable matters to a crisis, and that made them so lively in
wanting to destroy Ku Cheng. The country is in a
very unsettled state. This morning we all went to the

Chinese church at the College. Sixteen months **ago I
was** in the same **room** at a Chinese meeting, and didn't
understand a single **word**; now, **I** could understand it
all. The sermon preached **by Ding Sing Ki** Sing Sang,
the head of the College, **to my great** delight was quite
within the range **of my** understanding. His sermon
was, of course, about the **great** Sacrifice of our Blessed
Lord, and he spoke **so** beautifully about it. He chose
those **two** words (three in English), '**It is** finished,' and
spoke about the meaning of the words, explaining it
simply, yet clearly. One or two faces I knew among them,
in particular, Ding Tieng Ming (the Dong Gio curate), who
is doing his last term in the College preparatory to be-
coming a full-grown catechist; **and three** boys from our
Ku Cheng school, who were sent here last Christmas. A
good many of them took good stock of us in our Chinese
clothes, but not one look of disapproval was to be seen on
their faces. **I was walking with** Millie and Cassie (my
faithful companions) after the **service,** when, crossing
the courtyard, **I** saw **Ding Sing Mi** looking at me and
smilingly saying, ' **Ping** ang,' **so I** smiled back affably.
I **don't know him, but evidently he was not** afraid that
a **Kuniong in Chinese dress would** snap at **him.** He
asked me **a little about** Ku Cheng, **and if the two** children were **Mrs. Stewart's, and we** parted affably. **I do**
love the Chinese. Just **a** little **further** on, at the gate
of the boys' school, I saw three little persons awaiting
us—**of** course, our little boys **from** Ku Cheng, who
wanted to smile **at us as we** went by.

"Do all these little things interest **you, I** wonder ? I
suppose they do, but they **seem** awfully little to write

down, don't they? Of course, I could not do it to any one but you. Don't feel inclined to."

The proclamation of peace gave liberty to the missionaries to return—perhaps too soon—to their much loved work. One incident of the return journey, recorded by Nellie, is worth producing for the lesson it teaches. She was on board the house-boat travelling from Foochow to Sui Kan:—"As we sat there in the evening twilight among the group of rough sailors, all smoking their long wooden pipes, the Sung Cio (master mariner) entered into conversation with me about our doctrine. He is, like so many of the boat people, a Roman Catholic, but very ignorant; they teach them next to nothing. But his faith, though elementary in the extreme, seemed to me to be right as far as it went. He said he knew Jesus had died for his sins, and that he asked Him to forgive him his sins, so that he might go to heaven. Then I asked him if he believed he had that forgiveness, and he said, 'How can I know it, Kuniong?' So I told him then, making it as simple as I could, about the sacrifice for our sins, and that Jesus had promised that those who believe in Him should have everlasting life, and he listened attentively, never moved a muscle, but occasionally giving a grunt of assent, and I really had a very nice time with him. He said that he had been taught about Mary, but I think he has heard the pure truth from some one else, and just has a few ideas of it. But he was such a nice man; so honest and good he seemed to be. Then I was talking to the other men too, and they asked a few questions, but all of them seemed rather to despise the whole thing, and were more

P

interested in asking about our foreign country. But they were off and on, so that in between I had good talks with the Sung Cio, and one of the things he said to me was this : 'Kuniong, some of your foreign Sing Sangs are very bad.' So I sadly assented, knowing that he has, in all probability, seen and heard of the wickedness of the Tea Sing Sangs in Foochow; and I told him that all hearts in the world are wicked till changed by the grace of God. Then he said : 'Kuniong, I mean some of your Jesus Doctrine Sing Sangs are very bad,' and went on to tell me of a certain Sing Sang who had been so impatient with him when he was bringing him up the river once, and forced him to go on, he said, when the wind was unfavourable, and he had not many men, and he was obliged to put on one poor fellow who was sick to row the boat, because the Sing Sang was so impatient, and wouldn't believe his word. I would rather be *days* late than get a character like that from these Chinese that we want to influence. All your good talk goes for nothing at all in the face of what they see with their eyes."

The return to Ku Cheng was accomplished, and Nellie rejoices over it :—"God has most beautifully been answering our prayers about the whole trouble up here, and also about the Christians. We knew, of course, that there was no need for the work to cease while we were away. We are only necessary to God as long as He chooses to let us be so, and we prayed much that He would work on in His mighty power and do even more than He had done through us before. The prayers have been abundantly answered ; from so many places we have been hearing one way or another of God's blessing poured down. And in nothing more than in this—the devil this time has completely outwitted himself. No respectable heathen will have anything to do with the Siah Chai (Vegetarians); they are 'out of it' altogether. There has been a strong body formed against them, calling themselves the Lieng-Gak, who are sworn to oppose the Vegetables, right or wrong. Only heathen are in this, but all the 'best people' are in it. They have not asked Christians to join, because they know that already their church is opposed to the Vegetables, but the feeling is one of great friendliness between the Lieng-Gak and the Christians, and they are very ready to listen to the Jesus doctrine. They all say it is a very good doctrine. Alas! they, many many of them, still lack that *one thing*—not yet, *not yet* have their precious hearts been given to Jesus. We have prayed that the Lieng-Gaks may be led into the way of truth ; many are inquirers. It was lovely to hear the women talking about it. They said over and over again, 'Truly, prayer is of great use,' and kept on thanking God for His goodness in answering our prayers."

CHAPTER XVIII

TOPSY'S MARCH EXPERIENCES

Dr. Gregory in Sek Chek Du—A station class contemplated—The
fox-devil—Confidence in the mission—The poor demoniac—
Bad news from Ku Cheng—Unwillingness to leave—Departure
by water—Ku Cheng on the defensive—Discontent with the
authorities—A primitive garrison—Peace restored—Resuming
work—Topsy's reflections—Return of the exiles—Ordered off
again.

Topsy's experience of the troubles is so distinct from
that of her sister, that we give her account separately.
The news of danger came to her in the midst of work of
absorbing interest at her beloved Sek Chek Du, from
which the first part of her letter is written.

"They were all very pleased to see me back again.
They are such dears! Dr. Gregory is very busy superintending alterations to the house, which he thinks no
one but himself can do for us, and although he got rather
an important letter yesterday about his moving from here
to go to another district, he says he hasn't time to go in
and see about it this week, he has such a lot to do here.
I think Mr. Stewart has impressed him with the idea that
the Kuniongs are very precious and need looking after;
he is always saying that if we don't have proper foreign
things made to eat we shall get ill and be sent home,
and none of them appear to wish that. I got such lovely
purple flowers coming out on Saturday, like honey flowers,

so sweet; the whole place is looking beautiful with the trees coming into full leaf, and the orchard in front of our house looks beautiful now; the house can't be seen from the road, the trees are so thick. It is such a dear place, I wish you could come. My heart is locked up in it, and the people are getting so friendly and nice; they come now so much better on Sundays, and are learning rapidly. It has been decided that we shall have a three months' class here; the opportunity may never be so good again, as one Kuniong alone couldn't possibly undertake it. So we held a council on the subject, and the final arrangement is that we are to have the women for three months, with me to teach them; and every now and then Elsie will come in from itinerating and teach them, and I will go out, so that will make a change. You know it is rather hard work itinerating, sleeping in all sorts of funny places, and eating funny things, so it will be good for Elsie to have a change.

" 27th.—Things are going on here very well; a good deal of interest is taken in the station class. This week the 'names are open,' as they say, that is, every one that wants to come is supposed to send in their name. We haven't yet got answers from Lang Leng or Gang Ka, but they will probably be in by Tuesday. I gave the carpenter some home thrusts yesterday, which he took very well, and I gave him a card with a text written on it, which I told him to take home and digest.

"This afternoon, as we were thinking of getting ready to go out, one of our old friends came in—such a queer-looking old lady, whom we call 'the rag-bag.' She can't learn much in the way of character, but I believe her

heart is beginning to be touched. She came in with a
very important air, and began to tell us of some people
near us whose house is full of the fox evil spirit. Almost
the most dreaded form of devil possession is by this fox-
devil, of which the people never speak above their breath
for fear it should hear and possess them. This house was
troubled with it, and one man was very ill, so the people
had sent her to ask us if they might move into our house
to escape. They said that we were 'resting under God's
wing,' and that the devil would have no power here.
Wasn't that a beautiful testimony to God's house in the
midst of heathen darkness? So we talked with Sing
Ging about it, and prayed together, and then sent our
old friend off with a message to the effect that we should
be very pleased to see them. The afternoon was cold
and damp—such a change from yesterday's heat—but, in
spite of that, in about half-an-hour four or five men came,
bringing with them this poor devil-possessed man. We
gave them a room off the upper *tiang-dong*, into which
they took him, and presently his wife came, and then
they asked us to have prayer with them. I went downstairs to call the doctor, and we chose the 9th of Mark
14-29, and asked him to read it. There were about
fourteen of us, namely, five or six baptized Christians,
two or three inquirers, and the friends of the sick man,
absolute heathen, gathered in the *tiang-dong*. They
brought him out and he sat with us quite quietly at first.
He looked as though he heard nothing, and his face had
a peculiar strained expression, and every now and then
would tremble all over, and the muscles of his face would
contract. The doctor read and explained the words, and

impressed on the people that they must believe and leave
their doubts. While he was talking, the man sprang up
and tried to get away. It took four men to wrestle with
him and keep hold of him, and then we prayed together,
and still, even while we prayed, he seemed as if torn by
some strong force. It just seemed as though Jesus and
the devil were having a battle, a test of strength, and we
had nothing to do but pray. When we had finished praying he was quieter, and then they tried to get him back
again to the room, but it was dreadful to watch the
struggle. He had hold of the door, and lifted it off and
dropped it almost on us, only we caught it; and then
they got him into bed, and we talked to him a little, but
he didn't seem to understand a word. This evening we
had prayers just near his bedroom, and afterwards Sin
Ging was in there a long time, and has just been to tell
us that he is a good deal better, and can understand some
of what he said. It is so splendid that they look on this
place as devil-proof. Praise God. I feel like shouting
'Glory' all the time. There has been a special messenger
in to-day to summon the doctor and Sie Mi from Ping
Nang into a meeting at Ku Cheng about the Vegetarians.
They are becoming more and more numerous, and the
city gates are closed to-day, and no one is allowed in or
out. I believe wonderful times are near at hand for
China and all the world.

"*29th.*—Another day after yesterday's pattern—my
dear's birthday—the second birthday that we have been
separated. I asked God to be very near you to-day, and
I know He has been. The sick man is better to-day, but
he still looks just as though the devil was in him, and

when the fit comes on him seems torn by the evil spirit. The men say his heart is filled with the spirit, and he is so miserable. To-day he talked with us a little, and said he was very miserable, and wanted Jesus to give him peace. While we were talking to him his face all changed, and he simply yelled: 'Peace! Peace!' ever so many times, his eyes glowing like fires. He told us how miserable he was, and wanted the devil to go. We prayed with him a long time, and asked him which he wanted in his heart, Jesus or the devil? And he said, half Jesus and half the devil—true type of a home Christian—but we told him Jesus must have all or none at all. After some time we left the room and sat outside in the *tiang-dong* where it was cooler. The room was so hot and stuffy that they all followed us out, and we suggested praying again together, he seemed so much quieter. But as we were kneeling down, the devil seemed to force him up, and he ran across the *tiang-dong* and leaped on to the roof just over the weather well, almost slipping down, which would have been certain death, as it is almost twenty feet. The three men rushed after him, and we helped to hold him though he struggled dreadfully, calling at the same time for our man to come and help, and then they dragged him down and got him back again into the room. To-night he seems quieter and came in to prayers in the lower *tiang-dong*, but we have moved him downstairs in case of another attempt on the roof. The tiles were all smashed to pieces. He knelt for a long while after we had all got up, and has been quite quiet ever since. This afternoon we had our Friday afternoon prayer-meeting, in the middle of which a messenger came in with a letter from

Ku Cheng. We told him to wait till we had finished, but he seemed in such a state of fuss that at last we opened it. It was from Mr. Stewart, telling us to come into Ku Cheng at once, as the Mandarin had private notice of a rising amongst the Vegetarians. He says all the women must either come inside the city gates or go to Foochow. Our compound being outside the city wall, all our people have moved into the American compound, which is inside the wall. They got in by a ladder. Nellie also sent a line, saying she had packed all of our possessions that would go in one load, and the rest we must leave to the mercy of the 'Vegetables' if they attack our houses, which is what the natives seem to think most likely. Our messenger was on his way to Dong Gio for Annie, and as she can't be in much before ten or eleven A.M. to-morrow morning, we called a special man and sent him to Ku Cheng this evening, although it was so late, giving him some extra cash, to try and beg off going in. We can't make out whether the feeling is running against foreigners or against the whole of the government and church combined. If all come in for it alike, we would so much rather see it out with the people here; it seems so dreadful to leave them. If it's absolutely necessary to go to Ku Cheng we shall have a messenger back in the morning. They say the 'Vegetables' are 3000 strong in the city. One man here was in rather a way to-day, as he said there are ever so many of them up in the streets, so you see these are fairly eventful times for us over here. We don't know one minute what will happen next, but praise God for the peace that passeth understanding and the everlasting arms that are underneath. Sin Ging went in this morning, having been sent for yesterday to help in seeing what could be done. He told us we would probably be sent for to-day. We laughed at him, but his words have come to pass. The *huoi-in* went off with about thirty men to fetch his sister from a village some distance off. He was afraid to go alone. This will put a stop to our class of women now for some time, I suppose, unless this thing is settled in a few days, which is quite as likely as not. There have been a number of soldiers sent up from Foochow, but I shouldn't think they would do much in the way of protection. The doctor told us yesterday that people were all saying something must be going to happen to China, there are so many 'signs'— hail in the third month, Vegetarians rising, the war not yet settled, and a variety of other things, which they think point to a change probably in the government of China, and we think that it points to a greater change, even the return of our Lord, when wars and troubles will end in His presence. We've been holding receptions ever since 9 this evening, and it's 10.30 now, and the last one has disappeared downstairs. It was the *huoi-bah* who came to advise us to go in by the boat, as we should run less risk that way from the Vegetables, who would probably find us out if we went in chairs. The boat will take longer, but probably he is right that it would be safer. I hope to-morrow we shall get a letter in to say we may stay here.

"*Friday, 29th March.*—We had such a good time with the patients at prayers this morning, a good many being women. After that we doctored them, and then we went to see our poor sick man, but he was asleep. We are expecting the man in from Ku Cheng any time now, with a letter, to say whether we must go or not. Meantime Elsie has gone out to do some doctoring, and I am going to study. The people are rather excited about our going, and our nice woman came in this morning to know if it was settled. It was nearly 11 P.M. before we got to bed last night.

> 'God holds the key of all unknown, and I am glad.
>   If other hands should hold the key, or if He trusted it to me, I
>   should be sad.
>   What if to-morrow's cares were here without its rest?
>   I'd rather He unlocked the day, and, as the hours swing open, say
>   Thy will is best.'

"*Saturday night, 30th March.*—As we neared the city excitement reigned supreme. There were exclamations of—'Kuniong, do you see the lanterns on the wall?' Yes, one paper lantern, and, further on, the soldiers. Were they soldiers or chair coolies? The long bridge, usually such a busy place, was quite empty, and the river beach and the houses and streets outside the city wall were all left desolate, only a few people being left, who stared at us, and wondered why we had come to the city, of all places. The wall is about 15 or 20 feet high. The whole place looked quiet, but not peaceful. As we came near the city wall we saw a ladder let down, and men busy bringing in loads of wood. All gates are barred across and guarded. We landed and tried to get up the ladder, but they wouldn't let us, so we went on a little further to the Sang-Bo-dong (the chapel is just inside the wall) and then we saw friendly faces beaming down upon us, and presently a ladder was let down, and up we went, monkey fashion, and all our goods and belongings after

us, and went into the church.   Such a crowd of girls and
women and boys was there from the school; we hear
that our compound is quite deserted.   Sing-Mi was
sitting peacefully in the front *tiang-dong* getting shaved.
They told us the news, how that Mrs. Stewart and the
other Kuniongs had all started for Foochow, while Mr.
Stewart was stopping with Dr. Gregory in the American
compound, and we were to go up there.   We got thither
about 5.30 and had supper with them, and have just
come over to Mr. Wilcox's house to sleep—Elsie and I
together in this great place.   There is a guard outside
that will delight us all night with shouts and beating of
watch sticks.   There are two very strongly-developed
sides to the whole thing, one serious and the other comic
in the extreme.   We knew nothing of the real state of
affairs, or why we were summoned in, or what the danger
was, until we had a talk with Mr. Stewart this evening.
He speaks of it as a revolution in the country, not a
religious persecution or anything to do with Christianity
in particular.   The Vegetarians have grown to an immense
force of reckless, lawless men, incited by their leaders to
seek for plunder and rebel against all authority.   They
are gathering round the district in great force, our place,
Sek Chek Du, being one of the worst.   They have left
the city, and then by order the gates were closed.   Of
course it stands to reason the citizens can't stand that
long, as they must live.   Rice and food and wood, and
other necessaries, must be brought in from the country,
and tugging it up a ladder won't do for long.   Besides,
the city people are beginning to grumble, and have
posted up placards all over the place, to the effect that

when 'the rulers begin to persecute the people rise.'
The feeling runs pretty strongly against the Mandarin.
So, to-night, as far as we know, the best thing is for us
foreigners to leave the city as quickly as we can. Mr.
Stewart thinks we needn't go direct to Foochow, but go
round to another place a day's journey from here, Sang
Tong, where Miss Newcombe works, and perhaps stay
there a few days or so until this either blows over or
bursts. It may be the Vegetarians will come down at
any time and force the city, and then with several
thousand drunken opium-eating men, armed with knives,
sticks, and any sort of implement, the safest place for
us would be out of their reach. Sang Tong is away in
the east, and the danger is mostly threatening from the
north-west. We go through to Sang Tong on Monday,
and wait there for further developments. It is evident
the city can't stay in a state of siege long. The money
given out to the guards on the walls comes to 200 dollars
a day, which is paid by taxation and by gifts from the
gentry, and, of course, it can't last perhaps beyond
Sunday. Then the great question is—Will word go
round and bring in a swarm of Vegetables, armed with
certainly anything but nineteenth century weapons, but
still quite equal to being very unpleasant? There is
nothing for it but prayer, and God can dissipate the
whole thing as the sun breaking forth destroys the
darkness. The comic side is very comic. Even in the
midst of the trouble, all the others having gone off, and
Elsie and I finding ourselves the only Kuniongs here,
and with every prospect of trouble perhaps very serious,
it is impossible not to laugh and see the funny side.

Imagine the magistrate of a city of several thousand people coming for an official interview, and at the critical point asking if the foreigner had a gun. 'No.' 'Well, a cannon?' Please remember this, and advise all new missionaries to add a cannon to their outfit in case of need in a riot. And if you only saw the soldiers! There is a guard at every gate, and at our compound and the doctor's compound just outside his door. As we came in there were a dozen or so men lying about on the ground smoking long bamboo pipes, dressed in ragged clothes and straw capes, just like the chair coolies. This was the guard, if you please. They take themselves off at meal times in a body. Every now and then the Mandarin goes round to have a look at the defences; first come a few men straggling along anyhow, and then some gentlemen in red coats minus any attempt at weapons; then the great man in a chair. They told us how the other morning the Stewart children were outside when he went round, and guard and all stopped to stare at them, and even the old Mandarin himself leaned out of his chair to have a look at the foreign children. The Mandarin is afraid to write for soldiers from Foochow, because perhaps when they arrive the whole thing will be over, and then he may have extra expense, or some idea of that kind. It's like playing with fire though, for, unwarlike and childish in all their policy, as the Chinese are, yet very serious results might come from a rising.

"*Sunday*, 31*st March.* — Thank God we heard this morning that the gates are all opened to-day, a peace having been made last night between the head Vegetable and the Mandarin. The doctor sent a man to see while we were at breakfast, and he came back with news that two gates were opened. Of course, a great many tales go round, so one could hardly believe right off that all was settled. However, we went down to Sang-Bo-dong (the English church), and found that they all knew that peace was declared. Our gate was open and every one was rejoicing. The women all seemed so relieved. There are seven or eight women from Mrs. Stewart's station class, and a number of girls and boys, all crowded in at Sang-Bo-dong. We had a very good service. Every one was so happy and glad that now we shall be left to them. Mr. Stewart thinks that we need not go to-morrow, and has sent a speedy messenger after the others. He thinks we may wait a few days and see, so we will collect together our scattered belongings again. At dinner time Elsie and I went over to our compound to have a look at things, and see if we could get some dinner. One man left there in the house gave us some of his rice, and we found some condensed milk in an open tin in a cupboard, and some jam, and so we had a grand dinner. The houses looked so desolate. We went back to service in the afternoon, and told them we would begin school again to-morrow morning at Sang-Bo-dong. It is thought wiser not to take them over the other side for a few days, as we may not have seen the end of the trouble, although we do believe that God has just stopped it now.

"All the trouble is really just the overflowing from the war, and until that is settled some way definitely there will surely be no real peace. The whole nation is being stirred up. May the outcome of it all be better days for poor China, perhaps even the dawning of the day that knows no ending.

"So now, about 6 P.M. on Sunday night, after most exciting days, peace seems once more to reign. It's very sad that so many of the women and girls have gone home. It will probably be some time before they come back; but they simply went like anything, and could hardly be stopped from leaving in the night.

"*Monday evening, 1st April.*—At last sitting down to write up the various events of the day. We had breakfast with the doctor, and then came down to the Sang-Bo church, where the women and girls are all collected, or at least all that have not gone to their homes. Elsie had work to do here, so I took the women and girls in two separate *tiang-dongs*. They were rather amused at first at starting school so soon again, but soon got to like it. It was so nice teaching them.

"We moved our things over from the American compound, and Elsie and I have set up housekeeping in 'The Olives.' The others may possibly have got the letter recalling them, and so until they come back Elsie and I will stay in 'The Olives.' Mr. Stewart is 'one piecy man' in his own house. It's so queer living in this big house after our funny little Chinese abode, with no other Kuniongs. I came over to dinner, and went back again to teach the women afterwards. The girls wrote me a letter in school all about the events of this week, and described it so nicely. I think I will get one to-morrow and translate it and send it to you to show how well they can write Romanised, and their style of letter-writing. Began with a Bible lesson for an hour with the

church-mother. Such a splendid time we had together,
and I did feel the power of God as one only does when
He gives the message, and they did listen so attentively
and answered up. Then they did Romanised while I
went to the next *tiang* to see how the girls were getting
on. They learnt Matt. v. 1–16 by heart, and said it
without missing a word, almost every one, and then I
explained it to them. It was all very impromptu school,
but much better than letting them go about all day doing
nothing. You see, none of their things are over at the
chapel, and it is thought best that the girls and women
should wait there a few days longer, in case something
more turns up to do with the Vegetables. To-morrow
we will take their things over and have more regular
school; but though impromptu and a little irregular, I
think they all enjoyed it, and I know I did. It was
about 4.30 when I started to come home, with several
women as escort down to the river, including our own
special Sing Sang Niong (the doctor's wife), who is such
a dear little thing, and her little boy, Sing Buang, who is
a great chum of mine. So also is the baby, a fat mite of
about twelve months. Every time it sees me it begins
to crow and stretch out its arms, and will insist on my
carrying it. The river is always so calm and beautiful,
stretching away down ever so far, and the mountains
beyond, higher and higher, rugged and bare. At our landing-place is a splendid banyan tree near the city wall,
and beyond are the villages clustering all round, which
do go so to one's heart. I got back and had some tea
(missionary luxuries), which was most welcome, as I was
tired after all the fuss and excitement. We have been

'living in baskets,' as we call it, for about six months,
never keeping our garments in anything but our travelling baskets. After tea we invited the teacher from the
boys' school to come up to write a letter for us to go out
to Sek Chek Du to-morrow, to comfort the hearts of our
dear *huoi-mus*, and tell them we will be back as soon as
possible, but until the other Kuniongs come back we
must stop here. Then we went upon the hill to see if
we could see anything of the others, as they may possibly
have got the note in time, but no sign of them. Prayers
are over now, and I am sitting in one of the little studies
in 'The Olives,' finishing up the day's events and this
curious mixture of an epistle. It's all so quiet after the
disturbance, one feels at leisure to get unstrung, so to
speak. The window opens on to the main compound
path leading from the large gate up past 'The Olives' to
the Stewarts' house. The path is so pretty now, with a
pine hedge, and bamboos, and ferns covering the banks;
and now the crickets and frogs are having a concert, and
the moon is such a beautiful bright crescent, soft white
clouds dimming the brightness every now and then; and
the air so soft and warm and summery—how I do love
the warm weather, it makes one live again. There is
something so like death and pain in the winter, and now
it is all glowing life and beauty. But we couldn't do
without the cold dark winters in our seasons *or our lives;*
there would be no real joy in the sunlight if there was no
cold dark death.

> ' Life after death ; port after stormy sea ;
> Peace after war ; death after life ;
>   Doth greatly please.'

"Although we are all back again so quietly, still it doesn't follow that all danger is over. Peace truly is signed, if one may believe the natives, but the Vegetable force is just as strong as ever, and anything may make them turn disagreeable again. However, they are all under the sovereign will of our God. We were wondering last night if there have been any telegrams about this in the home papers. Some seeker of startling events in Foochow may have been kind enough to inform the 'other side,' as the Chinese call it, of the trouble in Ku Cheng. I know you trust God too much to feel any undue anxiety about it, even suppose you have heard rumours of trouble.

"*Tuesday*.—The others got back to-day, awfully tired and rather the worse for wear. Things are quiet now, but all the leading men seem to anticipate more trouble from the Vegetables, as it is hardly likely that such an insult to the Yamen as forcing them to close the gates can be lightly treated. However, they are such peculiar people there is no telling what may happen next. We are not to go back to Sek Chek Du just yet, as that is one of the worst places. All round that district is pretty bad, and then you know I told you the Du is in a great valley, a thickly populated place, and oh! so utterly dark, so wicked that any of the devil's devices find it a good nursery, and the people congregate there; hundreds of Vegetables were there last week under pretence of seeing the theatre which drives a lively trade down in the streets. These theatres go round at certain times of the year, in some way connected with the idols, and get money and all sorts of wickedness. They have a platform raised about 12 feet from the ground, on which about half-a-dozen men and women (or men dressed as women) walk about, beating drums, waving swords at each other, and going on in the most utterly stupid way. It is altogether the most sickening sight; crowds go to see and listen, and refreshment stalls, loaded with various delicacies, are provided for those who can provide the necessary cash. 'Apples, oranges, lemonade,' the old familiar cry, is here turned into 'meing, slugs, and periwinkles.'

"Down till to-day, Sunday, all is quiet, no more actual reason for thinking of them, except that the leading natives are very doubtful of how long they will keep quiet. The Vegetables have the upper hand with the Mandarin, and they like people to know it. Humanly speaking, a great deal depends on Japan. We are looking out for news by the messenger expected in to-day. Divinely speaking, and surely that is all we have to do with, the hearts of kings and Vegetarians are in the hands of the Lord, and underneath us are the everlasting arms. I know you will not have a particle of fear for us. Pray hard for those poor darkened souls in bondage to the devil. As this letter is so huge, I will just tell you that we have orders from the Consul to go to Foochow (this news came by the messenger)."

CHAPTER XIX

NELLIE'S LAST WORKING DAYS

Value of the day schools — Native hospitality—Terrors of a pith helmet—The dragon festival—Visit to Daik-Ing's family— Buying peaches—Drinking water—An interesting family— Daik-Ing's history—His brothers and their wives—A mixed marriage—Gospel fishing—A cured demoniac—An unwilling listener—Lodgings for the night—A hot morning's walk—Daik-Ing explains—The women reached -Neglected husbands— Crossing a bridge.

A VERY important branch of the mission work in Fuh Kien, and one we have not yet noticed, is the day schools. These schools only cost the Society £4 a year each, and their value is well explained by Nellie in the following :—

" The Lord has been very good, and we have much to praise Him for, and I think in nothing so much as for His answers to prayer for the day schools. There are many of these little lights for the Master shining in dark villages through these two districts, and it is beautiful to see how the Gospel is being spread, through their means, to many hearts, not only among the children. The number of bright, interesting little boys that one meets in these villages is something wonderful, and they are so eager to be taught, so quick in learning, and many of them such good little things that one wishes there were more advantages for them. It is utterly impossible to reach them all. Often an entrance to some house, quite hidden away in

the depths of some village or other, and hitherto quite
unreached, has been made through one of these children
who has come to the day school to learn to 'read book,'
and has there made the acquaintance of the Kuniong,
whom he immediately invites to 'come home and see his
mother.' The women are sometimes shy of asking one in
themselves, and often it is that they do not see one at all
to ask, because the houses are, many of them, not reached
till you have passed through half-a-dozen others. It is
next to an impossibility to find one's way about a Chinese
village.

"Calling at a village the other day, we met some women
who asked us what we had come for; and I told them—
'To preach the Jesus doctrine, to tell them about God.'
They said they had not heard anything about it, or at
least, only just the name; so when I asked if they would
like to hear they said, 'Yes, very much,' Here a man
who had been walking about in the *tiang-dong* (guest hall)
behind them carrying a baby, interposed, and not very
politely said, 'You are very stupid, why don't you ask
them in; they can't preach to you standing out in the
street.' They then hastened to invite us in and gave us
chairs to sit on. We sat down, the Bible-woman and I,
and were very shortly as much surrounded by women and
children as any one could wish to be, and they seemed so
nice; they were so willing to listen, and some of them
even asked questions about the doctrine, which is perfectly
wonderful in a Chinese woman.

"As the weather is very hot I was obliged to wear a
sun-hat, just an ordinary pith one—but the affliction that
hat is to me! If you have it on as you enter the village

most likely the children, and those of the women who have
not seen you before, will imagine it to be part of your
head, and avoid you with considerable shyness in consequence of the peculiarity of your construction. If you
carry it in your hand, they see at once what it is, but the
amount of talking about it, and your own internal agitation at seeing your poor hat going round being tried on
everybody's head, rather hinder the quietness of the congregation at first, till the excitement dies down. What
the people in English dress do I don't know ; I have never
been in the country in English dress, and hope never to
be ; but it must be very awkward for them, I should think.

"To-day is the fifth day of the fifth month (Chinese),
and in this province there are great doings in honour of
the dragon—old beast ! For about two days there have
been preparations, and the worst of it is that the idea of
festivity to be kept seems to creep in among the Christians.
I do not mean with any thought of worshipping, but they
seem to have an idea of a little feast or something on their
own account, just because it is a time when every one has
jollifications, without thinking of the dragon at all. But
it would be better for them to have feasts at another time.
Of course they have them at Christmas, but they seem to
want to do it at this time as well. So the first day we
all had an invitation to a feast at the Baby House. The
women in charge of it and the Bible-women gave this
feast and asked us. The Olivites went, but we did not.
The second day (yesterday) we were invited to another
feast at the Girls' School, but we did not go to that either ;
and to-day, when I was coming down to breakfast, I saw
Mrs. Ciong Ing Lau, the wife of the head teacher of the

Boys' School, who had come to invite us to a third feast in the Boys' School, but somehow we did not go, and now there will not be any more. This afternoon, when I went upstairs after dinner, I heard the most tremendous noise of beating gongs and shouting coming from the direction of the city ; so going outside on to our little roost I looked down, and there they were, the city wall lined right along with people, and the tom-tom men lustily beating away, and five or six dragon boats being paddled up and down the river. So Lena, Toppy, and the children and I betook ourselves to a more advantageous position on the Bannisters' veranda, and looked for a little while. Just think of the awful darkness and ignorance of these poor creatures, fancying that those horrid dragons can hear what they say. The row will go on all day, I expect, though it is so hot ; if any of us were to sit or stand about in that sun from twelve to three o'clock we should probably be very ill, even if we did not have direct sunstroke, but the Chinese seem to have very thick skulls, and can stand a lot more than we can.

"This afternoon I shall be having my fifteen young men from the city day-school as usual. I invited another young man to come with them ; such a dear little fellow ! He came to church last Sunday morning with an old woman who belongs to the American church (Ngo-bo-dong) ; ours is Sang-bo-dong, but, as she justly remarked, 'God is all the same, and if it is wet and I come and worship here, it is all the same as going to Ngo-bo-dong." I quite agreed with her, and as she was inclined to talk a good deal I let her do it for a while, and she told me about the boy who was with her. He belonged to a neighbouring house, and was very well inclined, and wanted to learn, though he knew nothing, so she brought him. He was the nicest little fellow you can imagine. I talked to him and told him about the Lord Jesus, and about heaven, and asked him if he knew what would keep him from heaven or from being Jesus' disciple, and told him 'sin' would. So he nodded his head solemnly, evidently not deeply impressed, though feeling probably that he ought to be. So I asked him, 'Do you know what sin is?' and he said, 'No, but you teach me—then I will.' Then I told him some of the different things that God accounted sin, and asked him if he ever was like that— did he ever say bad words or think them? With a look that reminded me of 'the Israelite in whom there was no guile,' he turned his sweet little brown face round and said, 'No, Kuniong, literary men don't use bad words.' Then I said, 'Do you ever say words that aren't true, or deceive anybody, or get angry with any one?' 'Oh no, Kuniong, literary men don't do those things, and never get angry.' To explain, I should say that the education of a Chinese literary man is one that teaches him to walk without any appearance of hurry, to speak in the same way, and, so far as I can make out, to tell a lie whenever he can, but without turning a hair. This mite has only just begun, but evidently ranks himself among the literary class. The books of Confucius, of course, say many good words without giving any power to carry them out. After a little while, I succeeded in showing him that everybody has the same kind of heart, and that all are bad till made pure by Christ. Talking with him, and listening to what he was saying, as I looked at his innocent little face, I thought of that young man of whom it says that 'Jesus beholding him loved him.' I could understand that verse then.

"I have been wanting to go to Dong Liang for a good while; you know I went there once before, with Elsie Marshall, to see Kuok's wife. Well, now it appears poor Kuok has gone silly—they all think through grief at the death of his little son. I want to see them very much, and I also want to see how the Gospel Band's wife is progressing. So, yesterday, when her husband was here, having ascertained from him that she is not coming in till after the summer, I told him I wished very much to go and see her. His eyes lit up, he was apparently very much pleased; they just simply *love* us to go to them.

"The Sing Sang Niong, from the school below, went with me. She did my hair for me first, and then, our chairs having come, we got in and proceeded on our way, the bell at the boys' school ringing for nine o'clock as we crossed the river. The heat was awful, but I had my Chinese padded *meing* (quilt) over the chair roof, and my sun hat and umbrella, and exceedingly few clothes on, so was pretty well off. They carried us through the street of the city out to the other side, and then, not forgetful of our dread of the sun, they put our chairs down in the shade and comparative coolness of the city wall, and went off to get something to eat. Considering that it was not very early, they kept us waiting rather a long time; but the monotony of sitting waiting was relieved by seeing all the different people going by, either out of the city to their fields to work, or coming in and carrying things in baskets to market. I must say the peaches in their baskets looked delicious, so that I felt inclined to buy some, but I had no money. However, a little later on, when we were resting in a village, a boy came through carrying his two baskets on a pole full of peaches, which looked so nice, though I knew they were not ripe, that I borrowed nine cash from the coolies and bought three peaches for three cash apiece, and ate one straight off. It was *so* nice. (100 cash is a little less than 3d. What would three cash be?) I have rarely felt so hot in my life as I did that day. After passing Lan-A we came to the liang. It is not a very steep one, but certainly it is 'long' (Dong-liang means 'long flight of steps'). The coolies toiled on bravely, and it was a great joy, about half-way up, to come on a little stream flowing straight out of the rocks and falling into a little basin of white sand. This water you can always drink, so we all refreshed our thirsty lips at this little spring. I think it is most trying when you are panting for a drink to hear (as you do all the way along the roads we travel) the clear tinkle of running water, and see the lovely little streams bordered with fern and grass among the mossy rocks, and yet know that you dare not drink a drop of it; *it has flowed through the paddy.* But a spring clean out of the earth you may drink of with a good conscience. The river water, though it makes you thirsty to see it dashing in bright torrents over the rocks and swishing by under the cool green trees, you dare not touch; all the paddy streams go straight into it. At last—nearly two hours later than we had meant to arrive—we came to Dong Liang Ding (the little village at the 'top' (ding) of the liang through which you must pass. There was still

another half-mile or so to A-Cie, where the Gospel Band's
house is, and we solemnly proceeded on after a short
rest, when the people, as usual, gathered round in the
kindly way they do, and one old gentleman presented me
with some arbutus berries, which are very refreshing on
a hot day.   They were so pleased when they saw I could
eat them.

"As we drew near the village of A-Cie, the coolies
asked me where the church was, so I told them there
was no church—we are going to Li Daik-Ing Sing Sang's
house; so a kind young man directed us, and presently I
found myself being carried round a wonderful sort of
corner, where I wonder I wasn't killed entirely.   I preferred to get out and walk the rest of the way, and so
lost sight of the Sing Sang Niong's chair; but as I
mounted a flight of steps I saw she had been carried
into a large *tiang-dong*, and as I passed the door to
avoid a heap of ashes right in front of it, I heard the
familiar tones of the Gospel Band's voice—'Kuniong!
Kuniong!   Come in here!'   So I went in, and there
was his majesty with a smiling countenance, sincerely
delighted to see us.   Then we were invited to take a
seat in the *tiang-dong*, and the ladies of the household
were not long in making their appearance dressed in
their Sunday best, because, of course, they knew we were
coming.

"It is altogether a very interesting family.   More than
twenty years ago the father became a Christian, in spite
of the violent opposition of all his relations and friends.
The first annual native conference in Foochow took place
some time after his conversion, and he, full of zeal and

enthusiasm, went to it. Mr. Stewart knew him quite well, and while he was in Foochow that time, away from his home and everything, he took cholera and died. His wife became in consequence more frantically opposed to the Gospel than ever; but, thank God! though she did everything in the power of a Chinese mother to do, she could not prevent her eldest son's conversion to be a true child of God. The father before his death had built a very nice church next to their house. The old lady has been dead some time, and now, of course, the Gospel Band (or Daik-Ing as I *should* call him), as eldest son, has no more of that kind of opposition. His wife, however, was a heathen, and her history I will tell you, as I have heard it from Hessie Newcombe. Eight years ago they got her to come and read in the women's school in Ku Cheng. Of course when her husband told her to come she had to obey, but there is an old saying about leading a horse to water that applied strongly in this case, as Mrs. Li Daik-Ing sat like a thunder-cloud and sulked, with her arms crossed, refusing to do a single thing. However, after a time she became softened, and was quite willing to be taught, and was actually preparing in a sort of way for baptism, when Li Daik-Ing had to go up to the N.W., and as she was not going with him she had to go home, and there the old lady had such an evil influence on her that she went quite back, and has only been reached at all since by being in Ku Cheng last year. She has been taught a little, and expressed her willingness and desire to be baptized, so she was baptized in February (this year) at the conference. The Gospel Band has three brothers, none of them Christians, nor in the least in-

clined to be, so far as I can tell; God grant I may be
wrong in that! The wife of the third brother was in
Ku Cheng at conference time, staying with her sister-
in-law, Daik-Ing's wife, and she came to church, and as
it was one of the first Sundays after I had begun to take
charge of the Sunday-school, I had a nice talk to her,
and took a great fancy to her, a particularly nice young
woman. Such a sweet, gentle face, I can see her now,
as she sat on a doorstep in the city chapel in her bright
festival clothes and with a prettily decorated crimson
tiara adorning her hair, which shone with oil and sparkled
with pins. Her little year-old boy, also highly decorated,
was on her knees.

"But to resume. We were greeted with great glee by
Daik-Ing's wife, in whom there is an improvement even
in the short time since I saw her last, and then the three
brothers' wives came out. The third one, as I told you,
I knew before, and the fourth one is the daughter of a
Christian couple in Uong Tung (a village six miles from
here, where I have been a few times), and she has also
been in the girls' boarding-school at Ku Cheng, and now,
at nineteen years of age, she is married to this heathen,
who is not the kindest of husbands. Poor child! it was
quite touching to see the joy with which she greeted the
Sing Sang Niong and me. While we were sitting in the
tiang-dong after the first raptures were over, the three
elder wives disappeared with the Gospel Band, and we
heard various scrapings and movements in the back
regions, which assured us of a Chinese dinner to come.
The little fourth wife, only married four months, sat with
us, and poured out all sorts of tales into the Sing Sang

Niong's sympathetic ear. I could not make out a quarter of what she said, for she talked in a whisper, and so fast that it was difficult even for the Sing Sang Niong to hear, but it was all about her husband (Diak-Ing's youngest brother). How he wouldn't go to worship God, and will smoke a little opium, and won't listen to her, and will scold her when she speaks to him. Poor child! it is a wretched life. Her name is Ging Leng.

"Before long we were escorted into the back regions, and at a beautiful clean table we were invited to take a seat and eat. Only the Sing Sang Niong (Bible-woman) and I sat down, while the others all stood or sat around looking on. It was too hot to eat much, but still I did manage to eat a little; they are so pleased if you do; and then I talked to the wives. The second one looked very nice, but she fought shy of me, so I found that I must 'fish' a little; so I preached no gospel for a bit, but only 'angled.' Presently the host came in and suggested a removal to another place which he said was cooler. (Probably the men wanted to come through these rooms, and would not while we were.) So we all went down to a lower *tiang-dong*, where it certainly was very cool. It is such a great big house and so nicely kept. They must be well off. It is by far the nicest Chinese house I have ever been in.

"It was rather disappointing at first, I thought I was never going to get an opportunity to speak to one of them by herself; but at last I did. I made great friends with the second wife over my sausage basket, and then I had a nice talk to her; she was quite unreserved, and I got a splendid chance to tell her as plainly as I could the story of Christ's love—it was so good of the Lord—He just did it all; I felt He was there doing it.

"It is difficult to know how to get to their own village to teach them; there are so few of us to do it all. About four o'clock we went out to visit some of the houses. Oh! I forgot to say that while we were sitting talking, who should march in but Kuok's wife, the little woman who was possessed with a devil: so bright and happy; Smiling Tom was nothing to her! I did not recognise her a scrap, till one of them said, 'That is Kuok's wife.' She looked so different from the thin wasted little thing I had seen before.

"We went out 'preaching,' accompanied by Daik-Ing's wife, Kuok's wife, and Ging Leng, and didn't get back till about 6.30. In the course of our peregrinations we only came on one thing that I will tell you; it was in the last house we went to, where we were specially conducted to see an old woman who has not been able to come and see us. She was a real old curiosity, about seventy-eight or so, an old witch, and didn't in the least wish to listen. An imp of a girl with bright eyes and a nice little face —I should say the old lady's great-granddaughter—sat beside her, eating some nuts, and having heard us talking all the afternoon, knew pretty well the sort of answers we wanted to our questions, which you always ask, to see if they have taken in what you have been saying. As it happened, it was the Bible-woman who questioned this old curio, and as she questioned her the invariable answer was, 'I don't know,' and the imp in a loud voice would prompt her, and she would innocently repeat the answer amid the shouts of the bystanders. It turned out that she was a friend of Daik-Ing's deceased mother, and was deterred from being a Christian at the time of his father's death, because they all felt that the idols had caused his death in revenge for his being a Christian. She was not a very hopeful subject.

"When we got back to the house we found our things all put in the rooms of the fourth brother and his wife—quite a suite of apartments. I suppose the fourth brother and Ging Leng, as being of the least importance, had to move for us. The Sing Sang Niong went and had tea with Daik-Ing's wife, but I had mine in our *tiang-dong* with an occasional admirer looking on. Daik-Ing's eldest son, Huai Gi, is at school in Foochow; his second son, Gieng Gi, is the head boy of the school—such a darling little fellow. Next to him is a little sister—a dear little girl about eleven years old: the Gospel Band is so fond of them, though he does not show it very openly, but it is nice to see his determined strong features soften and his eyes brighten when you speak of his boys, especially of Gieng Gi. After tea, Daik-Ing's wife and Ging Leng came and sat with us, and before long he came himself, and we had a long confabulation, he sitting at a respectful distance and talking to me while the others listened. He told me about the neighbouring villages that he wanted me to visit, and mentioned six (counting his own); but two were out of reach—I could not have gone there and been back on Friday night, which I had to do. But he told me of one, called Sa Kang, a mile from A-Cie, up a terrific liang where no foreigner had ever been, and he himself only about twice. I said I should very much like to go, and he said he would try

R

and see if it could be done. He wanted to know if I
could stay another night, but I was afraid I couldn't.
It was very nice in that awful heat to have a room to
oneself and be able to undress properly. Sometimes you
can't, and in the hot weather that is a great trial. The
family began stirring next morning about 5.30, and not
much after six they brought me a little wooden tub of
cold water; it was delightful to be able to have a wash in
cold water. I had my breakfast about seven, and soon
after Mrs. Daik-Ing took me to see the chapel: it certainly is very nice, but no one goes to church in it.
Dong Liang is rather a dead place. Daik-Ing came for
us at ten. He wears loose grey pantaloons and a loose
thin white coat and an enormous hat, and carried a large
umbrella. We then proceeded up that mountain to Sa
Kang. The road led up the perpendicular side of that
mountain, with sun baking down on us all the way
except where the trees met over our heads and protected
us. The poor Bible-woman turned black, nearly! and
perspiration was streaming down all our faces. I could
keep up with the master, but we waited every few
minutes for her to catch us up. He never looked at
her—they are so proper!—but he would call out en-
couragingly, 'There's no hurry, slowly, slowly walk;' and
once or twice laughed outright at me, tearing along to
get up as quickly as might be. A mile straight up—
not exactly the sort of trip you would choose for a
June day in China. Just before we got to the village
there was a short flight of steps in the shade of a great
big tree, so the lady and I sat down and rested, and
the master went on to the top, where he stood half in

shade and half in sunlight, his great hat on the back of his head and his umbrella up, talking to an old fieldman with the buckets on each end of his stick over his shoulder, and the queer-shaped roofs of the houses in the village beyond making a background for their figures —it was quite picturesque.

"Then we went on into Sa Kang, where no foreigner had ever been before. The men, who travel about a good deal, had seen Kuniongs before, and had also heard the Jesus doctrine, but the women had not. A man brought me a teapot full of icy cold water from a mountain spring, and I drank as much of it as I dared.

"The master sat the other side of the *tiang-dong* fanning himself vigorously, and conversing with three men who were there, answering all sorts of questions about me. 'No! she isn't married; foreign women don't have to be married, it is according to God's will for them whether they do or not.' 'Yes! she can understand what you say, and she can talk herself, too.' 'No! she doesn't get paid a great deal of money to come here; she came because she wants to teach this country's women about God,' &c.

"A crowd of women was in the meantime collecting at the far side of the *tiang-dong* gazing shyly and curiously at me, and they were moved to astonishment when I called out to them and invited them to come and sit down and talk to us. 'Ai-a! she can talk our words.' I did not expect that they would approach with all the men there, but I was hardly prepared for the friendliness with which they all replied, 'You come to the *tiang-dong* in the house the other side, and talk to us there.' So we

were not long, I can tell you, in getting up and going off
with them, and in that house had a very good time, if
it had not been a little spoilt by an atheistical young man
with but scanty clothing and a very long pipe, who kept
making uncalled-for observations the whole time.   We
were there for nearly two hours, I should think, and then
there commenced a great disturbance all through the place.
The lords of creation had come in and found that their
dinner wasn't cooked, and that their wives were all off
somewhere listening to the Kuniongs' 'talking-book.'
There was immediate scatteration, and shortly after that,
Daik-Ing came and said we must go back. They did their
best to get us to stay for dinner; some of the men caught
hold of Daik-Ing by every available bit of clothes, and
would hardly let him go; but it would be a very determined person indeed who would get the Gospel Band to
do what he had said he would not do.   So we went off—
by a different road, I am glad to say. 'Kuniong,' said
the master, 'if we go back this way there is a bridge; do
you think you could cross it?' So I assured him I could,
and the lady would not be backward in doing what I had
said I could do, so we went on.   It was nothing of a
bridge.   The man stood at the other end to save us if
we fell into the water, but as I walked straight across,
he said, 'Sik-cai! lots of women would be afraid to do that.'
Chinese men think women can't do anything; their own
women are so helpless and incapable that I don't wonder,
but it is the men who make them so."

CHAPTER XX

TOPSY'S LAST DAYS AT SEK CHEK DU

Unsanitary surroundings—A warm reception—Topsy's ideal of
life—A handsome church—A fire—Welcome back to Du—
Extempore prayer—Church mothers—Sunday congregation
progressing—Newly-ordained native pastor.

AFTER their return from Foochow, and before settling
down to work, Elsie Marshall and Topsy made a little
excursion round some outlying country parts of the district, from the accounts of which we cull the following:—

"The great difficulty of living right in among the
people is, of course, what might be expected—their sani-
tary arrangements. There are no drains, so, of course,
everything goes either into the streets or on to the paddy
fields, and the odours are great and many. Our one
room, though large and wonderfully clean for a Chinese
loft, we have to use for everything, and sometimes we
feel as though we could eat nothing. This morning we
went out for about ten minutes before breakfast. I think
the people thought we were mad when they saw us going
up the hill, but we got some fresh air, which was what we
wanted. I think that, with some improvements, which
are always made in a native house when the mission
takes it, it would be just lovely to live in one always, but
it is quite necessary to make some alterations. Yesterday
we went to a village five miles away, and, judging from

our reception, I should think we were the first foreigners they had seen. For some time it was quite impossible to say anything to them of the Gospel; the noise was so great that I could not make out whether the baby with its face all screwed up, quite close to me, was crying or not; and Elsie and I had to scream at the top of our voices when we wanted to say anything to one another. After a bit they quieted down, and then we talked to them. At the next village we had two meetings and found the people very ready to listen, especially two women who took in what we had to say splendidly, and explained to the others what they could not understand. We had really a very good time, and very much want to go there again soon. It was so very nice walking there through such beautiful country, up and down hills the whole time. We had a chair between us, but did not use it much. I had that hymn in my head that we sang at our last meeting at Moonee Ponds, 'Speed Thy servants,' and so on till it comes to—'Never leave them, never leave them, till Thy face in heaven they see.' It is restful to look forward to the time when all the former things shall pass away, and all things become new. We shall look back and think how small were the trifles that came between us and God, that seem so large now, don't you think? Elsie has gone visiting with the Bible-woman; I was too tired, so stopped in possession of the loft.

"We had quite a number of patients in this morning. My thoughts always go to the casualty room, where I do up legs and heads here. The baby is nearly well now, but it took me nearly ten minutes to wash the dirt off a cut this morning.

" 14*th*.—Started this morning for Gang Ka about 9.30,
Elsie going on first about 8.30 to do some villages on the
way, while I stayed to finish doctoring some cases, and
then came on. Such a lovely day, through country so
rich and fertile, everything nice but the spiritual darkness
of the numberless villages through which we passed. It
is a little bit of my dreaming realised, to be alone somewhere working among these people. It is so nice to feel
perfectly quiet, not a sound all round except natural ones.
When my dear comes and we set up a shanty together,
it will be so nice; such a liberation from the strife of
tongues; you will enjoy it so. My dear dirty old coolies
took such a paternal interest in me. When we stopped
for them to have their dinner, one came to me with some
awful-looking cakes and presented them to me with his
fingers; I said I had had my dinner, so he took them
away and really looked quite grieved, and then disappeared into a shop and brought me some tea, which I
was rather glad to get, but discovered afterwards that it
had been poured out of a teapot from which the other
coolie was drinking; but one smiles at these details! At
nearly every place the people crowded round to talk, and
either brought me cups of tea or asked me in. They are
such simple, kind-hearted people, and I think our native
dress shows them we want to be friends, and they crowd
round and are so nice; I never pass a village but I want
to stay and live there. At one place they simply made
me get out and go in, although we were in a hurry to get
on as we saw a storm coming on, and they brought me
tea and a fan. So in return I doctored a baby, and after
some amiable conversation I got into my chair again.

The storm was beautiful, coming along over the mountains, the black, heavy clouds almost touching the mountain-tops, broken with flashes of lightning, and all round at the base of the hills a strange brightness. And *such* thunder! The coolies were nearly scared to bits, and retreated under their immense hats; at last great heavy drops came very slowly, and then it poured, but they covered my chair with oil paper, so I kept quite dry. When we got within about ten minutes of the house they just planted my chair down and ran under shelter; poor things, they do so dread a storm. Well, home again now. I am afraid there will be no more excursions before the summer holidays."

Topsy's last days among her beloved country-people at Sek Chek Du are beautifully described in a letter to her mother, which we copy entire :—

"SEK CHEK DU, *6th June*, 1895.—My Dearest,—At the end of a long day's work I am sitting down to write to you, my own dear mother, from our little den in this corner of the world. You will have my letter about the expedition round the country by this time, and now I must just tell you how we got to Sa-Tong on Wednesday —that is another Chinese house, a little done up to keep out the inclemency of the elements, and having a little girls' school in one part and a women's station class in another. It is very happy work going round the stations; I have enjoyed it immensely. They took me to the church, which formerly was the dwelling of one of the richest men in the village. The whole house is most beautifully carved; the door panels especially I noticed. We should prize them at home; I should like to send

you a cast of them—a mass of flowers and birds, with
the petals and centres of the flowers showing up so well,
and each feather of the bird's wing most beautifully
done, and such an expression on the faces. All round
the square in front, surrounding the *tiang-dong*, there
is a beautiful carving of flowers and leaves. It was here,
some months ago, that a fire broke out in the village,
quite close to the Kuniongs' house. All the place was
in the greatest confusion, people rushing hither and
thither, trying to save their things. Most of them
brought all they could lay their hands on to the
Kuniongs' house, and piled it up in the *tiang-dong*.
All around the fire was raging. The women, with their
babies, sat in the *tiang* singing hymns. Towards morning
the fire went out, and next day they found that one
house was left standing in the place where the fire had
been on all sides; the others were gone, and this one
alone stood to bear witness—to what? An old woman
who believed in the Jesus doctrine owned the house,
and while the fire raged all round she went up on the
roof and said, so that all heard her—'Jesus, save this
house!' Who can say He didn't hear when the house
was saved—a fact to which the heathen bore witness?
We stayed here all Tuesday, and then on Friday Elsie
went off to a place called 'Ang Ciong,' and I went to
Ku Cheng to get some medicine for my Du patients.
On Tuesday I got back here, and began with work again.
They all seem so glad to have us back again; the women
were crowding in the whole afternoon in detachments,
and yesterday I went up to the little school at Liang-
Muoi, where we have a very nice school teacher and

about eight or ten children coming regularly, and getting on very nicely. She has also a few women that learn spasmodically, when they get away from their babies and the endless round of work. I used to go on Wednesday afternoon to have a class with them, and so yesterday began again. It was so very interesting; first I had the children and then the women. To-day I went to Ba-cho-die, the village where the woman with the bad head lives, and got a very good welcome there. The cut has healed long ago, of course, and looks splendid. Then we went on to the school—a boys' school, and one of those day schools for which Fuh Kien is noted—and there I arranged with the old teacher that I should come twice weekly and teach the boys—I shall love doing that —getting there at 1 P.M., for an hour or so twice a week. 1 P.M. seems rather a funny hour to go at, but you see this is summer, and they don't have their meals by clocks, but by the sun—that gets up much earlier—and they have breakfast very early, and dinner about 12, and supper very late, as it's light till nearly 8, and after supper they like to go to bed. I must say I wish the Christians wouldn't sit up so late; they're all talking and reading their Bibles at the top of their voices till ever so late; but I suppose we must be thankful that they do read them.

"Last night I had the huoi-in's up for a lesson, and then prayers, so that it was nearly 10.30 before I got to bed. We had prayers without a lesson to-night, so it's only just on 9.30; but I must go to bed soon, as I am so tired, and there is rarely time from morning till night to write. Some one is in all the time; it really is very

nice the way they all look upon my den as common property, and march in and out, and sit down and talk. It
surely is something at least to gain the confidence and
love of the people. I must go to bed; I'm aching all
round. Good night, dearest.

"To-day was spent in the morning much the same as
usual, *i.e.*, reading Acts, interspersed with a little doctoring. Fringey (my teacher) says that I should finish the
work in about four months, but I very much doubt it,
as I get only an average of an hour and a half a day,
and not always that straight ahead, but I couldn't leave
the other work just for reading. Then this afternoon we
had the usual Friday afternoon's prayer-meeting, seven
women being present, all Christians. The subject is
always on prayer, and this afternoon I talked to them
about two kinds of prayer, one that agreed with Jesus'
way and one that didn't; first, being not as the heathen,
using vain repetitions. Some of the old huoi-bahs and
huoi-mus, much like those at home, are given to inform-
ing God of a lot of unnecessary things in their prayers.
They generally begin with a preface to this effect:—
'Almighty God, sitting in the heavens, heaven and earth's
Lord, we are met together with the dearly beloved.'—
Here follows a list, mentioning all the celebrities present,
and running somewhat as follows:— 'Dearly beloved
Muk-Su (shepherd, the term given to ordained clergymen), Sing Sangs (teachers of doctrines, &c.), Kuniongs,
Sing Sang Niongs' (teachers' wives, who are always put
after the Kuniongs). I think they consider the Kuniongs
a superior race of beings, not of this earth at all, in fact.
One of the teachers once said he thought the 'Kuniongs

never had any temptations.' The list would be more
impressive followed straight on, Muk-Sa, Sing Sang,
Kuniong, Sing Sang Niong, huoi-ba, huoi-mu, thiang du
gauk neng (brothers, and all men)—that is the preface,
and then comes the prayer. As I talked about it one
old lady nodded her head over at another old lady on
the other side and said, 'Kuniong doesn't like long
prayers,' as much as to say, 'That's meant for you.' I
endeavoured to show them how short and to the point
were the prayers of the leper and the blind man, and
how our Lord's own prayers aren't much longer than
some of our prefaces, and yet so full of heart and desire
and longing. At first one seemed to think that I was
personal in my desire for short prayers, and she said,
'Kuniong is very tired and can't finish long.' But I
quickly showed her it was not so, and I think in the end
they understood. I want you to pray especially for these
women, who are mostly all doing work for God. The
eldest is the teacher in the little girls' school in this
house, Mooie Sing Sang Niong, and she is really quite
a character — a clever woman with quite a dignified
manner—and she sits and entertains any number at a
time, waving her specs in the air to emphasise her
remarks. The diong do huoi mu (preaching Gospel
Church Mother), as the Bible - women are called, is a
very lively little person, very tiny, and with a great
deal more to say than her office requires, but very good
at heart. They both live in the church with me. In
a village about three-quarters of a mile away is the Liang
Muoi Kuoi Mu, who teaches a school for children, and
has also a few women. That's where I go on Wednes-

days. She is a very nice, quiet, gentle woman, and gets on very well in her work. Then there are two younger ones from the 18th Du, former pupils of the Foochow girls' school—very nice girls who come regularly and teach classes on Sundays. Besides these, there are two or three inquirers who sometimes come. After prayer-meeting is the teachers' preparation class. We are going through the life of our Lord, as I think I told you, and talk it over together first. To-night I took prayers, which I do about two nights a week, on other nights asking my teacher or one of the huoi-in's who is intelligent. We have them upstairs now, and the baby organ is to the front. It is very popular. It takes my heart out a little to talk to those people; to talk to actual heathen is something to be thought of, but now it is actual experience. Some of them are Christians, but one or two aren't yet. Our coolie isn't—we had to send the last one away. It's such a plague having to go about with a satellite all the time, but it can't be helped. This one is such a nice boy, but an acknowledged heathen, which is almost better than being an indifferent Christian. I had a talk with him, and I am specially praying for him; will you too, please? Sang Du (Third Brother) is his name.

"*Monday.*—Sunday began with heavy rain, and we were afraid it would stop the people coming; but about ten it cleared up, and the folks began to come. My dear woman from Ba-cho, that had previously the bad head, came bringing another with her; and one by one the old faces turned up, till we had three classes of women, and one of the boys from the day school for Sunday-school. That took about one and a half hours; then a rest for tea and conversation, and then the forms were arranged in order for 'Church.' It is so nice to watch the progress of these our beloved ones in Jesus. At first it was such an impossibility to make them even all sit facing one way, or observe anything like silence as to singing or prayers. It was unheard of; but now we get on very well in the singing of two hymns—'Jesus loves me' and the 'Gate ajar.' We all sit in quite an orderly quiet manner. Some time ago they got as far as saying the Lord's Prayer together, and now, for the first time yesterday, we said the Creed together, they having previously learnt the characters and meanings. There are some things they must learn, of course, for baptism, and so we are 'slowly, slowly' teaching them, so that the meaning may dawn on them and they may grow. One of our very nicest women is growing so remarkably. I was round at her house to-day, and she was reading to me from the Ong Dalk—a kind of catechism on the doctrine, which she can read quite well and understands the meaning. After a while another woman came in, and she began explaining to her so nicely. She seems quite to understand that she is almost the only light round there, and that she has to teach the women and witness to them. The next-door woman, who used to be a great trouble to us, has improved so much lately. She cleaned herself and her children up for church last Sunday, and looked so nice. She is a really nice woman now, and comes to learn, and likes it. There are ever so many that I love, and who come up before me as I write of them to you; but they are so surrounded with heathen darkness and sin that only God Himself can cut a way through to their hearts and touch them, and gradually gather them out one by one. It is wonderful to see how they have changed to us. At first they were generally so hard and careless, but now so much softer. Praise God! Yesterday (Sunday) we had twenty-six of these inquirers in the afternoon. We always have Sunday-school. Most of the time they learn to read the Lord's Prayer and other things and sing hymns, and then one of us talks for a little while. Sunday is the most tiring day here; from morning till night they come streaming in, and a good many bring their dinners and stop right on. We would often like to ask them to stop for dinner and give it to them, only that spoils their motive for coming. We could get any number to come if we offered them a dinner. It does go rather to one's heart sometimes that it's impossible to give all one wants to the people, for their own sakes.

" *Wednesday*, 6 P.M.—Just got back from my Wednesday meeting at the Liang Muoi school. We had a really good time over the meaning of their books. They can all rattle off the character, but the meaning is quite another thing. The people are all rejoicing downstairs in the arrival of the Ling Muk Su, that is, Sing Sing Mi, the native clergyman at Sam Bo Dong, the city church of Ku Cheng. You know he was just lately made a full clergyman, equal now to Mr. Stewart in rank in the church; so every one talks of them as the 'Muk Su laing oi' (shepherds two piece). He is a very good man, and very simple; it is so nice to see him. This must get fin'shed to-night, as I leave first thing in the morning, and I can't let the messenger go down without any line to you. I had to come in from **Sek Chek Du** (Friday), as they make **rather a** fuss about **me** being out there long together. There are great blessings hanging **over** us ready **to** fall. He says, 'Bring the tithes into **the** storehouse.' That's **our** business, the blessing is His."

CHAPTER XXI

LAST LETTERS

Heat, thirst, and theatres—Migrating up the mountains—Cold water
on the way—Rest for the weary—Intentions of the Church
Missionary Society Committee—North-west extension—The
Australian Church Missionary Association—Lassitude after
work—Past experiences at Ku Liang—The Christians of Ku
Cheng—Boys' classes—Scenery of Hua Sang—Study and
needlework—A game of "Clumps"—Letters from Warrnambool—Topsy's medical work—A hopeful case—Love never
faileth—Photographs—Miss Marshall overdone—Danger of the
sun's rays—Regions beyond—A remarkable woman—A Buddhist priest inquiring—Answer to prayer—Letter of a Chinese
girl.

FIVE letters have reached us, written by our dear young
missionaries in the last month of their earthly life. We
give them almost in full, not merely because they are the
last, but because every line of them is intrinsically interesting. The first of these was begun in Ku Cheng
city, but finished at the Sanatorium.

Nellie to her mother:—

"KU CHENG, *3rd July*, 1895.—This piece of the letter
will not, I am afraid, be very legible, but we are on the
move again, and the things are all packed, with nothing
left to write with. This afternoon we are off to Hua Sang.
The last few nights here have been terribly hot. I never
remember, in the hottest weather at home, having to sleep
without even a sheet over me, but here it is as much as I

can do to endure the weight and heat of my cotton night-
dress. It is all nonsense about wearing flannel day and
night. I never think of doing so. If you are careful to
wear a cholera belt, and not leave it off day or night, I
don't think it matters about the rest. I have had prickly
heat all down my back and in my hair, which feels thicker
and heavier than it ever was in its life, and all round
under my chin. My face, too, feels like it, and I have
several times quite expected to see it all over my countenance, but as yet my friends are spared the pain of
seeing a speckled visage going round. I am not saying
this for complaining, but only to tell you how awfully hot
it is.

"Last night, after I had been asleep some time, I was
awakened by feeling a cold wind blowing in through the
window, which was wide open. The doors were open too,
and there was a good old draught, but I dared not sleep
in that wind, so got up and shut half the window, and lay
down again and went to sleep. Before long I was up
again. There was a perfect torrent of rain coming down,
and the most fearful crashes of thunder, which made me
start like anything, though I was waiting for the crashes;
yet, as they came, they were so loud and sounded so close,
that it was quite enough to make you jump. The amount
we continue to drink is something awful. We were having
a discussion about it the other day, and saying that when
you can eat so little, would it not be better to drink a
nourishing sort of thing that would not go off in such
waste? because we are dripping from morning to night.
We thought of milk, but you can't get enough of it, so
then Mrs. Stewart suggested cold tea in bottles, put on

the shelf to cool, and for us to drink at any odd times. Mr. Stewart thought this a grand idea—he drinks like a fish himself. 'First-rate,' said he, 'would it have milk and sugar?' But he said 'we would drink *buckets; bottles* would be no use at all!' Nobody has done it yet, however, and now we shan't need it, for Hua Sang is so very much cooler.

"There has been a dismal old theatre going on over in the city for the last week. I go to sleep every night to the sound of wild yelling and beating of tom-toms and gongs, and blowing of pipes and other instruments. The last scene is always a most awful row—killing the devil. Last night I *did* wish they would hurry up and finish him off. The noise was protracted and intense.

"I wrote all the above under some difficulties; and about eleven or twelve in the morning the old watchman was going backwards and forwards between our house and the coolie stand in the city, seeing whether the coolies would take us up or not that day. We wanted to travel in a new fashion. The distance between Hua Sang and Ku Cheng is a little over twelve miles; the last six going up, and up, and up liangs most terrific to behold and worse to ascend. But the coolies like to start about six or seven in the morning, and get us to walk up all the liangs, and as we don't get up to them till the very hottest part of the morning, we are nearly baked all the time. So we wanted them to take us to the foot of the place where the liangs begin—six miles from Ku Cheng—and not start till about four in the afternoon, so that we could go up the liangs in the cool of the evening. But the coolies wouldn't do this. They *would* start early, and Mr. Stewart would *not*

give in ; so all that could be done was to start off and
walk the whole way, which we actually did.   We had no
foreign stuff of any sort to eat, so we had a large bowl of
rice cooked in a hasty, soppy sort of way, and sweetened
with brown sugar, and we filled our bowls out of the big
one and ate with chopsticks.   When we had pretty well
filled the crevices we started off, each man with an umbrella, but we left all our hats to be sent up on some
future occasion.   Mr. and Mrs. Stewart and Toppy and I
proceeding at five in the afternoon to walk up to Hua
Sang caused great consternation among the few people
we passed.   The bridges were the worst part of the
journey.   I do *hate* Chinese bridges !   If my head is the
least bit shaky I cannot cross them at all.   But I daresay
our early habit of walking on the top rail of the paddock
fences, and up and down the flag-staff in the Marstons'
paddock, helped now to get us over these awful things.
I can manage pretty fairly when I can induce the others
not to get on the bridge till I am off.   About seven we
reached the foot of what we call the ' clay liang,' which is
just a mountain of red clay with steps cut in it, so forming a path up the side.   The rest of the mountain and all
around is thickly covered with bamboo, tall thick bushes,
with fern and grass and flowering shrubs.   We were
very, very hot, and (if the truth be told), after our three
weeks' melting-down, consequent upon losing of strength
in Foochow, not exactly spry to the extent of climbing
liangs.   Mr. Stewart divested himself of his coat, and
marched along in his vest, as he said it was dark and
didn't matter.   Toppy was in her Chinese trousers without a skirt, but Mrs. Stewart wouldn't take her skirt off,

and I wouldn't, as I don't wear Chinese trousers, and, besides, I am rather shy.

"It was a real funny experience — four benighted travellers mounting painfully up and up. The outlines of the great hills in the distance all round stood clearly against the clouded sky, for though the moon was not bright enough to cast a shadow, there was plenty of light to see our way, except at intervals, when a dark cloud would creep across the face of the moon, and the soft sighing of the night wind in the trees and bushes sounded so weird and ghostly in the semi-darkness.

"On arriving at the foot of the 'clay liang,' we had discussed part of the contents of a bottle of cold tea with milk and sugar in it. Now, part of the way up, we finished it, and then our hopes were centred on a certain little mountain stream, where we always stop for a swig on our way up.

"At last we got there, and there we sat—Mrs. Stewart and Toppy on a low bank by the pathway, and I a little further up on a stone—quite close to the little fountain of clear cold water, which was trickling down through the ferny rocks, in the hollow of which we could see little bright fire-flies darting about. Mr. Stewart got up on the rocks and filled my silver mug for us poor thirsty souls, and at the end we only got *one* mouthful all round. When we asked for more he wouldn't let us have another drop. 'Cold water is bad for you' was all he would say. I cannot express to you how refreshing that cold water was to us; we could get up and go on up those fearful liangs with renewed strength. At the top of each there is usually a rather flat place, and you can walk along on the flat for a short way. On reaching each of these places we sank on to a bank or stone in utter exhaustion, and begged for some of the water out of that bottle which Mr. Stewart had filled at the spring. We had a rest half way up *the* liang—that last and terrible one—and at last reached the top in a very exhausted state. The little wood through which we go to the little shanties that we look on as our summer retreat never was traversed by people gladder to get into it. It was about 10.30. A few minutes later we reached the house, and were welcomed by the children, who had stayed up to see their father and mother, and Miss Stewart and Miss Newcombe, who, with Miss Codrington, had been up about three days. One comfort of being in was the large supply of hot water with a dish of tea and a good deal of milk in it, which we imbibed like anything. We were in bed by about 11.30, and I, for one, slept like a top all night—I don't believe I turned once! Topsy was very tired, and reposed in bed for breakfast. When you are tired here you seem to be so cross. I feel quite different to-day from what I did yesterday and the day before, because I am a bit rested. After all, there isn't much to be gained in wearing one's self out.

"Of these two days I have nothing to tell at all; it has done nothing but rain since we came up, and it is nice and cool. Toppy has, I am glad to say, so far as I can see, made up her mind to be quiet, which is a blessing.

"*Monday, 8th.*—Raining like anything again! It rained nearly all Sunday, but still Mr. and Mrs. Stewart went over to the village, where they say they had a very nice time. In the afternoon we had our usual Church

of England service at five o'clock, **and just** as we had
nearly done I perceived **Dr.** Gregory looking round the
corner of the place at me—the only one he could see in
the room. Then **he came in and** stayed for the last
hymn, which I really believe I heard him singing! Then
he stayed for tea. He is so sensitively shy and reserved,
I feel quite sorry for him. It is great fun to hear him
going for Topsy about the eucalyptus; **he** pretends **not**
to believe in it an atom, and I don't suppose **he does**
much. He must be very lonely over there **all by him-**
self; he will think **it a** joyful **day** when **he can** say
good-bye to China for **good and all.**

"We have been in China eighteen months **now, and it**
is no more decided where our ultimate location is to be
than it was the first **day we were here.** But I suppose
God had **a** place **for us to** fill in the meantime in Ku
Cheng. **I am** glad that **the** committee **think we** are all
right in remaining there.

"Mr. Stock's plan **is for us to work as Church Mis-**
sionary Society **in Ku** Cheng (a Church **of** England
Zenana place), but this **Mr.** Stewart would oppose with
his dying breath—for good reasons. I would **not consent**
to do it myself. I would clear **out** of Ku Cheng altogether first! **It is not so** much that there would be
any difficulty in Ku Cheng, but **what is done in one**
district may certainly **be done in another, and it** would
involve many difficulties **in the** other districts. I don't
think I have told **you about a very** interesting thing
connected with the work **in the** Upper Hien (where the
N.W. people and **Mr.** Phillips are). It seems that there
are five great 'gaings' (cities and surrounding villages)

up there, five great walled cities, and innumerable villages! Foreigners have been for a day or so at a time into *two* of these cities, but the villages remain untouched. Last year I think you saw a letter written by Louie Bryer, telling how two of them went into Ching-Huo; of course, that was only like a breaking of the ice. Hardly any preaching could be done, except among a crowd of frightened women whom they saw for a short time, being most of their time concealed in the back rooms of the house. We have prayed constantly for this place, Ching-Huo, and, indeed, for all these places up there, and also have asked that a man might be sent there who could pioneer. Well, I think God has answered that prayer in a very beautiful way. A few weeks ago the 'Gospel Band' was talking to Mr. Stewart, and he began about this Upper Hien, and spoke of the great need there, and said that if the Muk-Su ('shepherd,' the title of foreign clergymen) was willing, and thought it was a good plan, he would very much like to go and try what he could do up there towards opening the way; and on Mr. Stewart raising the objection that he could not speak the dialect, Li Daik-Ing replied—'Oh! yes, I lived there for five years!' Does it not seem a wonderful answer to prayer? And when I was at Dong Liang that time he talked to me a great deal about it, and we saw how much he wanted to go and preach up there. He would in many ways be a splendid one to go. He is so energetic and determined, and so clever, and knows so well how to do everything; and, of course, he is an earnest Christian, but there is one thing lacking. Oh! he does need a deeper knowledge of the power of the

Spirit of God. I wish you would pray for him, and ask any one who you think is interested enough to pray for him too. Native Christians baptized by the Holy Ghost are what we want for the evangelising here.

"There is another rather important point to be remembered about the distribution of the Church Missionary Society and Church of England Zenana ladies' territory, and that is this, that the Upper Hien belongs to the Church of England Zenana; but Mr. Stewart doesn't think they can in a long time supply enough ladies for these parts, and for that reason, if for no other, would be very glad to have the Church Missionary Associations of Australia and Canada sending under the Church of England Zenana, so that those who like might go on up there. If God ever gives us the mighty privilege of going up there—but I scarcely dare dream of it; whatever He does is right and best. Just now I believe He is letting us have this rather trying business about the dress (the question of wearing native dress) to see if we will stick to our guns. I have been thinking much of that text, 'Let your *yieldingness* be known unto all men' (R.V.), but I don't know that it applies in this case. Mr. M—— says, how could we go and work in Chinese dress with two Kuniongs (both senior) working in English? Of course, we couldn't. And if Ning Taik has got two Kuniongs I don't see what it wants with *four*. No station has four Kuniongs."

Nellie to a friend:—

"HUA SANG, 15*th July*, 1895.—Thank you so much for your birthday gift that you sent me; it is awfully good of you, and I feel smitten in the conscience for the very meagre letters I send you. We enjoy your letters almost more than any others we get, because they are always so nice, and nearly always have a lot about mother in them, which pleases us extremely.

"We came up here about a week ago; it is quite as hot here as we have it in our summers in Melbourne, and no one thinks of going out in the daytime. From 10 o'clock till 5 no one stirs out; and yet we think it most lovely, because there are cool nights and a breeze morning and evening, and it is such a contrast to Ku Cheng. Anything like the heat of the last few weeks—from the middle of June right on—I never felt in my life. The Stewarts' English nurse was sent up here with all the five children about a fortnight before we came, and when she saw me she quite exclaimed. I must have lost several pounds in the heat; you are simply dripping at every pore from morning to night and night to morning. Toppy was with great difficulty at last persuaded by the consensus of general opinion, and the orders of the doctor, to come in from her beloved Du and rest. She came in on Monday, the 1st July, and we came up here two days after. The reaction from hard work to comparative inactivity is having its usual effect: she is dead tired out, and stays in bed every morning for breakfast, and scarcely reads any Chinese at all. But that is awfully good for her, and she will be quite another person in a week. She told me that she had a most lovely dream last night—that she was nursing a typhoid! I privately thought, rather lovelier for her than for the typhoid. The last time I wrote to you was from Foochow, when we had left Ku Cheng

after all the troubles; after about a week in Foochow
we found we could have the use of a sort of barracks
kind of house at Ku Liang, about four hours' ride from
Foochow, and so we resorted there. It was one of the
funniest experiences I ever had, and yet not bad; I
rather liked it the first part of the time. Mrs. Stewart
was housekeeping, and we with (most of the time) five
other single ladies, all the five children, and their English
nurse, were together—such a tableful! It was all right
though for me. I was studying hard and got through a
lot, so much so, that about a week after our return to Ku
Cheng in the end of May, I had my second examination.
I felt rather sorry for those who had not any very particular work to do, and were panting all the time to get
back. One thing we did that was afterwards proved
to have been of the greatest use was that we met about
three times a day all together for special prayer. I am
sure that it was owing to this that we had such a speedy
return to Ku Cheng, to find the Christians not any the
worse at all, but, on the contrary, thanking God for
having taught them to lean only upon God and not on
the foreigners in time of trouble. It was so lovely to
get back to Ku Cheng. For the first ten days I had
a little revising of all my work (Chinese reading for
my examination I mean), because travelling down from
Ku Liang to Foochow and up by boat and chair to Ku
Cheng takes a good while, and you can't study and
travel at the same time. Then I had my examination,
and from that on till we came up here have had my
hands full teaching two classes of boys every morning,
one from 9 to 10 and the other from 11 to 12.30, and

visiting villages three afternoons a week, and on Saturday
afternoons I have my little day-school boys—such jolly
little chaps. I have them in the Stewarts' Chinese
guest-room, and there they sit all round and give information *gratis* about each other's families whenever
I make the slightest inquiry as to their age or anything
of that sort. They answer exceedingly well. Isn't it
a splendid idea to teach the boys like that? There are
such lots of nice little boys, who are so quick and bright,
and it is such a pleasure to teach them. Almost everywhere you go there seem to be crowds of little boys,
but it is not everywhere that you find they are being
taught—only in the places where these little village
schools have been established. I had to examine one
the other day in the three months' course that they have
settled for them all. It was very nice except for one
thing, that one of the books was written in the classical
character, which very few of us learn to read, as it takes
up so much time from the work; we read colloquial
character, and the classical can be translated into colloquial, which is then quite easy. You may imagine my
feelings when they handed me this book, and the first
boy began rattling it off at such a rate that by the time
I had turned over about three of the dozen pages he
had finished! I had not to examine in the meaning of
that book, for which small mercy I was entirely thankful. With the other books I got on all right. We have
come up here for six weeks or two months; it depends
on how the heat lasts. It is such a lovely place. Very
few people in the mission have been here, and certainly
no foreigners except missionaries. There is a girl here

this time who has seen the lovely sights of Japan and other places noted for beauty, but she says she never saw anything so beautiful as this place. I certainly never did. Yesterday we went out for a walk, and, following the narrow little path that leads along the sides of the great mountains, we came to a place where the view is simply indescribable (certainly for a person like me). As far as your eye could reach, miles upon miles away, is a panorama of mountain tops lit up by the golden light of the sun (it was about five o'clock), and where that light did not reach, soft purple shadows contrasted with the sunlight. The mountains near us, all covered with tall feathery bamboos, were also partly in shade and partly in the brilliant light, making the most beautiful effect, especially where the lower portion of the mountain is in shadow and the sun has turned the tips of the bamboos (all it could reach) into golden feathers.

"Far down through a framework of rugged hills, softened with gold-tipped bamboos, there was a perfectly exquisite gem-like view of the city of Ku Cheng, with the pagoda on the hill that looks so high to us from Ku Cheng, standing sentinel over it. The river, like a silver band, lying close to the dark walls, and the little wood on the hill where our compound is, and bright green paddy fields, and the little villages dotted about, all came out as clear as a picture, lying away down there at our feet.

"It is very beautiful; I wish you could see it. I am reading Chinese most of the morning, and I generally rest in the afternoon, for I feel so done up after the heat.

"I hope you will write again soon and tell me all about the hospital. We do love to hear about it. What makes you think matron didn't approve of us? I don't wonder, but I should like to know why. Are F—— and J. P—— and K—— still in the land of the hospital?"

Nellie to her mother :—

"HUA SANG, 21st July, 1895. — I really haven't got a thing to say this time. I hated coming up here at first; it is so horrid having to leave the work and everything to come right away like this. We have had some lovely walks, and the doctor and Mr. Stewart have been very busy taking photos. It is much cooler up here; I should think ten degrees difference, but even with that I feel so exhausted after doing an hour's Chinese that I feel like a boiled owl. I am reading the school books for the purpose of examining, and it is rather nice; I don't read with Fringey, though he is here. I have Mr. Stewart's teacher, Ding Sing Sang, whom I like very much, and who is a Ku Cheng man, which is a great advantage. The poor fellow was very sick when we went away last March to Foochow, but now he is much better. I often have very nice talks to him, and he told me the other day that he would like to be baptized. It is so good of God to answer our prayers like that. I know it is entirely the work of God's Spirit in his heart, though there is a friend of his in an out-station who is a Christian, and a splendid man. The time really goes pretty quickly. I do some sewing part of the day as a change of occupation, and at present I am engaged in making the best part of the remains of a linen sheet into a pillow case, which will probably last a good while. The native washing is fearfully hard on the things, especially anything at all old. I have made a pillow case out of a piece of cretonne that we had, and I have darned I don't know how many pieces of stocking, so I am not idle; and though I don't much care for that way of employing my time, still mending has to be scratched in somehow, and, as a rule, the evening is the only time, and I have been keeping arrears of mending for weeks for this summer time.

"Last night Miss Codrington, who is of a very sociable disposition, gave a tea-party, and asked Mr. and Mrs. Stewart, the Doctor, and us two. Miss Hartford and five of our Kuniongs are already there, so with Millie and Cassie we were a large party, and after tea we indulged in the innocent pastime of 'Clumps;' and Elsie and I, who went out together, thought of 'the print in the sand, made by the second nail in the left boot of the first convict that landed in Botany Bay,' and it was guessed by the enemy! Just think of that! I thought that poor Dr. Gregory would certainly get an illness from the way he laughed. It was awfully funny to see the way he enjoyed himself.

"We have had some more letters from Warrnambool. A Miss Coleston heads the union down there, and she confides to me this time that she has taken an immense fancy to *me* for some unaccountable reason. She has seen our photo in Chinese dress (now, where could she have got that from?) and immediately fell in love with it (that last is my addition). But anyhow she seems to take a great interest in us, and me particularly, so I told her that if she happened to be in Melbourne any time to go and see you, and you could talk to her a bit. It is a consolation, when it is so hard to get time and energy sufficient to write a letter of any interest, to be told that your letters are doing good, even though it be but in a small way. As my head is very stupid and I feel cross, I can't think of anything more to write, so will shut up, hoping to write a better letter next mail. We are having what they call 'Keswick' this week; it begins to-day."

Topsy to a friend :—

"HUA SANG, KU CHENG, FOOCHOW, *22nd July*, 1895.— I have two letters and the copy of the nurse's photo to thank you for. Will you kindly stop making remarks about your letters being a bore, or too long? They aren't long enough, although I don't want to trouble you for more, but I am so interested in all your doings. We have all been up here in Hua Sang for the last three weeks, having a rest. It's frightfully hot down in the city. Elsie Marshall (the girl I work with) and I wanted very much to go up to a mountain village in her district, but the Doctor put his foot on my going on that expedition, and I was fished in about the beginning of this month, and Elsie had to go alone. It's very quiet at this place— we live like oysters—eating and sleeping and going for walks—there isn't anything else to do.

"The last triumph at Sek Chek Du in the medical line was an old lady with an awful boil on the back of her neck, so that she couldn't move her head. Her son came one day to me and asked for medicine to take to her, but I said I would go and see her, and accordingly we visited her for about a week. Elsie did that part, as it was nearly a mile walk and I wasn't feeling able for it, and she happened to be in for a few days just then. When she left Du, I had the old lady moved in to our house, and doctored her every day, and fed her up well, for she was so weak that her son had almost to carry her upstairs— such a tiny wrinkled little piece of humanity. Well, she got better, and we taught her a little, and on the last Sunday I was there, as we began singing in the service, out she came from the bedroom and crawled downstairs all by herself, because she wanted to come and *vai* (worship) for herself. Next day I had to go into Ku Cheng, and she wanted to know when I was coming back, and said—'You must come in the fifth month, for my pears are ripe then, and I want you to have some.' Elsie told me that the Sunday before last she walked from her own house to church, nearly a mile away, with three other women. I am so sorry about your nursing troubles that you told me of. It is so hard when you've done all for people that you possibly can to have ingratitude shown. The only cure is this—'Love . . . endureth all things, and love never faileth.' I've been learning some pretty difficult lessons on that subject lately for a long time, with no rest, and spiritual indigestion very badly, but God won the victory, and, though feeling very tired mentally from the contest, I am quite rested and happy. It is difficult to see where human love *must* fail and only Divine love —a gift—*can* avail. Human love is good, and the natural outcome of affinity with people, but when He talks about 'Love bearing, believing, enduring all things, and *never* failing,' 'all things' means '*all* things' and 'never' means '*never*,' to my mind; and that is utterly impossible when only human love comes in; so there must be a supply to

T

meet the demand.   Have you read 'The Land of Promise,' by A. B. Simson?   It's so good.   When it's God's time and way, He will send you if He wants you.   We must be content to wait His developing."

Nellie to her aunt :—

"HUA SANG, 28*th July*, 1895.—I feel that yours must be one of the first written of my holiday letters.   We were so pleased to get a letter from Aunt J.   We often thought of her and meant to write, but there does seem so little time for writing a letter worth sending that it gets put off; and we knew, besides, that she always sees the letters we write to you and dear Aunt F.   I have told everybody about the heat here.   We were nearly boiled—steamed alive!—in Ku Cheng the last three or four weeks.   The boys' school broke up the last day but one of June, and up till then I was teaching two classes every morning, and my day-school boys on Saturday afternoons.   On Saturday the American doctor, Dr. Gregory, came over and took some photographs; and as my little day-school boys were there, he and Mr. Stewart took a group of them.   If I can get a print I will send you one, and also a group of the whole family of the Stewarts and us.   I look like an idol in a temple in it, and Topsy is looking benignly on all around, as though she would say, 'Not a bad lot after all, are they?'   They took another group of some of the Kuniongs in which we are also depicted, Topsy standing up at the back; and Mr. Stewart says she looks like Portia just beginning a speech.

"It is a pity that we have to rest so long in the summer, but if the Chinese themselves can't go on, it is no wonder that we can't. They tell us that it is never under eighty degrees all night at Ku Cheng now, and stiflingly hot. One of our number—Miss Marshall, who works with Topsy at Sek Chek Du—is a very energetic girl, with the constitution, as she herself says, of a crocodile— a strong, big, English girl, who had never known a day's illness. She has only just come in, and for the last month has been going about taking great care not to be much in the sun, riding in her chair, covered with a padded quilt, whenever she went out, and not stirring without her pith hat and lined umbrella. Well, what is she like now? In spite of all her precautions, she is about half the size she was two months ago, and with great black marks round her eyes, and her nerves so shattered that she cannot talk on almost any subject without beginning to cry. So many of our best workers have either been invalided home, perhaps never to come back, through persisting in going on with their work during July and August. I think it is one of the trials that we must take as Hobson's choice, that we *must* leave off during that time. The sun seems to affect your *head* if it can shine on your *back* even! It is so funny. The other day I was travelling into the country (in the end of June this was), and as I was riding along I felt myself getting very sick, and a deadly sleepy feeling creeping over me. I couldn't think what was the matter with me, and hoped I should be all right by the time we reached the place where I should have to talk to the women. At last I thought, 'I believe it must be the sun shining in through some place in my quilt!' So, at the next resting place, I got out, and sure enough they had fastened up

the quilt so badly across the back of my chair that the
sun could shine in, but only on my back—it could not
shine on my head—but all the same it seemed to have
just the same effect. Was not that strange? It is still
unsettled where we are to be finally placed, but in the
meanwhile shall just go on in Ku Cheng. My sympa-
thies are very much in the other half of Mr. Stewart's
domain, *i.e.*, Ping Nang, away up to the north of Ku
Cheng. The nearest point to us is Dong Gio, where I
have been several times with Miss Gordon, who is the
solitary lady in charge of Ping Nang. There are two or
three other large towns or villages, which act as centres
for the hundreds of other villages round them, but which
of course she can scarcely even begin to reach. And
then there is the great walled city of Ping Nang, where
no foreigner has ever been yet. I once was with Miss
Gordon within nine miles of it in Dong Kan, the furthest
point that has been reached in Ping Nang. I just should
love to be 'let out' in Ping Nang! What lies beyond
the city of Ping Nang no one knows, except that there is
a great valley containing, as one *hien*, or prefecture, five
great walled cities, with their surrounding villages, and
countless numbers of inhabitants. The dialect is different, but oh! I would love to go up there. Further on,
several days' journey, you would come to the Nang Wa
district, where there are some ladies, and that is a different dialect again. They have been once to one of the
five walled cities I have mentioned, but scarcely dared to
move for fear of bringing on a row. We heard from one
of these ladies, who has lately moved to an hospital several
miles from Nang Wa, and near *another* great city named

Kien-Yang, that she and her companion have been more than once into this city, and walked quietly about, no one seeming to mind at all. It will all come in time; Ku Cheng was once like that. The first missionary in Ku Cheng was chivied out, and killed by having to run in the hot sun.

"Miss Gordon, who has just come in from Ping Nang, told me a very interesting thing about a girl up there, who seems a very remarkable sort of character. When she was only seven years old she unbound her feet, and declared her intention of remaining single all her days (a great act of virtue in the eyes of the Chinese) and she also became a Vegetarian (*another* great act). She is now about thirty, and has stuck to this all her life. She is a Vegetarian. I don't know that she has ever tried to benefit any one else by her virtue, but anyway her friends looked on her as a wonder of perfection. Well, when this lady first heard of the Christian religion she inquired into it a little—not much—and then decided that as a good Vegetarian she must not inquire into heterodox things, so she persistently refused to hear any one speak of it. Some of the people belonging to her house got interested, and persuaded Miss Gordon to go to their house, and they told her, among other things, of this wonderful woman. Miss Gordon said she would like to see her very much, but the woman would not come out. Three or four times that Miss Gordon was there, the woman always refused to see her. The Christian Chinese were much interested, and Miss Gordon and they together prayed for this woman. The fifth, or I am not sure that it wasn't the *sixth*, time that Miss Gordon went there, she said nothing about the girl at all, but just before she went away a message was brought to her from this very girl, asking her if she would go and see her in her room. Of course she went, and the girl told her she wanted to lead a good life, and how hard it was to do so, and she was not sure if she was on the right road or not. So Miss Gordon told her of the 'right road,' by which she could have assurance of forgiveness for her sins and peace of heart *now*, and heaven hereafter in the presence of the Saviour, and she listened to it all very eagerly, and said, 'They are good words! They are good words! I wish I had heard words like that before!' You may be sure that if she never heard them before, she certainly will again. The individual cases like that are always the **very** cases that one would most wish to follow up.

" Another day she was in one of the village chapels, just sitting talking to the women in the lower guest hall, when a Buddhist priest walked in. Some of these men take up being priests because they really want to seek after the truth, and I think this man must have been one of those; but getting dissatisfied, and seeing that the craving in their inmost souls is by no means satisfied, they give up and go along with the crowd, and just continue being priests as a means of livelihood. That is what this man told Miss Gordon he was doing. He told her that he was unhappy, and that he had heard of the Jesus doctrine, and now he would like one of the books about the doctrine, if she could give him one. She had some with her, of course, and immediately presented him with a little book which would tell him the way of life pretty plainly. He stayed a little while talking after that, and listening to what she was saying to the people there, and in the meantime his book was being handed about. She said to me, she wondered if he would remember, and get his book before he went ; but she needn't have been afraid. Before he went out of the chapel he went all round and found his book, and went off with it up his sleeve. Poor creatures ! Poor creatures ! They are *so dark,* so ignorant, and yet they have souls and hearts just the same as ours. I think I did not tell you of our return from banishment at the time of the row. We came back in the end of May. Oh ! it was perfectly lovely to get back ; and it was worth while being in church the first Sunday after we came back to see the faces of the people who knew us; they were *so* glad. The trouble seems now to be all over; only in one or two places has there been even the slightest disturbance. One of the Christian women, such a nice, bright little thing, said to me one day talking about it, 'Truly, Kuniong, it is of great use to pray.' It was only by prayer that we could help the work, while we were all away at Ku Liang, and we used to have prayer-meetings about it three times a day all together. The result of God working in answer to our prayers, though we ourselves were not there *to do anything at all,* has been seen by all, in a strengthening of the faith of the Christians, and in the spreading of a desire, greater than it has ever been among the heathen, to hear the ' Jesus doctrine.'

"We are now at Hua Sang. It is such a beautifully wooded place, and so cool—comparatively, that is—being much hotter than our summer at home. Every day at five we go for a walk. I am going to try and paint a little sketch of one or two of the views, but both that and my pen are equally inadequate to describe the wonderful beauty of the scenes.

"I thought you might be interested to see the enclosed letter written in Roman character (which we teach them, as the women would otherwise *never in the world* learn to write). The writer of this letter has just been married to a young Chinese doctor; I like her very much, and am much interested in her. She came to see me the evening before we left Ku Cheng, and on going away pressed this letter into my hand, and asked me to go upstairs and read it alone; her tongue could not say all she wanted to, so she had written this letter :—

"'*Ching-ai gi Sung Kuniong* (Dearly loved Sung Kuniong [my name]—

"'*Nu ming-dang gaeng Kuniong li Ko* (I to-morrow must take leave of the Kuniong); *nu ceng ma sia dek* (I very much cannot bear this), *ing mi ming dang* (because I to-morrow) *ia diong Ko Dung bang* (also return to Dung bang). *Nu ai-uong Kuniong* (I hope the Kuniong) *thain a Ko nu Dung bang kakdieu* (afterwards will come to Dung bang for pleasure. My heart will be very glad I also will pray for the Kuniong so that she, riding in a chair to Hua Sang to-morrow, may not be tired, but will peacefully arrive at Hua Sang; and please will the Kuniong take my greetings to all the other Kuniongs at Hua Sang). Good-bye.—The girl Daik Ong's letter.'

"Did you ever see such a funny letter? But I like getting them."

CHAPTER XXI

MARTYRDOM

Topsy's prophecy—A happy party—Flowers for the birthday—
Surrounded by murderers—"Kill all !"—A little heroine—Mr.
Phillips' narrative—Miss Hartford's escape—Dr. Gregory and
the Mandarin—The wounded and dead—Another victim—
Going down to Foochow—Conclusion.

THE tragedy to be told in this chapter shall be prefaced
by a remarkable passage from one of Topsy's last letters
to her mother. It is written from Sek Chek Du, and, in
the light of the terrible event that occurred scarcely a
month later, it reads like an unconscious prophecy :—

"Last night God gave me the key to a great many of
my problems. It was oppressively hot, and the house was
quiet, so I got into a dreamy state—not really asleep, but
too far gone even to fan myself. I don't know how it
began exactly, but I found myself going over again that
night in the Garden of Gethsemane—the Lord kneeling
there, pleading that if it were possible the cup might pass
from His lips. Oh, exalted human heart of Jesus! for
our everlasting comfort those words were wrung from His
aching heart. When no other word can hold one up,
those words surely are the light of life to heart-sick souls.
He said it—He who was divine, God and man, the highest
type. Is it then weakness for us to say it too? I think
that night was a crisis in the world's history. The hardest

part was over when Judas came to Him, and kissed Him and betrayed Him. He stood so calmly while they reviled Him. There was no anguish shown then, only patient calmness and forbearing love. And what gave the ring of triumph to those words, 'Thou couldst have no power at all against me except it were given thee from above' (John xix. 11), when Pilate was tormenting Him? Such a quiet, confident answer! He knew God; He knew the price for the salvation of the world. Even on the Cross there was room in His heart for others' needs—for Mary and those who had been with Him. Those thoughts came in as I lay there half waking, half sleeping, and it has answered one of my questions of longest standing —how things come to us? Do we get things only from God or from the devil too? How big a share has he got in the daily round of life? I began a Bible study on the devil, which has proved very interesting. His ways and means of working are certainly worth studying, especially when we come into personal contact with him. It is very interesting to read Job with that idea in view. The great thing that puzzled me was this: when anything happens, or goes wrong, that you can *see* could have been all different if only people had sense; it is all put down, in a canting fashion, to the will of God. You can't positively insist that it is not, but you do know that if people had only exercised a little common-sense it wouldn't have happened. And now I begin to believe it is like this— that God *has* to send pain and death, and the most awful trials, because nothing short of that will do; because sin has altered everything, and we have gone away so far that gentle, soft treatment wouldn't do. Jesus had to suffer

His greatest agony to win redemption for us, and we have
to go through the same fire in the process of sanctification,
which is the will of God, and the hotter the fire may be
the purer will be the gold. Amen. Lord Jesus, Refiner
and Purifier of souls, cleanse and make me holy for
Thyself; and in the trial of faith, which is more precious
than of gold that perisheth, we can remember that He
said, 'If it is possible, let this cup pass from Me.' But it
was not possible. If it had been possible where would all
those hosts be that will rejoice because their robes are
washed white in the Blood of the Lamb? And if the cup
could pass from our lips, we should go empty-handed to
the gate of Heaven, and we should never know the joy of
living alone with Jesus. He is unspeakably precious.
He comes so near. I love Him so. He draws me with
those bands of love that never fail—never break—never
hurt."

Happy soul! The Lord was preparing her, and others
with her, for a very early meeting with Himself.

The week from the 19th to the 25th of July, being the
season of the Keswick Convention, so dear to the hearts
of many Christians in England, was again this year devoted by our missionaries to holding a little "Keswick
Convention" of their own. "It was a most helpful time,"
says Mr. Phillips, who kept the "convention" with them,
"and we were indeed a happy party." In that happiness
they retired to rest on the night of Wednesday, the 31st
July, after having held a Bible-reading amongst themselves on the subject of the Lord's Transfiguration.

Of the two small wooden houses forming the Sanatorium, the one known as "The Stewart House" was

occupied by Mr. and Mrs. Stewart, their five children, Lena the nurse, and the two Misses Saunders; while the other sheltered the five ladies of the Zenana Mission, namely, Miss Gordon, Miss Marshall, Miss Hessie New-combe, Miss Codrington, and Miss Stewart (no relation to the head of the Mission). At about five minutes' distance, lower down the hill, was the house in which Mr. Phillips was lodging, and close to it another hired house, of which the only English-speaking inmate was Miss Hartford, of the American Mission.

At an early hour next morning the children, with the exception of the baby, went out upon the mountain to gather flowers to decorate the house for the birthday of little Herbert. They were not far away when the English houses were surrounded by a band of about eighty men, armed with swords and spears, and led by a man carrying a red flag. These men did not belong either to Hua Sang or Ku Cheng, but came from some villages at a considerable distance. As to what followed we have but fragmentary accounts, but the murderous work was all over in half-an-hour. The five Zenana ladies, after a futile attempt to escape by their front door, went out at the back of the house, and were immediately surrounded by the assassins. The latter at first said that they were only going to bind them and carry them away, but when they asked to be allowed to take their umbrellas this was refused. Some of the Vegetarians seemed inclined to spare their lives, and an old Hua Sang man (a spectator, apparently) begged hard for them, but the leader waved his flag and shouted—"You have your orders, kill all!" And then began a butchery from which Miss Codrington alone escaped. She was fearfully cut across the face, and left for dead, but she never quite lost consciousness, and when the ruffians left the place she crept away to the house of Miss Hartford. Her testimony is that she did not feel her wounds at all for the time, and that all (except poor Miss Stewart, who was nervous and timid) were quite calm, and looking forward to going into the presence of the Lord.

In the Stewarts' house the ghastly work must have been equally rapid. Mr. and Mrs. Stewart were probably killed in the first few moments of the attack. Kathleen, the only one of the children who was not wounded, behaved with great heroism; but for her presence of mind the other four children must have been burnt alive. We give her account of what happened, but some allowance must be made, we think, for the child's imagination, some of her statements being difficult to reconcile with other accounts.

"Last Thursday morning, 1st August, between 6.30 and 7 A.M., Mildred and I were just outside the house on a hill we called 'the garden,' picking ferns and flowers because it was Herbert's birthday, and we were going to decorate the breakfast table. We saw men coming along, and at first I thought they were *dang dangs* (load men). Milly saw their spears and told me to run, but I was so frightened I lay in the grass, thinking perhaps they would not see me. The men did see me, and took hold of me and pulled me by my hair along towards the house. Just as we arrived there I fell down. They then began beating me. I got away from them, and ran to the back door. I tried to shut it, but could not at first, as the men put

their sticks in ; but afterwards succeeded, and bolted it.
Then I went into our bedroom and got under my bed.
Mildred lay on her bed.   Soon the men broke open the
door, pulled off all the bed-clothes, opened the drawers,
and took what they wanted ; smashed windows and things ;
then began beating Mildred, and cut her with their swords ;
afterwards they left the room.   One man saw me under
the bed as they were going out, and gave me a knock on
the head with a stick.   We next saw Topsy Saunders with
her cheek very much cut, being walked backwards and
forwards by the men who were asking her questions ; and
if they were not answered quickly they dug a spear into
her. [We are glad to believe that this is an error. Topsy
only received one wound, which must have been instantly
fatal.]   One question we heard them ask was about her
money, and she told them that they had taken all she
had.   Topsy afterwards came and told us to go into her
room ; so we went and lay there on her bed, and she left.
We saw Nellie Saunders lying by the door moaning.
From the window we saw four men outside the back door
beating and killing the Kuniongs (ladies).   One Kuniong's
head I saw quite smashed up in a corner ; it was an awful
sight.   Very soon I heard a rushing noise like water, and
going out to see what it was, I found the house on fire.   I
went back to tell Mildred, and we went to the nursery,
where we found Herbert covered with blood, Lena lying on
the ground (I think she was dead—she was covered with
blood), with baby beside her, and Evan sitting crying.   I
screamed at Lena, but she did not answer.   I tried to lift
her up, but could not.   I took baby first and laid her down
outside ; then went back for Evan.   Then we all five went

down past the Kuniongs' house, which was all in a blaze, into the little wood. After waiting there a little while I saw Miss Codrington with a Chinese man. I called out to her, and the Chinese man came and carried Herbert to Miss Hartford's. I carried baby, while Mildred and Evan waited in the wood. I then went back and carried Evan to Miss Hartford's. As I was going back for Mildred I met her on the way trying to walk ; but she had only come a few steps when I heard a cracking sound in her knee, and she fell down. Then I beckoned to a Chinese man, and he came and helped Mildred to walk a little way, and then carried her to Miss Hartford's."

The statement of Mr. Phillips is as follows :—

"About 6.30 A.M. on 1st August, hearing shouts from the direction of the Stewarts' house, I went out, and at first thought it was simply a number of children playing, but I was soon convinced that the voices were those of excited men, and I started off for the house. I was soon met by a native, who almost pulled me back, shouting that the Vegetarians had come. I said that I must go on, and soon got in sight of the house, and saw a number of men, say forty or fifty, carrying off loads of plunder. One man seemed to be the leader, carrying a small red flag. I could see nothing of any Europeans, and as this was in full view of the rioters, I crept up the hill in the brush-wood and got behind two trees, from twenty to thirty yards from the house. Here I could see everything, and appeared not to be seen at all, and as I could see no foreigners, I concluded that they had escaped. To go down was certain death, so I thought it better to stay where I was. After a minute or two the retreat horn

was sounded, and the Vegetarians began to leave, but
before they did so they set fire to the houses; ten
minutes after this every Vegetarian had gone. I came
down and looked about the front of the house, but could
see nothing of any one, though I feared something dreadful had happened, as I heard the Vegetarians, as they
left, saying repeatedly—'Now all the foreigners are killed.'
I just then met one of the servants, who told me that the
children were in the house in which Miss Hartford, of
the American Mission, was staying. I found Mr. Stewart's
eldest daughter, Mildred, here, with a serious cut on one
knee and another severe cut. When I had washed these
and put what old calico we had to staunch the bleeding,
I turned to Herbert, who was fearfully hacked about
everywhere. Then Miss Codrington sent me a message
that she too was in the house. I found her in a fearful
condition, but with cold water and rags we managed to
staunch the bleeding."

Miss Hartford, of the American Mission, had a narrow
escape, and owes her life to a native Christian. The
following is her account :—

" 1st August, 7.30 A.M., heard shouts and yells; servants
rushed in shouting for me to get up, the Vegetarians were
coming and were tearing down the house on the hill (belonging to the English Mission). Two minutes later my
teacher came to my door and told me to run. I put on
my clothes and rushed out to the door, to be met by a
man with a trident spear, who yelled, ' Here is a foreign
woman,' and pointed the spear at my chest. I twisted it
on one side, and it just grazed my ear and head. He
threw me to the ground, and beat me with the wooden

end of the spear. A servant came and wrenched the
spear away, and told me to run. I jumped down an embankment, and ran along the road. A servant came and
pulled me along until I got up the side of the hill, where
I lay to recover breath. After resting, I reached a secluded
spot and lay there. All the while the yells went on, and
the two houses were burning to the ground. After a while
the yells stopped, so the servant went to see how matters
were. He returned in half-an-hour, telling me to come
home, that five ladies of the English Mission had been
killed, and some were wounded and at my house."

Shortly after midday the dreadful news reached Ku
Cheng, and was brought by a native Christian to Dr.
Gregory. He at once went to the Yamen (Town Hall),
where several hundred people were gathered. The district magistrate (Wang, of whom we have spoken as the
Mandarin) said he would himself go right up to Hua
Sang and take some sixty soldiers with him. He also
gave the doctor an escort of thirteen soldiers, and they
both arrived at the scene of the murder about the same
time. It will be clear from what has been related that
there was nothing in the least resembling a popular rising
against the missionaries, and that the city authorities of
Ku Cheng had no hand in the outrage. It was evidently
the work of a band of marauders, and the district magistrate seems to have done all that could be done under the
circumstances. As Dr. Gregory says, "No one in or near
Ku Cheng knew of the intended attack, which was as swift
as it was terrible." It is a merciful consolation to know
that the reports circulated about torture and outrage were
without foundation. The body of Miss Newcombe, indeed,

was found thrown down an embankment, and the four in the Stewart house were burnt almost to ashes, but Dr. Gregory has no doubt that this took place after death. Topsy was killed by a spear wound through the right eye. which penetrated the brain. The only victim who received no serious wound was Miss Stewart, whose death was probably caused by nervous shock.

The first work of the kind doctor was to attend to the sufferers, and then, assisted by Mr. Phillips, he had the bodies placed in coffins. Then, after " much effort," he "succeeded in getting the district magistrate to order the coffins to be carried to Suikow," the port of departure on the Min river for Foochow. The survivors of the party were carried in chairs, but poor little Herbert succumbed to his wounds before reaching the river. The baby has since died, thus making the eleventh victim of the massacre.

Dr. Gregory's account concludes as follows :—

"We left Hua Sang, August the 2nd, at 3 P.M., for Suikow, and travelled all night, arriving at the latter place at 8.30 A.M. on the 3rd, the saddest and most terrible procession ever formed in China.

"The magistrates, led by our orders, sealed four boats for us at Suikow, which we left for Foochow at 3 P.M. on the 3rd. On the morning of the 4th we met a steam-launch taking the Sub-Prefect up to Suikow. We boarded this, and insisted on the launch towing our boats with the wounded to Foochow. Soon after this we met Mr. Hixson, U.S. Marshal (Consul), Archdeacon Wolfe, and Rev. Mr. Bannister with a launch bringing supplies. These we welcomed with much joy, and arrived in Foochow at 12.30 P.M. on the following day.

"As to the cause of this unheard-of savage and cruel act I cannot form a good opinion, but believe the actors must have been hirelings."

Why was it permitted? Why were lives so valuable cut off in the midst of work so important? A few minutes' warning (which numbers of friends not far off would have flown to give) would have sufficed to enable them to escape into the surrounding jungle. A friendly shower of rain might have been enough to turn back Chinese marauders from their purpose. But it was not to be. This terrible thing was permitted by Him without Whom not even a sparrow falls to the ground. He had spared and preserved them many times, but He did not spare them now. Beyond all human and secondary considerations we believe He had some all-wise reason for this, but what was it? Was it in order that the cause for which they fell might be conspicuously brought before the eyes of the civilised world? Was it in order that a lukewarm Church might receive another electric shock to rouse her from the slumber of indifference towards perishing heathen? The fate of the Ku Cheng martyrs bears something of a miniature resemblance to that of the two witnesses in the Apocalypse—"And when they shall have finished their testimony, the beast that cometh up out of the abyss shall make war with them and overcome them, and kill them. And their dead bodies shall lie . . . where also their Lord was crucified" (Rev. xi. 7, 8, R.V.).

It may even be that the Lord will use these letters to carry a thrilling and effectual message to many souls,

who would otherwise **never have known** what can **be**
done, what may **be done,** what ought to be done **by**
Christians in **vast, dark,** unhappy **China.** With the
earnest **prayer that it may be so, these** letters are sent
forth.   **And as for our beloved** friends themselves—"I
heard a voice **from heaven** saying, Write, Blessed **are**
the dead which **die in the Lord** from henceforth : **yea,**
saith the Spirit, **that they may rest** from their labours;
for their works follow with them."

THE END

www.ingramcontent.com/pod-product-compliance
Lightning Source LLC
Chambersburg PA
CBHW060533030726
47498CB00004B/1179